Shepherds

James Brumbaugh

Published by James Brumbaugh, 2013.

Also by J. Drew Brumbaugh

Shepherds

The Galiwee Visions Series:

War Party

Bula Bridge

Foxworth Terminus

Ten More

Girls Gone Great

(A children's book co-authored with Carolyn B. Berg)

The Tirumfall Trilogy :

Fall of the Western Kings

Child of Evil

For more information go to:

https://www.jdrewbrumbaugh.com

Dedication

Thanks to my wife, Carolyn, who read the multiple drafts I always have to go through to finish a novel and to all my family who have given me untold support.

Prologue

When there is a significant decrease in the world's food supply, the situation leads inevitably to turmoil and conflict. In one possible future, this shortage has left millions of people without enough food to survive. Those without sustenance, the poor and the dis-advantaged, have rioted in protest and their violent search for food spills across international borders. Marauding bands have pillaged through the countryside, hungry for even meager foodstuffs. Old hatreds have resurfaced, border skirmishes have increased, and world stability is threatened.

The oceans, once an abundant source of food, have been over-fished and now only the wealthy can afford seafood. But mankind, ever ingenious, has resorted to radical science to solve the food supply problem and return the oceans to productive aquaculture. Bio-engineered mermen and merwomen, known as shepherds, aided by trained dolphins, herd huge schools of re-engineered tuna at the whim of multinational seafood corporations. Held by those companies in indentured servitude, these much-maligned "cowboys" live aboard submersible rafts in areas of the open ocean allocated to them by international agreements. Further complicating matters, the partitioning of the oceans into ranches has severely limited the ability of independent fishermen to make a living. Those that continue to fish legally have banded together to fight for their rights utilizing the world courts. Other fishermen have found more lucrative though less honorable work.

Desperate men do desperate things and the oceans are now filled with treachery, pirating, and worse.

Chapter 1

Olga belonged to the sea. It owned her as surely as solid ground owned the rest of humanity. On land, the lubbers ridiculed her and called her an abomination, an ugly "thing" born in a devil's laboratory. But here, swimming in the vast Pacific, her body was beautiful with a grace no lubber could match. She drifted along peacefully, cradled by the warm water. The rocking caress of the gentle swells brought a sense of comfort, of belonging, of home. She pulled hard, breast-stroking with webbed hands and shot ahead, rolling over on her back to look up at the dark vault of the night sky. Off to the east, the pre-dawn glow hung at the horizon so that, overhead, only the brightest stars were still visible in the gray that preceded sunrise.

She glided backward through the tranquil swells, listening to the dolphins blow and dive as somewhere ahead they circled the tuna herd like sheep dogs. Twenty meters behind her, she could see the red, green and white running lights of the submersible raft, Homestead, cruising on autopilot.

Floating in her reverie gave her time to think about the radio message Ni had given her yesterday. The crumpled paper lay on her bunk. Star-Kist had offered to send Olga home to Russia – as if Russia had ever been her home—to see her mother, a mother she'd never met. Why now? Did her mother ask to see her? Olga wasn't at all sure how she felt about meeting her mother. She'd thought about it before, dreamed about it, shed tears. And now to have a chance to visit her, to meet the mother who had sold her into servitude. For all of her life, Chloe, the housemother at the St. Croix dormitory, had been Olga's mother. It was hard to think otherwise. Mostly she tried not to dwell on it. Her first R&R was months away and nothing could be done until then, so there would be time enough to decide how she felt.

She took another long, strong stroke, her hands pushing the water backward towards her feet so hard that miniature whirlpools swirled in her wake. The momentum carried her over the next swell and down into the following trough, gliding like a shadow in the feeble light, through the dark gray water. She slid her hands down her lean, graceful sides, feeling the smooth, tanned skin, skin that would never wrinkle no matter how long she stayed in the water.

She was naked except for the triangular patch of cloth between her legs, and even that small concession to the lubbers social mores she resented. Out here she could be proud of her body. She was a woman, but a woman like no land-dwelling lubber. She had been redesigned for a life on the open ocean. The genetic engineers had molded her body, streamlining her breasts and shoulders for faster swimming. Her strong arms and legs rippled with genetically enhanced muscles. Her hands and feet had long, slim fingers and toes that, unlike the earlier genetic designs, were fully webbed from fingertip to fingertip and from toe tip to toe tip. Only her blond hair, which she kept cut so short it barely covered her scalp, and her blue eyes had not been altered.

Even internally she'd been altered. Olga's lungs and blood steam had been modified to carry extra oxygen and she could easily hold her breath for thirty minutes, maybe longer. She was proud of her ability to swim faster and stay underwater longer than her older, genetically less sophisticated shipmates. Sometimes she thought Ici and Ni, the first generation shepherd couple who ran Homestead, were jealous. Out here, away from the lubbers, her improved engineering was the one thing that gave Olga a sense of satisfaction.

Still, she envied the dolphins swimming beside her, their sleek gray bodies gliding effortlessly through the clear water, water that was changing from gray to blue with the increasing light of the coming sunrise. The dolphins could live in the open ocean on their own but without the Homestead and the regular visits from the factory mother ships neither Olga nor her shipmates could survive.

Homestead was the key. She was a forty-eight meter, tri-hulled raft built entirely of shiny, stainless steel. Homestead sat low in the water and waves often rolled across her deck. The twin outrigger pontoons were attached at the edges of the thick stainless steel main deck with the center hull forming a deep keel for stability.

A square-cornered cabin sat on top of the main deck slightly aft of center and directly over the keel. The cabin contained their living quarters, galley and control center. It was almost two-thirds as long as the hull. Three of the cabin's four walls were straight with the front wall slanted back to reduce drag while the raft was submerged. A steel-rung ladder went up the near side of the cabin and Olga could see it clearly now like dashed lines in a vertical row. Around the front half of the cabin roof was a waist high railing of welded stainless steel tubing. Along the side of the cabin ran a single row of four, small, round portholes that marked the individual rooms. The portholes were dark now except for the third one back. That was Olga's. Aft of the cabin, the low, round hump of the solar steam generator stuck up above the outer pontoon like a blister. Homestead wasn't much to look at but she was functional and submersible, capable of diving to 300 meters to escape storms. In the four months since Olga had joined Ici and Ni aboard the raft, it had come to feel like home despite the sterile, utilitarian accommodations.

Olga rolled and dove under the surface, took a couple of powerful strokes and resurfaced fifty meters from Homestead. Off to the east, the huge gold-rimmed tropical sun pulled its way upward out of the Pacific. Olga rolled on her back and let the brilliant glow of sunrise wash over her tanned body. She floated for a while, motionless. The rhythm of the long swells seeped into her existence, like the beat of a life greater than herself. Swimming free in the open ocean was what she had been born to do.

She gulped in air, held her breath, and dove beneath the surface again. Long strokes combined with strong kicks thrust her farther away from the raft. She built up speed until she reached her maximum velocity, then tucked her arms at her sides and glided ahead like a torpedo, suspended effortlessly in the crystalline water. Sparkling shafts of light glittered around her.

Suddenly Sheriff, one of the larger male dolphins in their pod, shot past her, his sleek, gray body a blur of motion. Olga felt the pressure wave brush over her as the dolphin darted by. She started to race after him but Sheriff made a tight U-turn and stopped nose to nose with her. Olga rowed backward furiously with both hands and barely avoided crashing into the dolphin. Once halted, she reached out and stroked his smiling snout, looking him in the eyes, eyes filled with warmth and intelligence.

The dolphin nuzzled her, begging to be petted. Olga was glad to oblige. In many ways, Sheriff was her only real friend. Often she imagined that Sheriff's squeaks and whistles were his way of talking to her.

Olga circled around the dolphin but he pushed her gently to a stop with his nose. Peering past Sheriff, she saw the vast bulk of the tuna herd, thousands of scaly, yellow shapes zigzagging back and forth in unison through the water directly ahead. She'd drifted dangerously close to them.

Olga arched her back, angling upward, and pulled her way to the surface. Breaching with a vigorous splash, she took in a breath as Sheriff surfaced next to her.

"Thanks," she said. "You know not to let me get into the tuna herd, don't you?"

Some of the bigger tuna went over 200 kilos and a quick flip of their tail could knock the wind out of her. Her body was made for swimming, not banging into big fish. Worse yet was to be caught in the middle of the school with sharp fins and rough scaly bodies crashing in from all sides. She knew to stay away from the school; she just hadn't been paying attention.

Effortlessly treading water with her webbed feet, Olga patted Sheriff's broad smooth head. "Too bad you're not a man. We'd make a great pair."

Sheriff rolled away, turning back to his duties herding the skittish tuna. Only the dolphins kept them from scattering to the far corners of the ocean. Like the best sheep dogs, the dolphins constantly circled the fish, keeping the stragglers close. Sheriff was an important part of the control and he had to get back to work.

With slow, lazy strokes, Olga swam back toward Homestead. It was time to wake Ici and Ni. They would take over the watch and Olga could rest, eat and sleep. Olga hadn't gotten used to sleeping during the day even though she'd been doing it almost from the time she'd joined Ici and Ni on Homestead about four months ago. At the St. Croix School of Fisheries she'd been on a normal schedule, classes and activities during the day, sleeping at night.

Thoughts of school reminded her of Maria. Like all the students at St. Croix, Maria had been engineered by the factory geneticists to live at sea herding tuna. She was dark haired, brown skinned, shorter than Olga, beautiful, and she laughed more. Maria had been the only other student near Olga's age. They'd stuck together all through school. Even now they stayed in touch by wireless Internet video. Since Maria worked day watch in the Atlantic and Olga night watch in the Pacific they were both up at the same time. It was the only good thing Olga could think of about working through the darkness.

The saddest day in Olga's life had been the day the two of them had graduated, received their work assignments, and headed for different oceans. Olga wished they could at least have been on the same side of the world. It wasn't fair. By now all of the St. Croix students were scattered around the world, indentured servants to the big tuna companies. Better that than a lubber, she thought.

Nearing the raft, she dove under the surface building up speed as she swam. Reaching her top speed at the bottom of her dive, she turned sharply upward, her powerful arms driving her toward the surface. With a final burst of energy, she shot from the water like a submarine-launched missile. Momentarily airborne, she easily cleared Homestead's low freeboard. Tucking her legs up under her, she landed lightly in a crouch on the starboard walkway next to the cabin. Olga felt the rhythm of the deck beneath her, then, sure of her footing, straightened to her full height. Nine-point-five for the landing, she thought and turned to watch the sun finish rising out of the Pacific. It was her favorite time of day. The sun's new glow brought life back to the dark world. Best of all, it signaled the end of her watch.

The second week she'd been aboard Homestead, Ici had assigned her the night watch so he and his wife, Ni, could have the day watch together. Olga hated to admit that the long, dark night shifts often left her feeling melancholy and lonely. Ici and Ni had each other. Olga had no one and she wasn't likely to meet anyone in the middle of the Pacific Ocean either. The prospects were depressing so she tried not to think about it.

The blazing sun was now completely above the horizon and had begun its steady march west. With full daylight Olga let go of her despair. Instead, she let her eyes take in the beauty of the dolphins gently rising, blowing, and rolling underwater again. They swam fifty meters off the port bow, circling the tuna, keeping the fish from scattering. There was Pungee, the biggest dolphin and pod leader, and Sheriff, and Kate, Gunslinger and Slim. Olga counted heads, finding fourteen when there should be fifteen. Where was Cowpoke? Oh, there, as the smaller dolphin leaped on the far side of the tuna school.

To keep Homestead from getting away from her when she was in the water, Olga had the raft throttled down to only about a knot an hour on a course that ran north, northwest. Since tuna never swam that slowly, the dolphins herded them around the raft in an endless circle, never far away, never slowing.

Homestead rose and fell with the low, regular swells imparting a sense of peace. The serenity touched Olga like a kiss from the Almighty. She felt good about her life. The perfect way to end her watch.

Olga strode to the aft cabin door. She needed to wake Ici and Ni, and then get breakfast and some sleep.

Chapter 2

Miles away from Homestead, Captain Victor Poddington sat in the comfortable, leather chair in his stateroom. This cabin was larger than the one he'd had on his old ship, big enough that he had his entire holo-disc movie collection arranged alphabetically in the bookcase against the outer bulkhead. He loved the old classics and they made up most of the titles in his library. Above his black metal desk hung his favorite fly rod and a motley assortment of flies he'd hand-tied years ago.

On the holographic monitor "A River Runs Through It," one of his favorite classics, played on unheeded. Usually, he loved the fly fishing scenes. They reminded him of his native New Zealand, though he'd done more fishing alone than with family. He had no brother and his father had never really liked fishing that much.

He closed his personal logbook, stood up and flicked the remote to turn off the movie. Today his mind was preoccupied with other things and he kept losing the story line. It was this new ship. He just didn't feel comfortable aboard an imposter. The name on her stern was Sunrise Savior, and to the casual observer, she would pass for the internationally known, floating environmental lab. But this Sunrise Savior wouldn't stand up to close inspection. Then again Poddington didn't intend to give any guided tours. Still, he was uneasy. Commanding a ship bearing a false name was a bad omen.

His mind returned to the business at hand. Poddington had been off the bridge long enough and it was time to get back up to the wheelhouse to see how the siphoning was going. He flipped off the lights and left his cabin, closing the bulkhead door quietly to avoid alerting the crew that he was coming. He grabbed the handrail and climbed the spiral, metal stairwell taking care to tread lightly.

Entering the aft, starboard side of the wheelhouse, Poddington quickly scanned the interior, noting immediately that everything seemed in order, the seldom-used chart table, the ancient oil-filled compass, the computerized positional tracking screen, the radar screen, the ship's wheel, and his own addition, the halo-monitor that allowed Poddington to watch his movies while on the bridge.

George Braxton, better known as Deep (for Deep Water), Poddington's long-time friend and first mate, stood near the radarscope, but Deep wasn't looking at the green screen, his concentration was on the main deck. Behind Deep, at his station, stood the wheelsman, Chip, controlling the ship's course as the Sunrise Savior cruised slowly through the plankton field. Otherwise the wheelhouse was empty. Poddington walked over to where Deep stood at the wheelhouse windows.

Deep nodded as he caught sight of Poddington. Above the first mate's serious gray eyes was the ever-present, faded red baseball cap pulled down low as if to shade the sun. A cigarette dangled from the corner of Deep's mouth, stuck to his thin lips like it was glued.

"How's it going?" Poddington asked his first mate.

"Seems okay to me," answered Deep.

Poddington turned and leaned out the window overlooking the foredeck. His squat, barrel-shaped body made it awkward and he pushed back his captain's hat so he could see better. Below him, the deck hands controlled the pumps and filters that sucked up the yellow-green plankton in great, throaty gulps. His eye was drawn to Sleena bossing the men of the pump gang. The black woman loved lording over the men in her crew, though most of them weren't too thrilled about having a woman in charge. Poddington didn't care. He liked the way she took charge, especially in his cabin at night. Just thinking about it started his pulse racing.

As much as he liked having her aboard, he didn't really know much about her. She'd signed on when Poddington had agreed to act as ship's captain for the new owners, a drug cartel. They'd needed crew to replace those who left when their duties changed from running arms to siphoning plankton. At first, Poddington had been reluctant to have a woman on board; but Sleena hadn't let much time go by before she'd convinced him otherwise.

Deep interrupted his thoughts. "How long are we going to have to stay on this bed? There's bound to be a swimmers' raft around here somewhere. They'll probably show up soon."

Poddington's head snapped around. Deep was half a head taller than Poddington and the Captain had to look up to meet Deep's gaze. Normally

Poddington wouldn't be bothered by anything his first mate might say, but right now idle banter irritated him.

"So?" he snorted.

"I'd hate to get caught on our first run."

"Caught stealing plankton? They can't arrest us for that."

"No, but if someone figures out we're not the Sunrise Savior, then what?"

"You're probably right. But swimmers are nothing to worry about. In fact, I'd welcome the chance to snuff a few. They're nothing but slimy mutants. Not worth letting live, if you ask me."

Deep laughed. "You'd give anything to try out the deck gun."

Poddington shrugged. "Well, I kind of wonder what that thing will do. Liberating it from that last arms cargo was brilliant, even for me. Course, now that we aren't in the arms business anymore it may be a bit tough getting shells for it. But we've got enough to blow the shit out of a few swimmers."

Deep scanned the sea around them. Poddington turned back to watch Sleena on deck. The dark green coveralls hid her physique but Poddington had it memorized. He could visualize her firm thighs, hard, muscular arms, and the strong sculptured effect of her breasts over a thick layer of muscle.

Poddington continued daydreaming at the window. He thought about the drug cartel submarine, lurking out there somewhere, waiting to take their cargo of drugs to market. The submarine was a symbol of the cartel's power and money, a reminder to Poddington that they were not people to take lightly.

Distracted as he was, Poddington failed to notice the squat box-shaped swimmers' raft surfacing a thousand meters off their port bow. The vessel's twin pontoons angled skyward, rising slowly out of the sea until the entire silver cabin was visible. Water streamed off her hull and superstructure in glistening sheets. Then gravity took over and the twin bows fell gracefully back to the sea. Within a minute the submersible craft bobbed lightly on the swells. Hardly bigger than the launch aboard the Sunrise Savior and with a much lower profile, the raft was nearly invisible as she rose and fell with the waves.

"Captain," shouted the watchman from the bow. "Swimmers!"

Poddington looked in the direction the watchman pointed. He immediately identified the small vessel as one of the swimmers' rafts. On the bow Poddington read "Oyster Bay" printed in large, black letters. He glanced around, looking for the mutants' dolphins and tuna herd. Forget the fish, he told himself.

"Man the deck gun," he shouted.

There was a flurry on deck as four of the deckhands ran forward and up the stairs to the forecastle. Sleena jumped to the motor switch and threw the lever to raise the gun from below decks. A hidden hatch in the foredeck whined open and the hydraulics moved the naval cannon up into its firing position.

Poddington checked the raft. So far no one had appeared and the hatches were still closed. He stepped out of the wheelhouse, leaned over the rail and yelled at the deckhands standing around below, "The rest of you scum buckets break out the rifles." He waited for them to obey and when they were too slow, screamed, "Now! Get moving!"

Behind the swimmers' raft an ominous black conning tower rose between the low wave tops. No doubt where the submarine was now, thought Poddington. He watched it swing around until the bow pointed toward the swimmers' tiny ship.

"What the hell are those idiots on the sub doing?" spat Deep. "They're supposed to stay submerged during the day. What if some spy satellite picks them up? The whole damn operation will be blown."

Poddington watched for a moment. In the crystal-clear water he could see the outline of the submarine's hull beneath the surface. Slowly, the outer torpedo doors swung open.

"Christ, no. They're going to fire a torpedo!" Poddington turned to Deep. "Get on the radio and tell them to lay off."

"In the clear?"

Poddington thought for a moment. Christ, who knew what ears might be tuned in.

"No, just tell them no fish today. Absolutely no fish."

Deep thumbed the radio switch and Poddington turned his attention back to the raft. He could see the antenna rising from the aft bulkhead, a thin sliver of black against the sea's blue background. He couldn't afford to have the mutants radio any reports of the Sunrise Savior. His crew would have to knock out the raft's radio. If necessary the Sunrise Savior's equipment

13

could jam transmissions with a static burst, but Poddington would rather not. Massive static might tip off anyone monitoring that something unusual was going on. In this business, deceit and invisibility were essential.

Now he saw the first of the raft's occupants coming out onto the aft deck. It was a tall, lanky male creature. The webbed hands swung on unnaturally long arms against his thighs and the feet flopped like a duck's. Just the sight of the mutant disgusted Poddington. Lousy bastards, he thought, and was filled with a loathing, an urge to kill it and any others on board. They had cost him his ship, his life as a fisherman, a life he loved. They had forced him to take a job running guns and drugs. It seemed a lousy way to end his dreams.

By now the small naval cannon was above the forecastle and a crew of three had it cranked around toward the swimmers' raft. How accurate the thing was, Poddington had no idea. On the other hand, he couldn't resist the temptation to try it out. "Fire when ready," he yelled. He felt a tingle of excitement course through his body. In his own mind, he'd have made one hell of a naval officer.

The lone swimmer looked at the ship menacing his raft. His eyes grew and Poddington could swear the mutant was looking straight at him. Fear was evident in his face, a fear that was only too human. The swimmer turned and scurried toward the backside of the cabin.

The cannon roared and a ball of fire erupted on the side of the raft's cabin. Metal twisted away from the roof and sides and shrapnel went screaming into the air and water. The male swimmer crumpled to the deck, rolled over, twitched and lay still. Poddington grinned. A sense of pride in his gunners swelled in his chest. It was all he could do to hold back a victory shout.

"They're on the radio," snapped Deep from behind Poddington.

"Well for Christ's sake, jam them."

"Already on it, Skipper," said the radio operator from his cubicle off the aft of the wheelhouse. "Nothing's getting through."

Poddington turned back to the raft. A tall female swimmer with short brown hair was dragging the downed male behind the steel cabin. For a split second he caught a glimpse of her streamlined torso, the way her bare breasts were molded to her body, the lean lines of her arms and legs. A few stray rifle shots sent little spouts of water hissing into the air around the pontoons but the swimmers disappeared from view behind the protection of the cabin. More bullets clanged against the bulkheads.

Poddington shook his head. Wasted bullets, he thought.

"Shoot the radio antenna. The radio," he shouted, leaning from the open window, pointing at the black mast that rose like a stinger into the sky.

A couple of the deckhands looked up at Poddington, puzzled expressions on their faces. He was about to curse their stupidity when Sleena ran to the rail and yelled at them to shoot the radio. Exasperated, she unslung the automatic weapon she carried and cut loose with a burst. The rest of the armed crew followed suit.

Up on the bow, the cannon boomed again and Poddington paused, anticipating the ugly explosion when the shell crashed down on the raft. Instead, the round went long and raised a mountainous pillar of water on the far side of the vessel.

"Damn it," he cursed. "Don't waste the shells."

All the while, the Sunrise Savior had been steaming toward the raft and the distance was closing fast. It wouldn't be long before they were close enough to put over the launch. Poddington spun around, grabbed his 9mm automatic and shoulder holster from the wall hook, and ran for the ladder that went down to the main deck.

"You have the bridge," he yelled back to Deep, as he hit the deck running.

The small arms fire from the railing was now an intense rattle. The hail of bullets was slowly chewing away at the radio mast mounting bracket, if not the aerial itself. As Poddington reached the rail, the antenna crashed into the ocean and the deck crew howled with satisfaction.

Poddington stopped at the rail and surveyed the scene. They were only a couple of hundred meters from the raft. Behind it, almost a half kilometer away, the submarine's conning tower loomed dark and foreboding. Its silhouette still pointed toward the raft but it made no move to take action. There was no sign of life aboard the swimmers' raft.

"Put over the launch," Poddington ordered. "Sleena, you and I will go aboard and finish them off. Lefty and Eric will stand deckwatch. Fellipe will come with us. The rest of you stand ready."

A couple of the deckhands ran to launch the small runabout from the aft davits. Oh, this was going perfectly. He'd get his revenge. It was a chance

Poddington had thought would never come. Those damn swimmers were going to pay for what they'd done to him and Deep. The cannon thundered again and Poddington flinched. They were so close to the raft that the gun barrel could not depress low enough to hit the target. The shell screamed away over it, landing closer to the submarine than to the swimmers.

"Cease fire, cease fire," yelled Poddington. Damned idiots were wasting precious ammunition. They would board the Oyster Bay and finish this thing personally.

The launch idled around and Poddington, Sleena and Fellipe scrambled down the ladder into the open cockpit. The coxswain gunned the engine and the boat rumbled across the short distance to the raft. Poddington wondered if the swimmers would put up a fight, or were they even armed? No one appeared as the launch approached.

With the engines thrown into full reverse to slow them down, the launch bumped into the port side of the raft. Poddington, Sleena and Fellipe jumped aboard the flat deck. There was no hatch on this side of the raft. But there was a hole in the top of the bulkhead and Poddington noted with satisfaction the twisted metal around the cannon's first direct hit. A thin bloodstain marked where the swimmer had fallen. Poddington ignored it and dashed across the deck to the other side of the cabin, yanking his pistol from its holster as he ran.

Turning the corner, he paused, wary of an ambush. The hatchway on the starboard side of the cabin swung lazily back and forth in time with the swells. He couldn't see inside. He felt Sleena behind him, her short-barreled automatic poking past his right arm.

"Do you think they're armed?" she whispered in Poddington's ear.

His pulse was already racing and her hot breath in his ear made him think for a moment of other times alone when he had enjoyed the sweat and fire pouring from her onyx body. He shook the thought away. "I doubt it or they would have already shot at us."

Still, there was a kernel of doubt in his mind. It made him cautious as he slipped up to the door and pulled it fully open. Expectantly, he held his gun pointed down the shiny metal-walled hallway in front of him. It turned sharply to the left after only a few meters. It was also empty and silent. He listened for a moment. Somewhere toward the aft of the vessel he could hear a thin, wailing voice praying to the radio for help.

It was the boost his courage needed. He boldly stamped into the hallway, reached the corner and turned to the left. The deserted stainless steel corridor stretched to the aft hatchway, which was dogged closed. On either side of the hall were doors, three on the left, four on the right and all closed except for one that stood open at the far end on the left.

"Search the rooms," he ordered, motioning the other two past him with a wave of his pistol.

Sleena rushed past, headed for the last door on the right where now Poddington heard the voice on the radio louder than ever. He decided to check the first room on the right and pushed the door open.

Sunlight washed into the room through the gaping hole in the bulkhead where the cannon shell had exploded. Poddington could see everything plainly. There were two swimmers in the room. The male lay face up on the floor, a widening pool of blood spreading around him. Bending over him, holding his head in her hands was the brown-haired female that Poddington had seen dragging the male from the deck. She was naked except for the triangle of cloth covering her pubic area, and for an instant, Poddington couldn't take his eyes off her small breasts. Though they were sculptured into her torso, they were still distinctly feminine. He found himself wondering what it felt like to have a swimmer.

As he entered she turned and looked him in the eye. Her face was as gray as granite. Shock and terror filled her blue eyes, and her lips trembled as she tried to speak.

"W-why," she stammered. "Why?" And still she cradled the male's head in her hands even as she looked into the barrel of Poddington's automatic.

For a second Poddington had to ask himself why. Her eyes pleaded with him in the bright sunlight. They were human eyes filled with pain. Poddington hesitated. He was prepared to kill alien beings from a nameless laboratory, not this. A scream pierced the air. It echoed down the empty hall, only to be cut off by the angry staccato of automatic rifle fire. That jolted Poddington into reflex action.

"Fucking swimmers," he snarled and squeezed the trigger. Once, twice, three times. Surreally, his mind slowed time and he watched the bullets blow mushrooming bits of blood, skull and brains into the air. There was something artistic about the splatters and the strange mixture of colors mingling in the air, floating in slow motion. Odd patterns formed on the walls and on the floor where they flowed together with the blood of the downed male. The female toppled in a heap onto her companion who groaned as her weight crashed on him.

Poddington bent over to see if the male swimmer's eyes were open and felt a twinge of disappointment that they were not. He stuck the gun close to the streamlined head, right under the molded nose, and pulled the trigger. The roar was deafening, but Poddington thrilled so much to the way the body flinched upon impact that he fired twice more before he turned back out into the hall.

Sleena was just coming from the aft end, a cruel grin on her face. "They won't be radioing anyone else. I wasted the bitch in the radio shack."

Poddington noticed her quick breathing and her breasts heaving softly up and down pushing against the tight coveralls. Little beads of sweat stood out on her forehead. The gleam in her eye said she wanted something more and Poddington hoped he would have time to find out what that something was once they were back aboard the Sunrise Savior. Without warning, she grabbed him and crushed her mouth against his, her tongue flittering wildly inside his mouth. She pulled back and winked.

Poddington was stunned for a moment. Just then, Fellipe charged out of an adjacent room and broke the silence. "Nobody left aboard," he said flatly. "Let's get out of here. I think she's taking water."

Indeed, the deck had taken a list aft and Poddington wondered about her seaworthiness. "Let's go, double time."

The three of them rushed up the corridor, turned right and exited by the starboard hatch. Out on deck it was an easy jump to the waiting launch. The coxswain gunned the motor and swung the boat away from the crippled raft.

They had drifted farther from the Sunrise Savior and now, as they cruised back, a dolphin suddenly appeared next to them. The graceful mammal leaped into the air beside the launch and seemed to hang suspended as it stared at each one aboard. Then it fell back into the sea. Immediately a second dolphin poked its head above the water to look at the launch passengers. It swam alongside, holding its head so it could see them. Several more joined in on both sides of the launch.

"What the hell are they looking at?" asked Sleena. "They give me the creeps."

Poddington didn't answer. He stared at the pod of dolphins now trailing his launch like a pack of wolves. It was then that he remembered John Him in Taiwan. How many times had he asked if Poddington could secure dolphin meat? It was a priceless delicacy in certain areas and worth a hell of a lot of money. His hand went to his pistol.

"Shoot them," he said and carefully took aim at the nearest gliding shape.

Poddington fired directly at the smiling gray head. The others fired only a fraction of a second later, filling the ocean on both sides of the launch with bullets. In an instant, the sea swirled red with dolphin blood. Poddington ignored the squeals of the wounded dolphins, intent on killing the ones close enough to shoot. Gray bodies marred by swaths of red littered the pristine seascape. In a moment, all the dolphins either floated dead or were gone.

"Get them aboard. We'll freeze the carcasses and sell them later."

They wrestled the half dozen dead dolphins aboard. Poddington looked back at the Oyster Bay and noted that the raft hadn't sunk, and didn't look like it would anytime soon. Several dolphins swam circles around it. He thought of going back to finish the job. Too risky. He didn't like the idea of staying around any longer than necessary. Someone might have picked up the distress signals. No, he'd let the submarine blow the raft up with that damn torpedo they were so anxious to fire and he'd get the hell out of there.

Poddington stepped to the radio, picked up the hand microphone and hit the talk button. "One more fish and the day should be over. Over."

"Roger," came the reply. "We'll set it to run on the surface."

Well, at least that would end it, he thought as he put the microphone away. Already the submarine was lining up for the final shot. Poddington heard the whoosh and saw a white streak as the torpedo ran toward the stationary raft. He waited, waited, then—instead of an explosion there was a tremendous crash. The raft shuddered. Nothing else.

"What the hell happened?" he asked.

Fellipe turned toward Poddington. "I think it was a dud."

"Oh Christ, just what I needed," said Poddington, rubbing his sweaty forehead.

"Captain," squawked the radio. It was Deep. "We're picking up something on radar. A ship's headed this way."

"What else could go wrong?" Poddington mumbled under his breath, then grabbed the microphone. "How fast is it coming?"

"Not fast, but it's headed directly towards us. It could be a UN frigate."

"How far away?"

"Nearly 50 miles."

The launch bumped against the side of the Sunrise Savior.

"We're coming aboard. Let's not wait to see who it is. Just get us out of here."

The crew scrambled to hook the launch into the davits and within minutes it was being hauled aboard. Poddington scrambled back to the pilothouse and glanced at the radarscope. The brilliant green dot signaled the ship approaching from the east. He wondered who they were, wondered what danger they might present. Taking no chances, Poddington ordered the Sunrise Savior to head off to the west at full speed. The submarine had already submerged before the Sunrise Savior started to make way. They steamed off leaving only the listing Oyster Bay to mar the endless stretch of blue.

Poddington could hardly control himself long enough to get the dolphins taken below to the freezer. Then he put Deep in command and headed below to his cabin where he knew Sleena waited. His pulse still raced but he wasn't sure if it was residual adrenaline or anticipation.

Chapter 3

Over the horizon, a trawler churned through the gentle swells on a heading aimed for that speck of ocean where the Oyster Bay lay wounded. The fishermen aboard went about their daily business unaware of the trouble they were approaching.

The ship's engines thumped rhythmically and Toivo Nurminen felt the vibrations through the soles of his rubber boots. He stood on a square metal platform that hung over the side near the bow. The platform was surrounded by a waist-high railing and suspended by thick steel cables that led up on deck through a set of pulleys to dual deck-mounted winches that could raise or lower it to water level. Toivo had had it fabricated so he could be closer to his dolphins. The platform now hung over the side, barely above the water, and Toivo leaned against the railing to steady himself. His ship, Sisu, was over 70 meters long and barely rose as the shallow waves swirled against the bow, the thin, white foam trailing off to the sides in long vees. A light breeze tickled his scalp through his short brown hair. The azure sea rippled off to the horizon and joined the blue, cloudless sky forming a continuous vault of color.

Ahead of the boat, a dolphin pair rode the bow wave. Intermittently one slipped beneath the surface to send sonar pulses exploring the waters around them. Toivo watched the dolphins working as a team. He listened to their squeaks, clicks and whistles, hoping they would locate fish.

"*Poika*," he called, whistling on the inhale to get the right sound and folding his tongue almost double to form the clicks in the back of his throat. "*Where are the fish?*"

"*No tuna*," answered the larger dolphin as he slipped under the next wave.

There is nothing out there, Toivo thought. Not even the dolphins can find fish. Maybe the shepherds and their factory-bred fish have taken over this section of the ocean, too. Where are the wild fish—the ones he could catch legally? All too often the bright yellow factory tuna had taken over vast areas of the ocean and pushed the wild tuna out. The thought of the genetically altered, goldfish-like factory breed disgusted him. They were more like pets than real tuna.

The worst part was that the factory herds were so successful that the increasing availability of fresh factory fish had steadily driven down the market price. It was hard to make a living even when he was catching fish. Maybe he should steal factory fish like some of the Chinese boats did. Naw. What was he thinking? Toivo did not steal.

Perhaps he should give up, sell the boat, or go under contract to one of the canneries. No. Sisu was a good boat, and Poika and Tyttö were good fish. He laughed. Dolphins, he reminded himself, were not fish. After all these years he still couldn't break the habit. He remembered when he and his family had moved from Finland to Hawaii. He had been seven. His father had taken a job with the Kewalo Basin Marine Mammal Laboratory to develop a computer program that would analyze and reproduce the dolphins' language. He could still hear his father scolding him for calling the dolphins fish.

Toivo looked across the open sea; she remained empty and barren. There were days he wished he had married Anja and stayed with the dairy in Oulu. He hit the button to raise the platform up to the main deck. The winches hummed faintly as they retracted the cables until the platform clicked into its locks, level with the deck. Climbing over the ship's railing he started back for the wheelhouse.

"*Ei kalaa?*" asked Wilho from his station at the wheel. The windshield was tipped open and the stocky man's voice carried easily to the bow.

"Nothing."

Toivo trudged back up the deck. He knew the crew was worried, especially Wilho. They should have had a hold full of fish and been back to market in Hawaii a week ago. Wilho had paid for his daughter, Enni, to fly there from Finland for a holiday with her father and now she was waiting in Honolulu. She wouldn't be able to stay much longer. Instead of enjoying a holiday in Hawaii, Toivo and his crew were still out in the Pacific with an empty hold. They had a few albacore frozen below but not enough to pay for the trip. The last two days Poika and Tyttö had barely been able to find enough small fish to feed themselves. Where were the damn tuna?

"It's days like this that make me wish I'd never let you talk me into leaving the papermill," said Wilho. His grim face and the worry lines crinkling his forehead reflected Toivo's own despair.

"Talk you into it?" Toivo shook his head. "You hated sitting behind that desk. You hated wearing a tie. And you weren't much of a salesman anyway. You begged me to take you to sea." How quickly people forget, he thought.

"It would be better than this." Wilho reached up and pulled the windshield shut.

Toivo chuckled. Wilho wasn't happy unless he was complaining. "If you think things are bad now," he said loud enough for Wilho to hear through the glass, "wait until tonight's chess game. You've left yourself no defense. You're finished."

Toivo hesitated at the door to the wheelhouse, his callused hand pausing on the handle as if opening the door was admitting defeat. He'd worked hard all his life only hard work didn't seem to be enough anymore. And wishing there were fish to catch didn't make it so. He pulled the door open and went inside.

The wheelhouse was small but not cramped. It sat squarely atop the aft deck with windows all round that gave a view of the main deck and the sea in every direction. Directly in front of the wheel, where the wheelsman could watch them, were the radarscope, the computer location graphics, and the sonar fish finder. To the left stood the map table, which had largely been replaced by computer location graphics. Like everything aboard Sisu, the wheelhouse was well lit and functional.

"There was a ship on radar ahead, but she steamed off," reported Wilho as Toivo entered.

Toivo nodded, then turned and walked pensively to the windshield looking forward. He stood for a while contemplating the sea ahead through the wide windows. It was fish that concerned Toivo, not other ships. With Wilho handling the wheel, Toivo had time to think. Worry was more like it. How could simply thinking figure out where the fish were? They had already tried every spot where they'd caught fish before. Now they were off to virgin territory, searching for tuna that probably weren't there.

At that moment Poika leaped out of the water beside Sisu, his head barely clearing the deck. He sprayed a mouthful of water at Toivo and fell back into the sea. The water splashed against the wheelhouse window, startling Toivo out of his reverie.

Toivo yanked open the door, leaped outside the wheelhouse and dashed to the ship's rail.

"*What is it?*" he asked, leaning over the gunwale.

The dolphin jumped, emitting a series of squeals. "*Fish! A school of fish this way.*" He dropped back into the blue water and raced away to starboard.

"*Voi, voi, voi,*" Toivo yelled to Wilho, "to starboard."

Wilho spun the wheel and the boat heeled over trying to follow Poika. As she turned, the swell caught Sisu abeam and she wallowed along on the course Toivo indicated. He strained to keep Poika in sight and called out headings to Wilho so the wheelsman could follow the sleek mammal's course.

"What is it?" asked Wilho, scanning the sea for signs of fish.

"Tuna," yelled Toivo, the sparkle back in his blue eyes.

Tyttö joined Poika and the dolphin pair breached in unison. They dove into the next swell and extended their lead over the boat. For a long moment, the two gray bodies remained beneath the waves. Then, farther ahead and more to starboard, they broke the surface again. Toivo pointed, and Wilho eased the boat around to follow.

The dolphins leaped clear of the water again, still farther ahead of the lumbering ship. There. Toivo caught the first flash of the big fish. He could see the ripple of fins ahead of the dolphins, the twisting wakes of fish darting back and forth. A small school, he thought. Probably tuna. He hurried back into the wheelhouse and closed the door.

"Tuna," he shouted into the intercom and heard the sounds of the crew scrambling to get on deck. Satisfied, he turned to stare at the spot where he'd seen the swirls, looking for evidence that would confirm his suspicions.

Though the school was still a long way off, Toivo caught flashes of brilliant yellow in the sun. Damn! Factory fish. Then where were the shepherds? Or at least their herd dolphins?

"Do you see a shepherds' raft?" he asked Wilho.

"No," said the wheelsman through clenched teeth, "and if I did, I'd pretend I didn't."

Toivo smiled. Wilho was getting desperate. "I don't see any shepherds either. And I don't think all of the fish are factory-bred. They must be strays."

"Then they are legal catch," whooped Wilho and laughed gleefully as he always did when they were in pursuit of tuna. Wilho threw the throttle to full ahead and the gentle thump of the engine increased to a low rumble. The boat lurched forward but the dolphins and the racing tuna pulled away.

Through the spray, Toivo watched the dolphins. Their breathing leaps were low, their flukes driving hard. Steadily they were overtaking the school. Soon they would pass the tuna and turn them back toward the ship.

Toivo looked out the aft window. The rest of the crew already had the nets out of the storage lockers and spread on the fantail. Gunnar was pointing for the running lines to be pulled into place, and even Helmar, who was on his first trip, was busy helping Pentii set the drop buoys. Everything would be ready in a few minutes.

Toivo turned back to gauge the dolphins progress. He spit into his hands and rubbed them together, a habit left from his long-liner days. Poika and Tyttö were only a few meters behind the school. It wouldn't be long.

"We're ready, Toivo," called Gunnar from the stern. The tall Swede stood poised by the net release lines looking to Toivo for the signal.

Toivo held his right hand up plainly where Gunnar could see it. The nets had to go over at exactly the right time. If they were early, the fish would be too far away and many would scatter before they reached the net. If they were late, the net would not be fully deployed.

Wait. . . the dolphins were abreast of the lead tuna, wait. . . now! He dropped his hand. Wilho laid the wheel over to port and Sisu began its swing. Gunnar fed the lines and the large net snaked out behind them. Helmar and Pentii funneled the purse seine overboard making sure the netting didn't tangle. The boat traced a huge semicircle leaving the net in an arc behind them. Now the dolphins had to drive the tuna into the net. The team of fishermen and dolphins had done it hundreds of times, but always split-second timing and smooth operation were essential. The tiniest mistake could foul the nets and they would end up empty.

Toivo watched as the boat turned. He heard the nets running into the sea. It felt good to be fishing again. Maybe there would be enough fish to break even.

Abeam now, the dolphins were turning the tuna. The school flashed around and ran toward them, closing at 30 knots. The rush of the tuna, streaks of gold, and the puffs of vapor from the dolphins breathing marked their progress. It was going to be close. The net wasn't fully extended yet, but here came the fish.

"Now," yelled Toivo. "Turn hard."

The boat heeled. Tuna plowed into the net. The ropes tightened against their winches. Wilho threw the engines to flank speed and boat lunged ahead to close the trap on the thrashing fish.

Toivo glared down at the mass of flailing yellow tuna.

"Voi, voi, voi," he spat. "Factory fish." He slammed his fist into the rail. If the shepherds came now he would have to release them.

"Where are the swimmers?" asked Wilho, stepping away from the wheel with the propeller in neutral and the boat drifting on the swells.

Toivo grimaced every time Wilho used the derogatory term "swimmers" and would have called him on it, but now wasn't the time.

"Maybe they are submerged," Toivo said, turning a full circle to scan the horizon. Any moment he expected to see the boxy, houseboat-shaped shepherd's raft bob to the surface. But none came, and there was no sign of the herd dolphins that always accompanied factory schools. He glanced down to assure himself that the fish bore the distinctive yellow sides. Yes, there was no doubt these were factory fish. But only a few thousand, less than a tenth of the smallest factory shoal, and there were a few dark, native fish mixed in. Strays he decided.

Toivo ran his hand through his hair and turned to look at the crew. They stood poised at the gunwale on either side of the loading ramp that bisected the stern, ready to haul in their catch. He hated having to make such a choice. Stealing factory fish was piracy with serious consequences. Catching a few lost strays wasn't.

"Get them aboard," he snapped. Maybe he was doing the wrong thing, but he couldn't give up what little profit there might be. He turned back to scan the horizon for shepherds or a factory ship.

Poika broached beside Sisu. Above the whine of the winches and Sisu's engines Toivo could barely make out the dolphin's voice. "*There are other dolphins nearby,*" he said. "*Over there.*"

The dolphin pointed with his beaked nose. Toivo squinted against the sun. Other dolphins so near the factory tuna had to be from the shepherds' pod.

There, off the starboard quarter, he finally saw the low silhouette of a shepherds' platform. It was the standard stainless steel cabin, twin pontoon raft that Toivo had seen several times before. This raft was closer than he expected and he wondered how he had missed it in his first search.

The raft dipped behind a swell and Toivo realized why it hadn't shown up on radar—it was lower in the water than the wave tops. It reappeared on the next crest and he noticed the unusual angle the twin bows made with the blue background of the sky. The aft end had settled below the waterline, almost as if it had begun to submerge. As he watched, the raft disappeared and reappeared behind the wave crests without noticeable change. A whistling shot of vapor brought his attention to the handful of dolphins circling the platform.

Toivo whistled at Poika. "*Go to them. See what they are doing.*"

#

Poika flipped his head, turned and charged off with Tyttö right behind him. At first the big bottlenose dolphin buried his flukes hard into the water in a burst of speed. Personally he was in no hurry, but he didn't want to disappoint Toivo. Humans were so impressed by "going there fast," he thought. Five hundred meters from Sisu he glided along, echoing both the strange ship and the dolphins circling it. He could see it clearly and knew no one on board was alive, not only because he could hear the other dolphins singing, but also because there were no heartbeats from inside the vessel.

He let his mind wander as his momentum carried him toward the raft. Memories were wonderful playthings, possessions he could examine over and over. Though years had passed, he could remember the day he met Toivo. It had been far out to sea. The pod had been chasing fish that day and Poika's mother had been caught in an abandoned drift net. Poika had been circling his mother's body trying to figure out how to free her, too young to understand that she was already dead when Toivo's ship had pulled up alongside. Poika had been unaware of the approaching vessel and it was just luck that it turned out to be a friend.

Toivo had come to the rail and called out to Poika in the language of dolphins. Poika had been stunned. How could a man speak to him? It had filled him with wonder. Surely this was some kind of a miracle. Men did not speak with dolphins. It just didn't happen. Not that dolphins hadn't tried occasionally to speak with men, men just didn't hear dolphins. Even more miraculous was to find out that the man was heartbroken over Poika's mother's death. Even now it amazed him to think about it. Humans never understood death nor the need to sing when one was around the dead. They had no sensitivity to the spirits. Except Toivo, though even he didn't really understand death the way dolphins did.

"*They have gone ahead,*" said Tyttö from behind him, and the images went back into storage.

Poika and Tyttö reached the platform. The factory dolphins circled tighter. Poika and Tyttö floated into their circle and nudged the edge of the nearest pontoon. No one came out.

"*The humans are all dead,*" said the largest factory dolphin.

"*We will join you in your singing,*" said Tyttö and took up station in the ring of circling dolphins.

The spirits had not departed yet, and though Poika wanted to stay and join the singing dolphins, he turned and swam back toward Sisu. Now there was reason to hurry and he pushed himself to reach Sisu before the crew had the nets up.

#

Anxiously waiting for Poika, Toivo checked his crew's progress. They almost had the tuna aboard. He wondered where the rest of the school was and why the shepherds didn't come to claim their fish. As soon as the catch was aboard, he was going to find out.

Toivo leaned as far over the rail as he dared. "*What is it?*" he asked when the dolphin's nose surfaced beside the boat.

"*They have gone ahead.*"

"*The men-who-are-fish?*" Toivo used the term the dolphins had given the shepherds.

"*Yes, the men-who-are-fish.*"

"*How did they die?*"

"*I don't know. The Pod sings to them and it is impolite to interrupt.*"

Toivo turned to Wilho. "Poika says the shepherds are dead. From what, I don't know but we'd better find out."

"Then the fish are ours."

"Christ, yes, but I don't like being relegated to taking fish from dead men."

"Swimmers aren't men," shot Wilho vehemently.

Toivo shook his head. It was true. The shepherds were not like ordinary men. They were part of the factory efforts to drive the independents, like Toivo, from the ocean. Still, they lived and breathed like men. Moreover, the shepherds had been changed without their consent, altered in a laboratory without benefit of a mother's womb. It reminded him that Poika had often expressed the opinion that the shepherds were the first good step mankind had made in a long time. But today was not the time to debate the shepherds' merits again. "Take us over there as soon as we have the nets aboard."

Wilho nodded then sauntered back to the wheel. Toivo watched from the deck railing as the nets were reeled in. Though it seemed to take forever, within minutes the nets were aboard.

Without a word, the wheelsman brought the boat around and headed for the platform. The half-sunken raft still rode low at the stern, the twin pontoons stabbing upward to the sky. On the raised bow Toivo read "Oyster Bay" painted in black block letters.

He eyed the dolphins circling slowly, their slick gray skins glistening in the afternoon sun. An occasional flash of sunlight reflected off the metal tag at the base of the dolphins' dorsal fins. From that he knew they were animals raised and trained by the factory to assist the shepherds with tending their tuna school. The tag carried a serial number that identified each mammal and the company that owned it. Owning dolphins didn't seem right. Slavery was wrong and the dolphins were as much alive and intelligent as most people Toivo knew.

"Easy," he said to Wilho as Sisu slid up against the port pontoon.

Toivo climbed on Sisu's special platform and thumbed the button that lowered it over the side. Once the platform neared the tops of the waves, he leaped over the rail and jumped aboard the raft. He landed gingerly on the wet metal deck, his feet slipping due to the incline, but Toivo managed to maintain his balance.

Below the pumps labored against the slosh of the sea. The shepherd's platform had settled low enough that the aft door was awash. Fortunately, that hatch appeared closed and should still be watertight. Toivo inched forward until he saw a jagged hole blown through the steel plates of the cabin. The twisted metal peeled back like a fragile banana skin. He knew only a naval cannon of some kind could cause that type of penetration and the skin on the back of his neck itched like it had in the forest during his wartime Army days.

He scrutinized the deck for some other clue. A faint red stain trickling over the barrel-like floats caught his eye. He stooped to look closer. Nearly invisible red wisps eddied away in the water. Blood. It should have brought sharks. That explained why the dolphins circled the platform. They were still protecting their shepherds.

He crossed to the starboard pontoon and, leaning against the angle of the deck, sidestepped down to the hatch. It stood open like a black hole into some unearthly mine. A wave sent seawater splashing inside and Toivo heard it slosh down the impenetrable darkness of the hallway beyond.

"Get me a flashlight," he yelled to Wilho.

While he waited, he knelt to check the deck and floats. Here and there he saw strange little dark puncture wounds in the metal. These holes seemed so alien out here on the vast lonely expanse of the Pacific that at first his mind refused to register their source. Suddenly it hit him, shrapnel holes from cannon fire. He shivered involuntarily.

As he started to get up from the deck, his eyes strayed along the pontoon floats. A rounded, dark shape with squarish metal fins stuck from the pontoon he stood on. Christ, he thought, an unexploded torpedo!

Involuntarily he took a step back away from it. What if it blew up?

He heard Wilho behind him. "I'm not sure I want to go in there," Toivo said, knowing he had no choice in case Poika was wrong and someone was alive. He took the offered flashlight.

"What's happened? Is that blood back there?" asked Wilho, pointing over his shoulder to where the red stains had been.

"I think so. There's cannon holes in the cabin and a torpedo stuck in her side." He indicated the near pontoon. "Who would do this?"

Wilho's eyes widened as he glanced around. "Jesus!" he whistled.

Toivo stooped to enter the hatch.

"Toivo," said Wilho, grabbing him by the arm, "Don't do it. This thing's ready to sink."

"What if someone is alive?"

Wilho shrugged.

Carefully Toivo stepped through the doorway. The faint smell of death tickled his nostrils. He forced his mind to ignore it. The floor was slippery and angled down about ten degrees. Not too steep yet but the raft wouldn't have to settle much more by the stern before he'd never get back out. The flashlight sent an eerie spot of yellow around the inside of the cabin. The bulkhead had been pierced in several spots by cannon shrapnel but most were above the waterline. Distinct little water spouts marked where shrapnel had penetrated the hull below what was now sea level. Still, the pumps kept her afloat.

Toivo inched down the hall until he reached the first door. It gaped open. He peered in, cautiously avoiding sticking his head in too far. A pungent smell assaulted him, bringing a wave of nausea. He gagged, cupping his hand over his mouth. He stepped into the room. A huge hole in the wall let in plenty of light for him to see the grisly scene. Two bodies lay crisscrossed on the floor. They had been shot several times, and were barely recognizable as male and female. Toivo gagged again. This time he vomited. He struggled backward out of the room, the awful taste of it in his mouth.

His feet slipped on the wet steel deck and he staggered on to the next room. The platform shuddered. Toivo fell against the bulkhead, catching himself with one arm. He waited, poised for flight. The boat steadied. He heard Wilho's calls echo down the metal corridor. He ignored them.

The next room had been quarters for one of the crew. The bedding had been stripped off and it floated leadenly in the seawater. What remained of the furniture was smashed and heaped in a pile. There were no more bodies.

He crept farther down the hall. The open hatchway he'd entered through was around the corner and now only a faint glimmer of daylight filtered over his shoulder. He came to the last room and pushed the door open. The yellow circle from the flashlight passed over instruments that were broken and dark, jagged pieces of plastic and glass. The radio was riddled with bullet holes. He aimed the light toward the floor. A broken, bloodstained body lay face up beneath a bent stool. A bullet had blown away half of her face.

Toivo pulled back into the hall. His stomach revolted. For a long minute his knees went rubbery and he had to brace himself against the bulkhead to keep from falling. Who would do such a thing? He forced down the nausea, held his breath and looked back into the control room.

In an instant his mind recorded every detail. She had been young, tall, with the webbed hands of the shepherds. Short brown hair covered what was left of her head. She might have been beautiful, but the body's grotesque position and the blood made it hard to tell.

The platform shuddered again and Toivo heard one of the pumps screech and stop. He lunged up the hallway. The platform settled lower. The seawater was gaining on the remaining pump. A wave slid through the open hatchway, and surged against his ankles. He tried to run, but the water clutched at him. Another wave rushed in against his knees. He heard Wilho yelling. Poika and Tyttö had joined in, adding their frightened whistles.

Toivo dove for the door, half swimming, half crawling. His mind blazed with a kaleidoscope of surrealistic images – water mixed with blood illuminated by shafts of sunlight and the bodies. He had stopped thinking but survival instincts carried him onward. Grabbing the lip of the hatchway with his left hand, he pulled himself through as another wave crashed in. He struggled through the wall of water into the sunlight. Instinctively he dashed across the short, flat section of deck to where Wilho leaned over the rail from Sisu's platform, his arm outstretched. Toivo grabbed it and swung across to the metal scaffold. A gurgling hiss roared up behind him, almost as if the factory vessel were a living thing grasping for one more victim. A geyser of trapped air spouted from the open doorway as the sea rushed in and the raft settled beneath the waves. Wilho already had the winches hauling the dolphin-watch platform back up to the main deck.

"Full reverse," he shouted, but Gunnar already had the engines churning in reverse and the sturdy fishing boat backed away from the sinking structure.

"*Poika, Tyttö*," whistled Toivo. "*Are you all right?*"

In unison the dolphins leaped above the gunwhale, somersaulting back into the sea with a towering splash.

Wilho eased Toivo down until he sat on the deck. "Are you all right?"

Toivo shook like a wet puppy. "Yes, I'll be okay. But the shepherds were—murdered. Shot."

Wilho blinked in disbelief. "Shot!" Then his face hardened. "It was bound to come to this sooner or later."

Toivo looked hard at his friend, trying to penetrate Wilho's granite mask. "Do you think the Guild did this?"

"Why not? The swimmers claim our fishing territory, push the wild fish farther from fertile feeding grounds, try to take away our life. Eventually someone was going to fight back."

"But the IFG agreed to fight in the courts, not out here. What about the Chinese? Or the Russians?"

Wilho threw up his hands. "You always blame the Russians. This isn't between the Russians and the Chinese. It's between us and the factories."

Toivo knew there was no point in arguing further. "It doesn't matter. We must report it to the U.N. Fisheries Council. This is piracy. Radio it in now. There were three of them, two women, one man. The vessel was the Oyster Bay. And you can report the school lost, except for the few fish we netted."

"What about the factory dolphins?"

"They can stay or go as they want. Poika can find out what they want to do." Toivo turned and yelled up to the wheelhouse. "Gunnar, make sure the catch is frozen."

The big Swede nodded as he stepped out of the wheelhouse. He swaggered down the steel steps to the deck and headed aft.

Wilho bent to offer Toivo a hand, but Toivo waved him off. "Let me rest a few minutes."

"Okay," said Wilho and started for the wheelhouse.

Toivo turned his eyes to the sea. For a long moment he said nothing. Finally he yelled, "Wilho, keep someone on the radar scope at all times."

It wasn't long before Toivo had the U. N. frigate on the radio. After he'd explained what they'd found, the UN Captain ordered Sisu to wait the two days it would take for the frigate to arrive.

Toivo stayed on the bridge for a long time pondering the ominous events that had taken hold of this fishing trip. Finally he went down the ladder to his quarters, not sure if he could sleep. It was going to be a long night and two days wasted waiting. And once the UN ship arrived who knew how long the questions would last. This had not been a good trip.

Chapter 4

Captain Poddington leaned on the railing outside the wheelhouse and allowed himself a moment to admire the beauty of the rolling blue Pacific. For once, he'd taken off his white captain's hat and dangled it over the rail in one hand allowing the wind to ripple through his thin red-orange hair. The bright tropical sun beat down on his face and arms, browning the exposed skin except for the pair of tattoos on his left arm. On the forearm was a tuna with over-sized teeth. On the biceps a naked woman straddling an anchor was half-visible from under his short, white, shirtsleeve.

Time slowed while Poddington waited to see if the other ship found the Oyster Bay. They had tracked the bigger vessel's course on radar but the raft was too small to show up so there was no way to actually know if the raft had been found or not. Perhaps it had sunk. Poddington hoped so. So far there had been no reports that anyone had sighted the Oyster Bay.

Waiting left too much time to imagine trouble coming. He tried to tell himself that things were going well enough. He forced himself to think of more pleasant things, like the fact that soon they would be making more money than he'd ever dreamed of. Still, he missed being a fisherman. It occurred to him that maybe he wasn't cut out for this kind of work. He shifted his concentration back to the company business. It wouldn't be long before the chemists aboard had enough PXC synthesized to load the submarine. Then she'd be off to the United States, smuggling her cargo in where U.S. Customs would never be looking for it.

Then, too, there was his Chinese contact, John Him, who'd promised to pay in cash for the dolphin carcasses. Easy money, and a lot of it. It was amazing what breaking the law did to the price of an otherwise cheap commodity. Maybe he and Sleena would take a little vacation to Singapore. He'd always wanted to see more of the Far East. Why not? He'd leave Deep in charge for a couple of weeks. What could go wrong?

He thought about the swimmers again. Why couldn't he get them out of his mind? He could still see the woman's eyes pleading, looking at him. No, he would not feel sympathy. They were mutants who'd put him out of work. They deserved to die.

Deep stepped out of the wheelhouse to join Poddington at the railing. Right behind him stalked Luis Jones, a short, stocky man with black hair, dark eyes and a darker personality. Jones, or whatever his real name was, was the second mate. He had been assigned to his position on board by the drug cartel that leased the ship. He was not someone Poddington trusted, and even if he did, Jones didn't know the first thing about running the ship.

"Captain," said Deep, with a furtive glance over his shoulder at the second mate, "we just picked up a radio transmission—they found the Oyster Bay. They saw the dead swimmers before the raft went down."

"Damn. Well, at least the raft sank. Did they identify themselves?" demanded Poddington, spinning around from the rail.

"A fisherman. The ship's named the Sisu. Finnish, I think."

"Not that idiot with the pet dolphins." Poddington thought about it for a moment. He remembered seeing that boat many times. Always with a full hold. And, according to the scuttlebutt, all because the Finn could talk those dolphins into helping him find fish. Envy? Yes, Poddington had envied the fisherman. Now there were other things to consider. "Who was he calling?"

"He called the U.N. frigate that's out here chasing illegal whalers. The frigate told him to hang steady until they get there. Two days, they said."

"Well, that'll teach me to think things are going smoothly."

Luis Jones shoved past Deep. "We will have to make sure this Finnish fisherman isn't around long enough to become a problem." The short man's dark eyes held a fierce light, almost daring someone to argue.

Deep's forehead furrowed. "You mean you're going to kill another fisherman?"

"Might have to make them disappear," said the second mate, the insinuation clear.

Poddington watched the horror crease his first mate's leathery, wrinkled face. He couldn't afford an open conflict between Deep and Jones.

He started to interrupt the conversation but Deep cut him off. "Why? They've already radioed what they know. These fishermen can't do us any more harm."

There was some truth to his friend's words, but Poddington knew the people he worked for now didn't take chances with loose ends. It didn't matter what he thought, the fisherman had to go. But how could the Sunrise

Savior be connected to the murder? Perhaps they could just move off, disappear themselves for a while.

"What are you waiting for?" asked Jones. "We've got two days to get this done and get out of here."

"So why not just get out of here?" asked Deep.

"They saw the bodies. They saw the swimmers were shot. They can testify that it was murder. Without any witnesses, there hasn't been any murder. And now that the raft's sunk, no one will ever recover the bodies."

Deep shook his head. The crow's feet around his eyes stood out. "I don't like it."

Poddington looked at this friend and first mate, "You knew this might happen when we took this job. And you know there's no turning back now. We've got to protect ourselves."

As he talked, Poddington watched Luis Jones for any sign of softening. The black-haired man was unreadable.

Deep turned back to the wheelhouse, stopped, then turned back to look Poddington square in the eye. "Pod, ever since you took up with that black bitch you've changed."

The muscles knotted in Poddington's jaw. The blood vessels in his neck bulged thick with rushing blood. Involuntarily he drew back his fist. He gritted his teeth, fighting the urge to slug his only friend. Slowly he lowered his fist.

"Don't ever say anything like that again."

Deep had retreated a step or two. His face was gray-white like fireplace ash. "Okay, Pod," he muttered softly. "I don't like it but I won't let you down. We've been shipmates too long to ruin it now."

Poddington forced a smile. "That's it, Deep," and he slapped his first mate on the shoulder. "We need a plan. Some way to take out the Finn's boat."

Deep stood silent.

"And we need it done before the frigate arrives," snapped Jones.

"We've got two days. Then it's too late," retorted Deep.

"He's right," said Poddington, glad to support his first mate on at least one issue. "I'm not taking on any warships in this tub."

"I don't care how, just do it," said Jones, his thin lips tense and hard.

Poddington exhaled slowly, trying to stay calm. "We could rush them right now."

Deep looked grim. "It'll be dark soon. That deck gun isn't radar controlled, you know."

It was almost as if Deep hoped the fisherman would escape during the night. "And we don't know how fast they are."

Poddington found himself wishing he didn't have to kill these fishermen. The look in Jones' eyes said different. Tomorrow, they'd do it tomorrow.

He wiped his forehead with the back of his hand. "We'll work in on them tomorrow. Maybe we can catch them with their nets out. Use the signal light to let the submarine know what we're up to."

Poddington watched Deep shuffle to the port signal light mounted on the rail. He's a good man to have around, he reminded himself. But a fisherman at heart, maybe not up to the kind of life Poddington had gotten them into. Then again, ever since his son died in that hunting accident, Deep had been a quieter, less aggressive man. Poddington could remember more than a few bar fights around the world where he was damn glad it was Deep covering his back. He'd even seen Deep take a knife away from a slant-eyed squirt in Beijing and slit the little shit from ear-to-ear. They barely beat the law getting out of town that time.

In fact, it was Jones that bothered Poddington. He couldn't be sure what the second mate was up to. It was obvious he didn't have much sea experience. Poddington would keep his eye on him.

What had seemed like such a good deal when he'd lost his fishing trawler to the mortgage company was fast becoming too complicated and dangerous. When it put him at odds with Deep, there was something very wrong.

Chapter 5

Toivo sat with his chin cupped in both palms staring at the chessboard. He had no interest in the game tonight. His mind was filled with images of grotesque bodies, of seawater mixed with blood. Who had done this? He hated to think Wilho was right. When he had joined the Independent Fisherman's Guild it had been to pressure the World Courts into keeping the open ocean free for anyone's use. More than once he had heard talk in waterfront pubs about driving the swimmers and the factory ships from the ocean by force. It had seemed like drunken talk at the time. Now he wasn't so sure.

"Are you going to move?" asked Wilho, leaning back in his chair.

Toivo refocused on the pieces. His knight had been poised to put Wilho's king in check. He couldn't remember Wilho's last move. Already his friend had slipped out of the trap left from the night before. Unable to think, he moved the knight ahead.

Wilho put his half-empty beer bottle on the corner of the table. "Thank you very much," he said and slid the waiting bishop into the square holding Toivo's knight.

Toivo stood up. "Enough for tonight," he said, stepping back and sliding his chair in.

"Thinking about the swimmers?" asked Wilho, scraping his chair across the steel deck.

Toivo turned his back to his friend and peeked out the porthole at the black, night sea. Ripples of moonlight traced the dark swells and a blanket of stars drew upward from the edge of the horizon. Toivo didn't like to hear Wilho call them swimmers, like they were less than human. But murder made name-calling seem so trivial. "Killing is wrong, no matter what justification you use. They didn't ask to be what they are, no more than we asked to be men."

"Toivo, my old friend," said Wilho, gulping another swallow of beer, "it is done and you cannot change that. Thank God it was not us."

Toivo heard his friend's voice go hard, taut. He turned to face him and saw the familiar wrinkles etched around the eyes like tooling in old leather. "Is this what it will come to? War between us and the factories?"

"Maybe, unless the courts put a stop to it. Men who loose their livelihood become desperate. There are a lot of boats worse off than we are. If it weren't for Poika and Tyttö who knows how badly off we'd be. Maybe you'd feel differently if they were going to repossess Sisu?"

"Sisu is paid for," snapped Toivo, but he knew that wasn't what Wilho was driving at.

"But we have food, money in our pockets—well, not so much money this trip." Wilho laughed at his own joke and Toivo couldn't help smiling for a minute. The wheelsman ran both hands through his hair. "If we don't stop the damn factories soon, there won't be enough fish for us either."

Toivo shook his head in disgust. It was true. The factories took the most fertile ocean areas, pumped them full of fertilizer and bait fish, then stocked them with millions of hatchery-raised tuna yearlings that gorged themselves on every baitfish for miles until they forced the wild fish out. Still, once in a while the fringes around the factory areas provided prime growth zones for the wild tuna where they got fat on the spillover from the factory program. It wasn't often. Actually it didn't matter. The factories expanded their areas all the time; soon there would be nothing left.

"No," he repeated, realizing he was rationalizing the problem away. "Killing is wrong. There are peaceful means we should use. Maybe it wasn't the IFG."

"Maybe not, but if not it should have been. We have the most to lose."

"No," said Toivo, gritting his teeth. "It's got to be the Russians. They have nothing to lose by killing, and it is something they know all too well."

Wilho wrinkled his nose. "You only wish it was the Russians because you hate them so much. But you forget, they're not like they used to be."

Images of gunfire, of looted farmhouses, of peasants armed with bolt-action rifles and pitchforks raiding across the border into the Finnish farms flooded Toivo's mind. He'd been in the Army when hordes of starving Russian peasants had stormed into Finland hell-bent on taking whatever food they could find. At first the thought of shooting them had made him sick, until he'd seen what they did to the Finnish farming families they had overrun. He remembered one little red farmhouse in particular, with neat white trim around the windows, sitting on a marshy bay. The mother had been shot in the back of the head, the father strung up from a tree and stabbed countless times. They had found the two boys pitchforked through their chests and left to bleed to death in a shit-filled stall in the barn.

"No," he said, shaking off the memories, "they made a mess of their country and they tried to ruin Finland too. That time they found we were ready for them. I'm beginning to think that they are the ones trying to take control of high seas fishing."

"Then we should help them."

Toivo felt the blood rise in his neck. "I'll never help a Russian, not now, not ever." He turned and looked back out the porthole. His teeth clenched so tight they hurt at the fillings. He should let the U.N. handle the matter. After all, he and Wilho were fisherman, not soldiers.

"I'm going to bed," said Wilho.

He heard Wilho tramp to the ladder and bounce down it to the lower deck where their cabins were. Toivo stayed for a long time at the porthole.

#

The five Factory dolphins from the Oyster Bay swam alongside Poika and Tyttö. In the dark behind them, Sisu churned steadily over the swells. Poika echoed ahead, but the ocean ran empty except for a school of fry and the fuzzy smear of plankton floating off to starboard. Deeper, the echoes bounced off the underwater waves riding the thermoclines. Not since Poika was a youngling was he fooled by these softer pings. The other dolphins were silent tonight. He had waited respectfully until they had finished their spirit song and had eaten well, diving for many-arms. Now Poika hoped they could talk more about the men-who-are-fish.

"*I am the-male-who-speaks-with-man-friend,*" he said to the factory pod still not sure who spoke for them.

The largest female turned a wary eye toward Poika. "*I am she-who-was-tagged-first. I am proud to lead this pod.*"

"*What became of the-men-who-are-fish?*"

"We went to the plankton beds as we have done many times only this time men were there in thunder-ship. Not a ship-that-pulls-fish-catcher but one that rumbled with death. Thunder-ship made the water explode, then came alongside and some men forced their way aboard. More thunder came from the ship of the men-who-are-fish. The other men left us and a boat rose from undersea to shoot metal fish at the ship of men-who-are-fish. We were left to sing with the departing spirits."

"Did these men from thunder-ship take anything?"

"Yes, the thunder-ship dragged the food-beds for the yellow plankton with pipes that sucked up the sea."

Poika swam silently for a short time, wondering at the things men found of value, the objects and the intangible "money" as Toivo called it. Poika still could not comprehend what money was worth. His thoughts returned to the new dolphins. *"Where will you go?"*

"It is unclear to us now. If we are not intruding we will swim with your pod for a time. We would like to study more about the way men think."

"Stay as long as you like. If you have questions for the men I will ask Toivo for answers, but I must warn you that his answers defy logic."

#

Toivo stood near the bow, feeling the early morning sun on his face. As he watched the dolphins he thought about the U.N. vessel still a day and a half away. He hated to waste the time but they had been ordered to remain on site. He scanned Sisu. Gunner squatted on the fantail teaching Helmar to mend nets. Wilho stood, legs spread, at the wheel. The others were below at the endless card game.

They were a good crew. Even so, the meager catch was hardly fair reward for their efforts. It was barely worth selling. Still they needed to get them to market. Maybe the price would be higher than the last time. Besides Wilho had to get to Honolulu before his daughter left.

Poika rolled over and swam on his back, looking up at Toivo. *"Fish,"* he whistled, and raced away to port.

Toivo squinted against the glare, but couldn't see the tuna. Nonetheless he yelled "Tuna," and pointed after Poika.

"I knew our luck would change," shouted Wilho from the wheelhouse. He snapped on the intercom and relayed the message.

Toivo spit in his hands and rubbed them together. Now he could see the fins knifing the water as the tuna ran from the dolphins. Poika, Tyttö and the five factory dolphins raced after the fish, gaining as Toivo watched. It wasn't going to be long before they caught the school, a good-sized school from the look of it, and no sign of yellow.

"Ready on the nets," Toivo commanded, but Gunnar and Helmar had the nets almost in place as the rest of the crew dashed up on deck. "They'll turn soon."

The crew scrambled to their duty stations. The coils of ropes thumped on the deck, the faint squeak of block and tackle, the swish of the nets, all of it music to Toivo's ears. They pulled nets from the twin lockers near the fantail, joking and laughing as they worked. Toivo felt their hope. Like a well-orchestrated team they set the nets, ready for the turn. Toivo judged the dolphins' progress, gauged their intercept time, and waited for the precise moment.

"Now," he shouted, dropping his hand.

The net spilled over the side. Wilho automatically began the turn to align the half-open net with the onrushing school. Already the tuna had circled, heading for the boat. The dolphin herded them straight for the nets.

"Steady, here they come."

Poika leaped high in the air, as if trying to see the boat. As he landed the big Bottlenose corrected his course to push the tuna toward the middle of the net.

"*Good boy Poika*," called Toivo, using the back of his tongue against the roof of his mouth to cut the clicking noises at the precise intervals.

The tuna surged into the net. Their weight sent a shudder through Sisu. The lines that held the nets sprang taut popping a mist of fine droplets as the strands twisted under the pressure. Wilho gunned the engines and Sisu raced to complete the circle.

Some of the tuna wheeled to flee, but the factory dolphins forced them back into the net. Sisu closed the net. The crew set themselves to pull the catch aboard up the stern ramp.

Wilho stepped down out of the wheelhouse and strode to Toivo with a detectable swagger, the boat idling in place. "It'll be a good trip after all."

"Yes," said Toivo, for us, he thought. But his mind ran flashes of the dead shepherds. It hadn't been good for them. Somewhere out there the murderers roamed, maybe to kill again.

"Enni and I will have a good time now. There will be money enough to enjoy a holiday." Wilho eyed Toivo for a minute.

"Yes, we're all ready for a holiday. This has been the toughest trip yet. I don't look forward to putting out to sea again." Toivo scratched his head and looked at his friend. The smile was the same, but the weather had put extra wrinkles in his dry skin, wrinkles that wouldn't have been there if Wilho had stayed in the city. Maybe Toivo should quit trying to play out his fantasy and sign on with one of the canneries. "Sometimes I think it would be easier if I went under contract."

"Work for a factory! The sun must be getting to you. Sisu would be little more than a bus. We'd be hauling fish from the factory schools, and bait fish for the tuna, and plankton fertilizer. You'd miss the chase, the freedom. The money isn't enough."

Leaning on the rail, Toivo turned back to look out to sea. "You're right. There's still enough fish to make a living."

"Besides," said Wilho, slapping Toivo on the back, "now we have seven dolphins to hunt tuna."

"Yes. For as long as they stay."

"Look there." Wilho pointed at a dark silhouette against the distant horizon. "It looks like a tanker. What's a tanker doing out here?"

Toivo squinted at the distant shape. There was something familiar about the outline, something that tickled his memory but wouldn't come to his consciousness. The black form on the horizon sat like a blotch on nature's order. For several long minutes Toivo watched it before he realized it was either stationary or moving very slowly. If it was having trouble why weren't there any distress calls?

He turned and saw his crew just beginning to winch the net aboard, the fish fast disappearing down to the lower deck where they were gutted and frozen.

"Get those nets aboard," he encouraged the men. "Wilho, what do you make of that ship? I'd say they're dead in the water."

"Yes, I think you are right. But what is it? It looks like a cross between a coastal tanker and a suction dredge."

"I don't know. Bring me the binoculars."

As Wilho dashed to the wheelhouse, Toivo looked for Poika. The dolphins were nowhere to be seen. Strange, he thought, usually they hung around close during a catch. The men always tossed over strips of tuna while they cleaned the big fish. Now the dolphins were gone.

The dark silhouette hung near the horizon. Wilho returned and Toivo pressed the glasses to his eyes. He blinked away the initial vision, and looked again. The ship was broad and squat, more than twice as long as Sisu. She had a raised forecastle that dropped sharply to the long main deck, which carried a maze of piping and valves. A triple-decked aft cabin sat squarely on the stern. Large twin pipes ran down over the side into the ocean amidships. He could not make out any of the crew at this distance.

"Wilho, as soon as the nets are up we're going to see if they are having trouble."

Wilho squinted from the sun's glare and stared at the distant vessel. "I don't like it. There is no reason for such a ship to be here."

"Maybe not, but we're going to find out what they're up to," said Toivo under his breath. Subconsciously he was gauging the time it would take to get the fish aboard.

"I'll be standing by in the wheelhouse," said Wilho and he ambled off down the deck.

Toivo took another look around for the dolphins. They were still missing. Too many strange things were going on—dead shepherds, disappearing dolphins, factory tuna aboard Sisu and tankers adrift in the fishing zones. He thought about the old days when they only worried about catching fish.

Sisu's engines raced, throwing a boiling white froth behind her and Toivo realized the nets were aboard. The tuna boat shuddered and lunged ahead. Toivo checked the stern and saw Gunner and Helmar with their fillet knives out dropping down the ladder to the freezer deck.

Toivo turned back to the tanker. It was no longer stationary. The strange vessel was closing fast and already he could see the men scurrying across the deck. What he saw next made his heart stop. The strange vessel was turning toward Sisu and a half a dozen men were struggling to open a hatch in the foredeck. As he watched, the hatch swung back and a naval gun turret rose out of the forecastle. The men clambered through the hatch and the cannon barrel swung toward Sisu.

A silent prayer whispered through dry lips, then he yelled to Wilho, "Hard to starboard. Flank speed."

Wilho spun the wheel and Sisu heeled over as she swung to starboard. The wake behind them marked their turn but it seemed too slow, the curve too gentle. Behind them, the other ship was making way now and she followed Sisu with increasing speed.

There could be no doubt. These men were after Sisu. Visions of dead shepherds blinded him for an instant. These had to be the men who murdered the shepherds. But what could they be after? Surely not the tuna. There had to be something else.

The other boat was closer now and Toivo could see the men on deck. The grisly barrel of the main turret tracked Sisu like an ominous finger of death pointing straight at them. From the main deck a forest of skeletal rifle barrels bristled in the hands of the men gathered at the rail.

"Wilho," shouted Toivo, "have Pentii send an S.O.S. Tell Gunner to get the shark rifle." Toivo felt his stomach twisting up in knots. He saw the fear in Wilho's eyes. It mirrored his own. This was impossible. There was no reason for any of this. Yet it was happening.

Toivo ran to the wheelhouse. "Wilho," he said once inside, "get out the flare gun and anything else we can use as a weapon."

Wilho's face was white. "It won't be enough."

Toivo wiped the sweat from his forehead. "Probably not. But we will put up what fight we can."

"Captain," said Pentii from the cramped radio room behind the bulkhead, "they are jamming us."

"Try another frequency, but keep trying. Maybe the U. N. will hear us though it won't do much good unless they can send an airplane right this minute."

Pentii ducked down behind the bulkhead and Toivo could hear him frantically repeating, "Mayday, Mayday. This is Sisu. We are under attack. Mayday, Mayday."

"Get off the deck," yelled Toivo, leaning out of the wheelhouse door. Half of his crew stood huddled around the fantail gawking at the closing vessel. They dashed for the gangway below. In a minute the deck was clear.

Gunnar came up the stairs to the wheelhouse and stepped up behind Toivo. "Here's the rifle."

Toivo took the bolt action .30-06 from him. "Get below."

Gunner looked Toivo in the eye. "Nope," he said and pulled a worn revolver from his belt. "I'm not going out without a fight."

"Good man," said Toivo and patted the Swede's right arm.

There wasn't much they could do but stare at the threatening cannon's ominous muzzle. An orange flame belched from the cannon barrel. The whistle of the shell rushed at them and a huge geyser leaped skyward just behind Sisu. Toivo winced.

A moment went by and the cannon roared again. The eerie whistle and the bellowing explosion seemed to come at Toivo out of a dream. Sisu's stern erupted in a ball of fire and twisted steel. The engines whined upward as they free-revved, suddenly unencumbered by a propeller. Sisu drifted, rudderless and dead in the water.

Toivo wiped the tears from the corners of his eyes and forced himself to watch as the strange ship neared. Still several hundred meters away, Toivo's heart stopped. He saw the men kneel at the rail, sighting down their rifles. The unmistakable flashes of gunfire made him flinch. Bullets splattered the water around Sisu. A couple hit the cabin bulkhead, whining away as they ricocheted off the steel plates.

Toivo clutched the rifle in his hands. It wasn't much but it was all he had. He looked at Wilho, who huddled below the window beside him, the flare gun tight in his right hand. Toivo's stomach twisted in a knot and beads of sweat trickled along his palms. He made a silent vow to kill as many of them as he could before they got him. He pulled back the bolt and rammed home the first brass round in the magazine.

The dark vessel pulled closer, the roar of her engines rattling the windows in Sisu's wheelhouse. The knife-edged bow slicing through the wave tops headed straight for Sisu. It was only a matter of minutes.

"A city job wouldn't look so bad now," he said to Wilho.

Wilho's face was drawn tight. His mouth quivered but he didn't say anything. Toivo slapped him roughly on the shoulder and turned to open the rear wheelhouse window. He slipped the rifle barrel out the opening and rested it on the sill.

Gunner crawled to the other window and aimed the pistol out through the opening. The sinister ship roared nearer. The men on her decks held their guns loosely. A couple of them fired wildly from the hip, the rattle of automatic weapons unmistakable.

When less than 50 meters separated Sisu from the other ship, Toivo laid the sights on a burly man near the bow. His mouth went dry. He had killed before and the memories of it brought bile to his throat. His rage forced it down and his mind went cold, as if someone else pulled the trigger. His mind recorded every instant and locked it in his memory. He squeezed the trigger and felt the recoil. The bullet struck and the man staggered, falling over the side, his gun splashing into the sea with him. The armed tanker never slowed. Those still on deck dove for cover.

Toivo fired again but the bullet whined off the steel deck. He rammed home another cartridge, but held his fire until he had a good target. There weren't many bullets and he didn't want to waste a single one.

Just then a hail of gunfire rained on Sisu. Bullets shattered the glass in the wheelhouse and whined around inside the metal bulkheads. The massive ship bore down on Sisu, her bow racing ever closer to Sisu's stern. At full speed the intruder rammed her. Metal screeched as the hulls ground together. Toivo fired, and another man screamed and grabbed his chest. Gunnar's pistol went off beside Toivo's ear.

Toivo worked the bolt to chamber another bullet. As he put the rifle up to the broken window, Wilho pulled the gun away from him.

"Get out of here," his friend said, nodding toward the sea.

"Are you crazy? You'll be killed."

"I'm going to die anyway." Wilho choked, and for the first time Toivo noticed the blood oozing from his mouth. Two bright crimson patches stained his shirt. "Get out. Maybe they won't see you."

Toivo started to protest, but Gunner grabbed him by the shirt and shoved him through the door farthest from the knot of armed men swarming aboard Sisu. Toivo stumbled as he tried to regain his balance, his arms flailing for a handhold. Gunner pushed him over the cable railing. Headlong, Toivo toppled into the sea. The crack of gunfire rang in his ears as the warm salt water closed over his head.

He surfaced, sputtering for air. Bullets splattered against the metal wheelhouse, sending tiny shards of steel into the water. Gunner fell in a flurry of bullets, little red puffs blossoming from his faded blue shirt. Wilho fired the 30-06, recocked it, and then fell backward as the automatic weapons found their mark. Through the open door, Toivo could see Wilho's dark silhouette slump down inside the wheelhouse.

Toivo swam away from Sisu, his frenzied strokes thrashing the water. More gunfire. He dove as deep as he could. Bullets sputtered where they struck the water, a horrible reminder of what would happen if he got too near the surface. Suddenly he felt a nudge. Poika was beside him, sliding his head up under Toivo's hand. Toivo grabbed the base of Poika's dorsal fin and the dolphin forged ahead with his powerful flukes. The water rushed past Toivo's face, pulling at him. He grabbed Poika with both hands and held on for as long as his lungs would allow.

Toivo let go of Poika and drifted to the surface. His head bobbed clear and he gulped in the air as he looked back at Sisu. The half-frigate, half-tanker had drawn up abeam of her. Toivo studied his adversary, memorizing every detail. He noted the name, Sunrise Savior, on her bow. Now he realized why the boat had seemed familiar. Sunrise Savior was a research vessel that was supposed to be monitoring pollution on the high seas for some worldwide environmental group. He had seen her once or twice in port somewhere. And this was not she. So what ship was it? And why would she attack Sisu?

But that wasn't all he saw. A short distance away, the low silhouette of an ancient submarine's conning tower rose ominously from the sea, the periscope a dark mast against the blue sky. Her bow was aimed at Sisu and

Toivo knew it was only a matter of time before they put a torpedo into his fishing boat and sank her. The ache in his heart grew.

On board Sisu, men were busy emptying the tuna from the hold. Others stood around the railing peering into the water, but their guns hung loosely from their slings. The shooting had ended. There was no sign of his crew. In his heart he knew they had been killed to the last man.

Memories of the dead shepherds rushed back, only instead, he saw Wilho's face on the corpse, and Gunner's, and Helmar's. Tears burned their way down his cheeks. He remembered his father telling him that Finnish men didn't cry, but he couldn't stop.

Poika stuck his head up next to Toivo. "*Bad men send Wilho ahead before his time?*"

"*Yes*," choked Toivo.

Poika nodded in his strangely human manner. "*I am sorry we could not do more. We went to learn more about the strange ship and could not return fast enough to warn you.*"

Poika sank below the surface without a ripple. Toivo felt the nudge and knew the dolphin wanted to get farther away from the killers. Almost without thinking, he grabbed the offered dorsal again. Flanked by the rest of the pod, Poika swam hard for a half hour, coming to the surface only often enough for Toivo to breathe. Shortly after the sun went down, Poika stopped and left Toivo to tread water while he and the other dolphins hunted fish.

Exhaustion finally overtook Toivo and the night assumed a hazy dream-like quality. For what seemed like a long time, the dolphins didn't return and he assumed they were not having good hunting. Then again, maybe they weren't gone that long. Panting for breath, trying to wipe the salt water from his burning eyes and still stay afloat, Toivo finally wished he had been smart enough to grab a lifejacket.

His muscles dulled as the hours wore on. Treading water became a mechanical reaction. The dolphins returned but Toivo couldn't be sure how often. Their hunting took them deep and far but they stayed with Toivo between dives. Poika and Tyttö spent part of the night cradling Toivo between their bodies like a piece of meat between two slices of bread in a sandwich. For a few minutes he slept. Eventually the dolphins left to hunt again and Toivo struggled alone.

SHEPHERDS

With the initial glow of sunrise Toivo saw the first shark fin circling only a dozen meters away.

Chapter 6

On the Homestead, Ici sat cross-legged on the flat roof of the cabin. Today was the 4th of July. It was his favorite holiday, even better than Christmas. He loved the fireworks. As a kid on Guam, he had never missed a Fourth, always finding a place on the beach close to the display, usually with Ni. Nowadays he put on his own fireworks show and tonight would be the best one yet.

In a way, it was a chance to show off his resourcefulness. He had gone to a lot of trouble getting fireworks in the middle of the Pacific. At first it had been hard to find crewmen on the factory ship who would bring what he wanted. Now he could always count on Jimmy Mandel and Petey to have a cache on board.

Too bad Michael had been transferred to Turtle. He'd enjoyed the fireworks almost as much as Ici. But, Ici reminded himself, it was better for Michael to command his own raft. He wondered if Michael would have fireworks on board Turtle.

Ici's mind returned to the business at hand and he looked out through the iron railing. The dolphins were keeping tabs on the tuna school about a hundred meters off Homestead's bow. He followed the fish by the distinct yellow flashes where the sunlight reflected off their scales as they circled Homestead. Tomorrow they would rendezvous with the factory ship, Martin B. and together they would harvest the larger tuna. The fish would be hauled away to the Star-Kist cannery and Ici's credit account would grow. He hoped it would be a heavy count, maybe enough to wipe out his debt. Hoping was one thing; the reality was that there weren't enough big fish.

The swells licked gently over the twin prows of the pontoons. They were riding with only minimal positive buoyancy right now, and the craft sat unusually low in the water. It made her wallow in the troughs. To Ici, the ride was comfortable.

The wind gusted through his straight black hair and the sparkle of the sun off the water made him blink. A few high cirrus clouds stood out like single brushstrokes of white on a blue canvas. He knew these clouds forewarned of a storm brewing miles away, but today it was beautiful and tonight would be clear. He loved sitting in the sun. Normally just being on deck on such a nice day would have been enough. Today, however, he couldn't forget the radio transmission they had intercepted yesterday. He couldn't believe the Oyster Bay had been sunk and that Lisa, Vern and Wing were dead. It had to be a hoax. But why didn't they answer Homestead's radio calls?

He stood, flexed his knees twice to loosen them, and dove off the roof into the blue-green water. Down he went, pulling himself under with his partially webbed hands, kicking with webbed feet. The quiet enveloped him. The buoyant feeling of the warm water blocked out everything else. Pencil beams of golden sunlight danced through the wave crests forming ever-changing patterns. He loved the feeling of freedom.

Now however, he had work to do. Breast stroking hard, he easily outdistanced the raft and soon found himself looking at the bright yellow tuna, the broad sides of the big fish forming a solid wall of living flesh. The dolphins turned them, herding the school in gentle switchbacks and circles, keeping the school of speedy fish from outdistancing the shepherd's raft.

Ici swam closer, examining the mature fish, his experienced eye checking for signs of sickness, and more importantly right now, judging the time left before the roe would have to be harvested. He reached out one hand and gingerly stroked the side of a passing female. She was over 200 kilograms, yet with a flick of her tail she shot away. Ici knew she was almost ready.

For a moment Ici forgot himself and his work. He rolled into a ball and let himself sink slowly into the depths. The streaks of light twisted and bobbed as he tumbled, filling him with a warm glow. A few more minutes, then he'd need a breath of air and would return to Homestead. The tuna flashed overhead, dark shapes passing between Ici and the sun, like miniature storm clouds, trailing their shadows across him. The longer shadows of the dolphins floated by overhead and the school turned away to the left.

Ici pushed once hard toward the surface and glided along, drifting upward toward the raft. Two hundred meters later he breached. Homestead glided past and he swam hard until he caught the rail and pulled himself aboard. He looked over his shoulder at the blowing dolphins. If only he could swim like they did.

He shook the water off and climbed the stainless steel rungs on the cabin face, up to the roof. For a long time he sat just feeling the sun warm and dry him. Daydreams of being a dolphin swam through his mind.

He heard light footsteps on the ladder and turned to see Ni's lithe, bronzed body snake up through the hatchway. She wore only the bottom half of a skimpy bikini and her small round breasts drew his eyes immediately. He never tired of looking at her graceful, slender body. She was a delicate work of art.

They were both genetically altered for their role at sea. "Shepherds" was what most people called them. "Cowboys" they more often called themselves. For now, he liked the idea of being a cowboy; there was something romantic about it. At least for Ici, the idea of living on the frontier, herding livestock, being in the open and free seemed to fit. They were the new cowboys of the ocean. Actually though, Ni was as different from him as he was from one of the "lubbers." He was first generation, the initial experiment that had succeeded. Ni was second generation. She had more fully webbed hands and feet. Her head and shoulders were more streamlined to allow her to swim faster and her lungs had increased capacity that was better suited to underwater work. On top of all that, Ici loved her.

"I thought you were coming aft to help me with the steam generator," she said, squatting down next to him.

"I am," Ici replied, letting one hand find its way to her thigh. "I was just trying to decide how much this harvest would bring."

She stood, shading her eyes to look at the tuna school. "There's more big fish this time, but the rendezvous is tomorrow. Today we need to get the generator running again."

"Are you sure it isn't a software problem?"

"Positive. The program works fine. It's probably in the stepper motor again."

"Could be," he said, using the rail to pull himself up to his knees. "But I just changed it the last time the factory ship was here, what, three months ago? Sometimes I wonder where they get the spare parts. It takes forever to get them and then the stuff falls apart. The people running things for the factory don't give a shit. We're the ones floating around in the middle of the

Pacific, our lives depending on some asshole lubber to put in the requisition. Just one time I'd like to meet the jerk responsible."

"Forget it," she said, rubbing his shoulder. "We're almost to the plankton fields."

"I just hope the bait fish are more plentiful there than they have been the last few days."

He put his arms around her thighs, hugged her and buried his face between her legs. "Let's make love," he whispered, "Olga never comes up here during the day."

Ni pulled away. "Not now." She turned and retreated to the ladder, then grabbing both rails, slid down through the hatch. "Come on," she said, her voice echoing up the metal well.

Ici stood, took one last look at the tuna to assure himself they were still headed for the plankton field, then went down the ladder. At the bottom of the ladder he stood in the middle of a short, narrow, dimly lit hallway formed by the stainless steel bulkheads of the rooms on either side of the corridor. It led from starboard to port across Homestead's beam, then made a left turn about two meters from him and continued on down the center of the raft's cabin. On his right was the watertight door that led to the head, showers and the forward storage area. The patter of Ni's bare feet drifted to him from around the corner and Ici hurried to catch up.

Ici turned the corner and noted that all the watertight doors on both sides of the hallway were closed, including the one to their quarters. So much for his romantic daydreams. It appeared Ni really did intend to work on the steam generator.

Ici hurried down the stainless steel hall. Ni was at the end of the passage and already had the aft door open. She stepped out through the doorway onto the stern deck. He rushed to catch up. As he passed Olga's cabin, he noticed the door was shut. The tall Russian was probably sleeping as she usually did in the afternoons. Even though she had only been on board for four months, she knew what she was doing and Ici had decided to put her on night watch alone. Ni kidded him about pushing night shift on Olga so they could be together. Ici chuckled to himself. She was right, though he never admitted it. He certainly was not a chauvinist.

He stepped out into the sunlight, blinking to allow his eyes to adjust. On the stern deck sat the clear plastic blister that housed the solar steam generator. The generator produced low-pressure steam to run the turbines that powered the twin electric motors that turned the propellers. At the same time it recharged the batteries stored forward. After passing through the turbines, the exhaust side steam was condensed for drinking water.

Ni was already bent over the deck panel that housed the controls for the mirror arrangement. It was supposed to concentrate the maximum sunlight on the steam dome. She spun off the last thumbscrew and lifted the panel aside, then set it gently on the deck.

Ici stepped up behind her. As he leaned over to get a better look at the electronics, he let his hand caress Ni's buttocks.

"Hey," she squealed, jumping to her feet. "Not now."

"Why not?" he pouted, trying to cuddle up to her. "Let's make a baby."

She sat down on the deck, hard. "Not that again. I told you I am not having any kids out on this Godforsaken platform. As soon as we pay off Star-Kist, then we'll have kids."

"And when will that be? Five years? Maybe seven or eight? What if I can't make babies then? You know what they say about our fertility rates not being very good. Michael says the males will go sterile by age twenty-five. I'm already twenty-four."

"I don't know," she said, slumping down with her back up against the rear of the cabin. "They're only rumors. Nobody knows that. Nobody's twenty-five years old yet."

"Not any of us. But some of the earlier experiments produced people who were changed and Michael says not a one of them is still virile. Maybe we'll be the same. I can't afford to wait to find out. The gene tampering may have shortened our fertility span—maybe our life span, too."

He kneeled in front of her, leaned forward and wrapped his arms around her. Gently hugging her, he let his lips sneak up to meet hers, kissing her softly on the mouth. She kissed him back. He wanted her now. He was filled with lust. Thoughts of making a child were gone. He slid his mouth down over her chin, kissing her as he went, licking her neck, kissing her neck and ear.

Finally he mouthed her smooth breasts, first one then the other.

Her breathing quickened. He kissed her harder, gently biting her erect nipples.

Desire seethed within him. He slid his hand inside her suit bottom, letting his fingers explore. Ni moaned as he began the steady stroking that he knew would culminate in an explosive climax. Her hand was inside his swimming suit, caressing him.

"Jesus Christ!" Olga stepped through the doorway, almost tromping on top of them. "Don't you guys do anything useful?"

Ni pulled her hand back. Ici jerked up. His face burned red. He tried to hide the bulge in his tight bikini briefs by folding his hands in front of himself. He rolled to one side and glared up at the tall, blond Russian. Cold as hell, he thought. She hasn't got a clue what a man is for.

She waved a stack of computer printouts at the pair. "Have you been watching this storm center?"

Ici got to his feet, the flush that reddened his cheeks forgotten. "Of course we've been watching the storm front. It won't hit until day after tomorrow. We'll probably catch the edge of it. We'll meet the factory ship tomorrow, finish the harvest and head south. We'll ride the storm out submerged. It won't be any problem."

"No problem? Have you seen the latest tracking projections? The FARSTAT package estimates the epicenter will pass no more than eight miles north of our rendezvous point. Winds are over 70 knots and still rising."

Ni stood and took the printout from Olga. She scanned it, nodded knowingly several times, then handed it back.

"It hasn't changed since this morning."

"Then we are in trouble," snapped Olga, folding the printout with both hands.

"No, we aren't," said Ici, and smiled the "know-it-all" smile he used to irritate the Russian. "We radioed the Martin B. earlier and moved the rendezvous and departure times up by six hours. We'll be a hundred miles south of the storm by the time it gets here."

"Well I'm glad to see you've done something useful today. Are we going to be submerged during the storm?"

"Probably."

"Can we try the sonic herding experiment then?"

"No," said Ici. "We are not running any experiments while there's a storm." The tall woman turned and started back into the cabin.

"One other thing," said Ici. Olga stopped and turned to face him. "During your sleep hours, you should be asleep. I'm not taking your watch tonight because you stayed up all day."

"And I'm not doing your work tonight just because you spent all day screwing around." She turned and disappeared into the cabin.

"We better get the solar generator fixed," said Ni. She took him by the arm and led him to the open access panel. "We're short on drinking water now and the storm is going to make it hard to replenish."

Ici grumbled his agreement and bent to the task. It didn't take long to verify that the stepper motor that was supposed to keep the mirrors aimed at the sun was no longer working. The generator was limping along at about thirty percent and they weren't able to get much more out of it without manually aiming the mirrors.

He disconnected the motor and pulled it out of the compartment. "Forget the mirrors," he told her. "I'm going to try to fix this thing myself. Will you radio the Martin B. and make sure they have a 1864601 DC on board? I bet the assholes don't have it."

"They'd better. Things are bad enough on this barge without the water being shut off."

"And without the steam generator we can only make about half speed. If this thing doesn't get fixed, we're going to be a lot closer to that storm than we want to be."

He headed into the cabin. Ni followed on his heels. At the first doorway on the left, she pulled him up short with a tug on his arm. Through the open door, Ici could see Olga intent on the color weather CRT in the control room.

Ni put her lips up near his ear and whispered. "I'll radio, but then I'm going topside to watch the tuna. Come up and keep me company when you're finished with the motor."

"Sure," he said and hurried off to the end of the corridor where they kept the modest supply of spare parts. They were leftovers from other things that had broken but Ici never threw out anything that still had working parts.

SHEPHERDS

#

It took Ici a lot longer than he intended, but he finally got the motor glued back together. How long it would work was anybody's guess. At least for now they could produce fresh water and the Homestead could run at full power. As soon as he had the generator running again, he headed topside. It was late and the sun was low in the sky. Not as much time to desalinate water as he would have liked, but it would have to do for today. Tomorrow would be better.

He went up the metal ladder to the cabin roof. Ahead of Homestead, the dolphins' heads rolled out of the water just enough to blow and breathe. Then they went under again, pushing slowly ahead, forcing the tuna to stick to the heading. Ni was asleep on her stomach near the forward rail. Her back was smooth bronze.

He tiptoed over to her and lay down. Lightly he put his hand on her back and snuggled up beside her. It felt good to hold her, like he was comforting her, protecting her. It made him feel like a man, a real man. Not some genetic freak made to farm the oceans for the starving millions ashore. Not that he minded feeding the lubbers. It wasn't their fault that he was what he was, and actually life wasn't that bad. At least he didn't have to live in a lubber's city and work packed in with the mobs that called that living.

Out here he was free. Well, someday he would be totally free. For now he still owed Star-Kist nineteen grand. And now that he and Ni had gotten married, they had combined their debts. He'd made it through five years, the first two with a lubber biologist on board, the second two with Michael for a raft mate, and finally, with Ni. With her as his wife, Ici knew he could make it through a few more. And then what? Retire and become a lubber? Or stake out a section of ocean and farm it himself? It was a question he wrestled with almost every day, dreaming of being free and worried about what he'd do when he was. Lately he'd been leaning toward trying to buy an ocean front house somewhere and farm fish closer to shore. There was something about the security of having a stable home, and access to medical care for Ni and the baby that they would never be able to get out here that appealed to him.

Ni stirred next to him. She rolled over and fluttered her eyes until they cleared. Brown and beautiful, thought Ici. He loved everything about her.

"It's almost dark," she said propping herself up on one elbow.

"Yeah, it took longer than I thought."

"You got the motor fixed?"

"Of course. Did you get a nice nap?"

She smiled. "Martin B. has the DC. You can fix the generator properly tomorrow. But one thing," she started, shook her head as if to clear the sleep from her mind. "It's probably nothing."

"Tell me."

"There was a garbled radio transmission. A Mayday. It sounded like a tuna boat was being attacked. There was too much static to understand."

Ici cocked his head to one side. "I wonder if it has anything to do with the Oyster Bay. Remember the broadcast we picked up from that tuna boat that reported finding Lisa, Vern and Wing's bodies? Maybe it is true."

"Could be, but I don't see the connection."

"Probably nothing." Ici sat up. "I keep telling myself it's only a hoax."

He stood and helped Ni up. "How about dinner? Olga's cooking, though I wish you were making one of your squid specials. Afterward I'm going to put on a fireworks display like you've never seen."

"Okay," she said, "I'll put up with it today but you know how I hate loud noises."

"It won't be too loud. Most everything I have will go off a long way from the boat."

She wrinkled her nose. "I've got to check the radio log and go over the weather videos before I take a shower. Then I'll be ready to eat. Did you take your shower yet?"

"No. I was waiting for you."

"Perfect."

She skipped down the ladder, Ici right behind her.

Meanwhile, Olga worked in the kitchen making dinner, her mind on her loneliness.

Chapter 7

The next morning was clear. The turquoise sea ran in soft rolling swells and a light breeze flicked across the wave tops, leaving mere ripples as it passed. The Homestead picked up speed as the light from the rising sun brought the steam generator up to power, pushing the twin electric motors to their maximum. Olga, Ici and Ni had eaten breakfast together. Afterwards Olga went to her quarters hoping to get a quick nap before they would begin harvesting the roe. But sleep had been hard to find, her mind a turmoil of questions about her mother, about the fate of the other rafts. She finally gave up and got up to help Ici.

Meanwhile Ni went to the control room to radio the Martin B. to confirm the rendezvous coordinates and Ici, grabbing his binoculars, climbed the ladder to the cabin roof to watch for the first signs of the factory ship. At least that was what he told Ni. Actually he made any excuse to get up on deck early to experience the birth of a new day. It was a fresh start, a new future, and he loved to feel the warmth of those first rays of sunlight on his skin.

He still felt the afterglow from his fireworks show. It had gone wonderfully, though he had cut it short. Ni's delicate ears could only take so many aerial bombs; the ones Ici liked best. They were so loud you felt the concussion right in the middle of your chest. He still had plenty of them left, but they would have to wait for another day.

Now that the sun was up, it was time to go to work. Looping the binoculars' neck strap around the railing, he left them swinging on the rail and dove gracefully into an oncoming wave crest. Ici sliced into the water and with an exhilarating bite, the ocean swallowed him. The feeling of weightlessness surrounded him and filled him with a euphoric sense of freedom. Spreading his fingers to get maximum force from the webbing, he thrust himself downward with strong strokes. A cascade of bubbles flashed past as Olga dove in beside him. Her streamlined physique cut through the water at an amazing rate and in a moment she outstripped him.

They both went deep, the water cooling as they passed through the thermocline layer. The harsh surface light softened and for a long moment they circled in the hazy blue-green of thirty meters down. They were in no hurry to get to work. Instead they enjoyed the moment, buoyed by the sea. It was the kind of time that Ici could share only with another cowboy. He watched the Russian sail gracefully through the water, even faster and better than he. He envied her abilities, but at the same time, he never stopped being thankful that he was a cowboy himself and not a lubber.

Slowly he rose to the surface, savoring each minute, not wanting to end the joy of swimming free. His lungs still needed to breathe and that need forced him upward until his head bobbed into the air and he exhaled explosively. A few short breaths later Olga surfaced next to him. They had to harvest the tuna roe today though he would have put it off if he could have. And he'd rather be working with Ni though the Russian woman had to do something to earn her keep.

"Ready to go to work?" he asked.

She nodded and they dove toward the tuna herd. Ni jockeyed the Homestead alongside, the plastic catch sack deployed off the stern. Pungee, the largest dolphin in their pod, cut the first breeder cow from the school and herded it to the waiting pair. Ici grabbed the tuna by the tail and slipped the noose around it, holding the big fish fast. Then he and Olga pushed along the sides until the eggs were jettisoned into the sack. The cool, silky sides of the tuna held the promise of unborn life. It reminded him of his own longing for a child, someone to pass on his legacy. Instead, he worked to insure the birth of millions of tuna.

By the time the first big mother tuna was stripped, Pungee had another one ready and waiting. That one became another, and another and soon the process became mechanical. Attracted by the hormonal signals from the females, the males swam by and released their sperm. Ni hauled up the plastic sacks full of fertilized eggs and lowered a fresh catch bag in its place.

Three hours later it was done. The tuna were again being herded toward the Martin B. and Ici and Olga swam to the side of Homestead. Ici hated getting out of the water. As he pulled himself up the droplets that ran down his legs seemed to pull at him, urging him to return to the warm womb of the sea. Later, he promised.

Olga leaped on deck beside him. "Done with me?" she asked.

In the binoculars, the thin wisp of smoke stood out against the blue sky, little gray puffs hanging in the air like a trail.

"There she is," he shouted. He pointed and held up the binoculars for her to see.

"Yes," she said, handing the binoculars back. "They're still running back and forth laying the fertilizer. It won't be long."

Ni went back below to maintain radio contact with the Martin B. while Ici climbed over the rail and down the hand rungs on the side of the cabin to the narrow pontoon deck. The Homestead was riding high in the water now. Even so, an occasional wave sloshed over the deck. The warm saltwater soothed Ici's bare feet as it ran ankle-deep along the cabin sides. The ocean caressed him and Ici felt the familiar call. Soon he would be back in the water.

He made his way to the bow, kneeled down and grabbed the handhold. The nylon strap was anchored to the deck to keep him from being thrown off as the bow rose and fell with each wave. He bent down until he could reach the water, then slapped hard three times with his cupped palm to produce the correct hollow sound. Within a minute, Pungee surfaced alongside the bow, the perpetual smile frozen on the dolphin's face. Ici reached out and patted him on the head, being careful not to come too close to the blowhole.

"Good boy," he said. Then he made a motion in the air with his hand, knifing it in the direction of the factory ship. Back and forth a half dozen times he motioned. "That way," he said, more to himself, because the dolphins couldn't understand the words.

Pungee shook his head up and down, then rolled and dove into the crest of the next wave. Ici watched as the big dolphin surged toward the tuna school. Oh, to be able to swim like that.

Pungee's whistles echoed through the Homestead's hull. Already the dolphins were correcting the tuna to run straight for the Martin B. Ici stayed on the bow. He would need to be there when they got to the factory ship. The dolphins knew their job but he still liked to supervise.

By now, the factory ship was a large black silhouette crawling back and forth across the sea in front of them. The multiple spray units discharged the fertilizer mixture on the water. Ici noticed an unusual orange tint to the spray and wondered if that could be the new plankton strain.

"They are almost done." It was Ni's voice over the loudspeaker. She was still in the control room, but with the forward video camera she could see everything Ici could from his spot on the bow. "Captain Jurgensen says he will empty his bait tanks at the same time he releases the tuna weanlings. He's laying the nets now. It will be on his count, eight minutes from. . . a pause. . .now. Get the D's ready."

Ici slapped the water three times again. Pungee and two other dolphins, Sheriff and Slim, appeared next to the bow. Now came the hard work. The school of tuna was generally stratified by size and only the largest fish were ready for harvest. Some of the dolphins would have to split out the bigger fish from the school and drive then into the nets that the Martin B. hung overboard. At the same time, the factory ship would be emptying one of her holds of the baitfish she'd brought. As soon as the baitfish were loose, they would empty the other holds of the new hatchery-raised tuna that were between three and eight kilograms.

A second group from the dolphin pod would be poised to round up the weanling tuna as they swam down out of the Martin B's holds, and drive them along with the baitfish away from the nets and the larger tuna being harvested. When they were far enough away from the nets to be safe, the tuna weanlings would be combined with the smaller fish from the original school. This new school would then be allowed to gorge itself on the feeders. Done right it was the most efficient way to get it all accomplished, though Ici hated the factory dictated demand for efficiency. Done wrong, it could turn into a disaster. If the big fish ran into the small tuna, all hell would break loose as the adult fish attacked the weanlings in a feeding frenzy. There were no second chances.

Ici made the sign of the boat by cupping his hands together with the fingertips touching. Then he showed the dolphins the flurry of little fish by waving his fingers in a downward notion, followed by the roundup command signal, circling the index finger in the air. Pungee shook his head up and down and Ici knew he understood.

The dolphins started to roll away from the Homestead and Ici slapped the water three times to let the dolphins know there was more. They stopped and looked up at him. Ici made the sign for the school, waited for Pungee to acknowledge, then split his hands apart. He circled the index finger to show herding, and the boat sign. This was the combination of signals that told Pungee to break out the bigger fish and herd them to the factory ship. Pungee nodded a half dozen times, rolled and was gone.

Sheriff and Slim were right behind him. Ici hoped they understood. They had only messed it up once. That was because a great white had shown up for lunch just at the wrong time. The dolphins got carried away chasing the shark while the tuna school split. Most of the bigger tuna got away because there weren't enough dolphins to keep them herded up. Not today, he prayed, not today.

As Ici watched, Pungee raced for the tuna school. His shrill wails and those of the other dolphins made the Homestead's hull ring like a symphony of chimes. Through the clear azure water Ici saw the dolphins splitting the tuna into two smaller schools. Seven of the dolphins drove the school of bigger fish toward the nets already laid out behind the Martin B. The other eight dolphins rounded up the smaller fish and drove them away from the big fish toward the Martin B.'s bow.

"Two minutes," came Ni's voice over the loudspeaker.

Ici watched. The school of smaller fish churned toward the factory ship. The big fish headed straight for the nets. Unconsciously, Ici swept the water for shark fins. Nothing.

"One minute."

Ici scanned the sea again. Everything was going fine. The larger tuna hit the big purse seine and the sea boiled as they struggled to escape. Tails and fins thrashed the water into a white froth.

"Now."

Amidships on the Martin B. the watertight hatch doors opened like bomb bays and water swirled to the surface all around the ship as she disgorged her cargo. At the same time, the smaller fish from the tuna school charged into the baitfish, immediately joined by their freed brothers from the hatchery. All around the Martin B. the water boiled in a feeding frenzy as the tuna relentlessly pursued the plentiful baitfish.

In a few minutes it was all over. Ici watched as the powerful winches hauled the bulging nets up to the Martin B. He tried to gauge the weight by the size of the mass of fish in the net. Not as good a crop as he had hoped. It would bring their debt down, although at this rate it would take a few more harvests before Ici and Ni's debt was cleared off the factory's books. He clenched his teeth until his jaw muscles hurt. Damn it, he had wanted it cleared this time. Now he would have to shelve his plans for a while longer.

A couple of the dolphins were circling the new school of tuna, keeping them away from the Martin B. while the rest of the mammals chased down the remnants of the bait fish school. Ici would have to see if Captain Jurgensen had some reserve baitfish for the Homestead to keep as a reward for the dolphins.

"I'm running over to the Martin B.," said Ni. "We've got to settle the weight, get treats for the D's and get out of here."

"I'll swim over. Don't forget, I want five hundred in cash," said Ici and dove off the side.

He swam with powerful strokes, his partially webbed hands and feet driving him ahead. Pungee was beside him almost as soon as he was in the water. They swam together, dolphin and man rolling to the surface to breathe, then back into the cooler underlayer. By the time he reached the Martin B., Homestead was tied off at her side. The shepherd's pontoon boat looked so small, so insignificant next to the massive factory ship. Olga stood on the cabin roof, pulling supplies out of a net that had been dropped by several of the factory ship's crewmen. Ici pulled himself up onto the Homestead and mounted the ladder to clamber up to the main deck of the Martin B.

Ni was already talking to Captain Jurgensen when Ici hoisted himself over the railing. The captain's bulk dwarfed Ni, his massive barrel chest pushed against the buttons of his white uniform. It made a stark contrast to Ni's brown, bare chest and black suit bottoms. Ici watched the captain's eyes, but they were focused on the horizon somewhere and not on Ni. Ici had seen Captain Jurgensen before and he had changed little in the last year. A tuft of thinning reddish hair peeked out from under the cap perched on the right side of his head. With his chin tucked down, his round face seemed to perch directly atop his wide shoulders. The affect made him look even larger than he was, and he was plenty large.

Turning his attention to Ni, Ici saw she already had the weight printout in her hand and was flipping through the figures while the captain waited.

"A little over five thousand tons," she said, handing the printout to Ici. "I checked it over and everything looks okay."

Ici scanned the listing quickly. Not a good harvest. In fact only about half what he'd like to get. He scanned the printout. The tare weights and net weights seemed to jive. He let his eyes run down to the listing for the supplies they were taking onboard. Staples, mostly. A few personal items, bait fish for the D's, and there was a DC board for the generator.

"The price for the bait fish is a little high isn't it?"

Captain Jurgensen nodded. "Supply is short right now. It costs money if you want to feed the dolphins."

"Okay," said Ici, knowing it wouldn't do any good to argue. The prices were set by the fisheries, not the ship's captain. He would have to file a complaint via Internet to Star-Kist directly. He took the pen offered by Captain Jurgensen and signed the original copy of the document on the last line, then handed it back.

"The weather is going to get nasty soon," said the Captain. "I suppose you'll want to be on your way as soon as the supplies are loaded."

"Yes," said Ni and started for the ladder. "One other thing. Have you heard anything about outlaw ships? We received a garbled radio transmission yesterday about a tuna boat being attacked. And there's a U. N. frigate just over the horizon looking for survivors."

"Not to mention the reported loss of the Oyster Bay," added Ici. "What is going on?"

Captain Jurgensen's brow wrinkled. "I knew Stockholm was nosing around looking for poachers, but who would attack a tuna boat? This is the twenty-first century. How much money can they make stealing tuna?"

"The rustlers seem to do all right," said Ici.

"Those are tuna fisherman down on their luck," said the Captain with a wave of his hand. "They don't attack ships, nor sink platforms. They don't have weapons for doing it either."

"Have any of the other shepherds said anything or mentioned being attacked?" asked Ni.

"No. Not that I've heard. We've kept every appointed rendezvous and nothing has been amiss."

"When was your last pickup with Oyster Bay?" asked Ici.

Captain Jurgensen pushed his cap back on his head. "It must be almost four weeks ago. That was our first trip delivering the new plankton. I could check the log if you need to know exactly."

"Have you heard from them since?"

"No, they were our last pickup that trip. We've been back to Hawaii since then."

Ici and Ni thanked the captain and went back down the ladder to Homestead. After they helped Olga stow the supplies, Ici took the $500 from Ni and slipped back up to the Martin B.'s main deck to buy his latest shipment of aerial bombs from Jimmy. He managed to lower the small crate to the Homestead's deck and pay Jimmy without being seen. Then, as he was about to go back down the ladder, Jimmy touched his arm.

Jimmy leaned over and whispered, "What do you know about this new plankton?"

Ici saw fear flicker in Jimmy's eyes then die. "Nothing," he said and put one foot down on the next ladder-rung. "Why?"

"I'm not sure, but I think something is wrong with it. Our last two trips, we've had a bunch of weirdo scientists aboard checking it out. One of them was from the World Health Organization. Why would they be interested in plankton?"

"They probably are required to check out anything that is being fed to food stock animals. It doesn't mean anything."

"Could it be poison?"

"No, don't worry about it," said Ici and started down the ladder.

Jimmy ducked back under the rail and disappeared behind the deck cargo.

Olga was waiting for Ici when he reached Homestead's deck. "What did he want?" she asked.

"He thinks something's wrong with the new plankton. Like we don't have enough troubles," snapped Ici.

"We've all got troubles. Right now I just want to go to sleep. Okay?"

"Sure. I'll wake you when it's your watch."

Ici headed for the bow. Maybe he should give her a little extra sleep. He and Ni could stay up a bit longer.

Once he was on the bow he ordered Pungee to start the school south again, away from the storm. They would run as far as they could and when the swells got too big they would submerge and ride the storm out 50 meters down. And though he didn't like it, he supposed they would have to try the underwater herding experiment that Olga was so insistent on. He just hoped the speakers mounted on the outer hull and the microphones worked okay. Whether the dolphins would be able to make any sense out of the electronic squawks that were supposed to be dolphin words remained to be seen.

The motors purred as the Homestead pulled steadily away from the Martin B. Everything was going as well as could be expected. Before they got busy he was going to call Michael.

He headed to the control room. As he passed her cabin, Ici noticed Olga's door was already closed. He hoped she was actually sleeping. He certainly wasn't taking her whole watch.

Ici turned into the control room. Ni sat at the console.

"Hi," he said, stopping in front of the radio console. "I'm calling Michael. Any word from that frigate?"

"Nothing. Tell Sandy I said 'hi' when you reach the Turtle. I'm going across the hall for some coffee."

Ni slipped out the door and Ici sat down at the control chair. He adjusted the frequency and flipped on the microphone.

"Turtle, this is Homestead. Come in Turtle."

"Yo, Ici," came Michael's voice, "this is Turtle. What took you so long to call? How was the harvest?"

"Okay, nothing to brag about. Less than half what we harvested last time. I'm a long way from clearing my debt. I'm still in for nine grand. "

"Don't sweat the small stuff. Are you going to change your life just because you don't owe the factory anymore?"

Ici laughed. Michael's philosophy was that all cowboys were meant to be at sea and that no cowboy would ever be happy on land. Ici thought it was nonsense. He was beginning to think a big house on the shore would be just fine. "Michael, have you talked to Vern lately?"

"No, the last time I tried to contact them I never got an answer." A serious tone crept into Michael's voice. "Has something happened?"

"I'm afraid so. We received a couple of radio reports. First that a fishing boat had found Oyster Bay and there were three dead cowboys aboard. The position they gave was about right for Oyster Bay. Now it looks like that tuna boat is missing."

"Where did all this happen?"

"I don't know exactly, not too far from us. There's a U.N. frigate prowling around right now looking for survivors from the tuna boat, but the chances of them finding anyone out here seem remote. Worse, with the storm coming if they don't find them today, they won't be around to find."

The radio channel remained silent for a long moment. Then Michael came back on. "Maybe it was an accident. What could Oyster Bay have had that somebody would want bad enough to kill for?"

"Hell if I know. It doesn't make sense. I think we're missing something."

"Maybe. What about us? Are we in danger? And what type of ship should we watch for?"

"No idea. It's a mess. Just play it safe. Don't trust anyone."

"Thanks for the advice. We'll be careful. You do the same. I'll talk to you after the storm."

"Right. And say 'hi' to Sandy from Ni. Homestead out."

Ici clicked off the radio. The soft green glow of the radar screen showed two bright blips. One was the Martin B., the other was the frigate. There was something ominous about the frigate's presence, something that broke the routine. Ici could only hope that by the time they rode out the storm, the frigate would have caught whoever was responsible. In the meantime, he had enough to worry about. Surviving the storm would be a good start.

Chapter 8

Toivo watched the circling ring of deadly sharks. He had been expecting them, though not quite so soon. Massive fishing efforts had reduced these ever-hungry predators to a protected species in many large international oceanic refuge areas, so with this depletion he thought the sharks would have taken longer to find him. Still, in the open ocean, they were always present, searching for food, scavenging, cleaning up. He wasn't bleeding—or was he? He tried to see in the water around him but there was no telltale crimson stain.

"*Help. Danger,*" he called in dolphin whistles. The saltwater had already cracked his lips and it was hard to make the dolphin's words.

Poika, Tyttö, and the other dolphins had to be close. Toivo watched the sharks circle, one fin dipped below the surface, then another. He felt imaginary teeth ripping at his feet. He tried to pull them up, curl them against his body to protect them. It was only a matter of time before these eating machines ripped the flesh from his body, killing him.

A large triangular fin darted in and a surge of water swirled around him as a twelve-foot tiger shark rushed past. Another shark took up the challenge and cut out of the circle, rushing toward Toivo. It turned aside at the last instant.

"*Help,*" he whistled again. Stay calm, he told himself. Thrashing will only increase their frenzy and entice the sharks to attack. Every nerve in his body screamed out to run, to hide. But there was no place to go. He could only pray that the dolphins hadn't gone too far. "*Poika, where are you?*"

Another fin darted below the surface, a smaller white tip. It bounced off his leg, nudging him but not biting. Toivo kicked out involuntarily, his foot scraping the shark's back, its sandpaper skin rasping against his shin. With a quick thrust of its tail the shark shot away.

Where were Poika and Tyttö? Had they abandoned him? Ever since he'd found Poika, the dolphin had never gone far. When Sisu was in port, Poika and his mate had even ventured into the harbors to be near Toivo. Where were they now?

"*Help, help,*" he whistled over and over, his lips burning with the effort.

The circle tightened, the fins dancing ever closer. Toivo wanted to scream. He was helpless. He was going to die, he knew it. No, no, no. He wasn't giving up, and he wasn't letting some stupid fish beat him. Not Toivo the fisherman.

Another dark shape surged past, only inches from Toivo's legs. He kicked out, too late, and his foot felt the eddies of the shark's passing. Suddenly, to his left, a shark body exploded from the water in a geyser of spray. Poika's nose was buried deep in the fish's belly. The dolphin had driven upward from beneath the shark so hard that both of them had flown straight out of the water.

"Thank God," yelled Toivo, his face lifted to the sky.

Now the water around him erupted in a flurry of fins, flukes and swirling eddies as the dolphins charged into the sharks. The pod rammed shark after shark, driving the predators away from the tired fisherman.

In a few minutes the ocean calmed along with Toivo's heart. Much to his relief, the fins disappeared and it was Poika's slick gray face that surfaced next to him.

"*All is well,*" said Poika, his smile fixed on his toothy beak. "*The eaters are gone.*"

"*Thanks,*" said Toivo. "*Where were you?*"

"*Feeding. Many-arms is deep here.*"

Squid, thought Toivo. The dolphins loved squid and when they found them, they would dive to extreme depths to get them.

"*Are you full?*"

"*Don't worry. We will not leave you alone again.*"

Poika nuzzled against Toivo, cradling the man with one flipper and letting him drape over the dolphin's back. "*Rest now.*"

Held thus, Toivo slept. Exhaustion would let him do nothing else.

#

When he awoke, Poika had been replaced by one of the factory dolphins. The sun was sinking behind a low bank of clouds on the horizon. His stomach growled, empty as a new grave. What was he going to eat? Or drink? What were his chances for being picked up? Not good. Only a few fishing boats out here. He was nowhere near any of the shipping lanes. His only chance was the migratory shepherds that watched their herds of factory tuna. His mouth tasted like stale garbage and burned of salt.

He stretched his neck up to get his head higher out of the water and blinked to clear his sight. With his eyes inches above the surface, the horizon appeared to be only a few hundred meters away. He pulled himself up onto the dolphin's back and looked around. The ocean lay flat and empty as far as he could see. He lowered himself back into the water.

"*Poika, can you hear any ships*?" asked Toivo even though he was sure the dolphin would have already told him if he had heard one.

Poika surfaced a few meters away. "*No, no ships. Eat now.*"

Tyttö bobbed up next to her mate. She had a small bonito in her beak. Side-slipping over to Toivo, she extended the fish. He took it, not sure he wanted it, the salt content likely would make his thirst worse. He'd eaten raw fish years ago when he had worked on the Chinese tuna boat, but there he'd had no choice. Here he had no choice either, except that here he had no knife to clean it, scale it, or cut it into strips.

He bit into the side of the fish, got a mouthful of scales and spit them into the ocean. What had he been reduced to? It seemed a strange irony that a fisherman should suffer such indignity!

"*Not good*?" asked Poika.

Toivo ignored the dolphin knowing it would be hard to explain his reluctance to Poika who ate raw fish all the time. Toivo bit into the fish again where he had pulled off the scales. He took in as big a mouthful as he could manage and chewed carefully, aware that choking on even one bone could be fatal. After mashing the complete chunk of flesh into a pulp, he swallowed.

Not bad. He took another bite. Then, wedging his fingers under the bonito's skin, he ripped the skin back from the flesh, striping off the scales with it. He ate the rest of the fish, slowly grinding up each mouthful, always wary of bones. His stomach felt better, but the salt burned like strong acid, crusting the insides of his mouth. It made him thirstier than ever and left him desperate to have a drink. He decided to forego any more fish unless he could be absolutely certain it was not contaminated with salt water.

The sun went down and the night breeze rippled the sea. Stars twinkled overhead and a slice of crescent moon shone through high wisps of ice clouds. Toivo tried to lie back in the water, to float and conserve his strength. The dolphins huddled around for a few minutes, talking in low whistles. Toivo was too tired to pay any attention.

Tyttö took over, acting as Toivo's personal floatation device, and the tired fisherman spent the night in fitful sleep. His dreams were tormented by black figures with guns shooting at him, shooting his friends, killing, killing. He awoke so many times he almost dreamed that he was sleeping. All night long the dolphins took turns keeping his head above water while the rest of the pod circled nearby, guarding.

#

The next day passed slowly and Toivo grew weaker as the hours passed. The dolphins gathered ever more frequently in groups, too far away for him to hear them discuss their growing concerns. Nonetheless, they continued to rotate the duty of keeping the fisherman's head above water. The salt water had already caused his feet to swell and his mouth to blister around the lips. Toivo felt older than he should have. His body hurt all over and his guts felt like there was a knife stuck there, twisting so the pain made him grit his teeth to hold back whimpers. He ate another small bonito. This time he forced himself to lick the blood from its ribs. It seemed to help though a part of his mind still revolted at the thought of raw food.

Night came again. The breeze stiffened and the swells began running higher. Now Toivo fought to keep his head above water. Without the dolphins help, he would have gone under. His arms ached. His legs cramped into knots that wouldn't go away. His stomach burned like it had been impaled by an ice pick. At times he thought about letting death take him. But Poika, Tyttö and the other dolphins were there, encouraging him, and he fed off their strength. Toivo would not give up. Life was too dear. He wanted to live. And he owed Wilho, owed Wilho's daughter an explanation for why her father hadn't come home.

#

Night dawned into the next day. Toivo could remain afloat only on a dolphin's back. The waves crested like mountains over his head. The dolphins changed more often. He knew they were working hard fighting the swells, even without carrying his weight.

Plumes of spray stung his face. The effects of the prolonged saltwater exposure were magnified by his lack of sleep. Open sores burned on his back and shoulders. His lips ballooned until he could hardly open them. Toivo sagged deeper into the water. Even his grip on the dolphin's dorsal fin was precarious.

Another mountain of water raced toward them, lifting them skyward. Tufts of whitewater whipped away off the peak. Over the crest, they plunged down into the huge chasm between waves. The wind continued to rise.

Soon it took two dolphins to keep Toivo afloat and even then, the salt spray and the curling wavetops constantly forced water into Toivo's gasping mouth. With one dolphin on each side, Toivo used both arms to keep his head as high out of the water as he could. The dolphins changed frequently. They tired quickly fighting the towering waves, working to keep the man's weight suspended above the water. The other dolphins dove and stayed below the surface as much as possible to conserve their strength.

The hours dragged on. The wind continued to build, pushing the waves ever higher, their massive power slamming into man and dolphin. The dolphins were exhausted. They changed every ten minutes or so, diving out of sight as soon as they were relieved. Toivo sputtered and choked constantly. His only thought was to breathe, get air into his lungs. His arms slipped off the dolphins now and then, but the dolphins would slide underwater, pinch in against his ribs, and push his head back out of the water. Time lost all meaning. How many waves had crashed over him, how many times had the dolphins changed, how long could he hang on?

At last, Poika took over for the factory dolphin under Toivo's left arm. The other dolphin slipped away beneath the waves. Now Poika and Tyttö held Toivo up. Toivo wanted to thank them, but he didn't have the strength to talk.

"*Toivo*," whistled Poika. The sound he made was so far from human speech that only Toivo could recognize it as his name. "*You are a brave being. Perhaps it is time for you to go ahead.*"

Toivo heard but it took a moment to sink in. Was he ready to die? His body cried out for peace, for rest. It would be easy to let go of the dolphins, to sink beneath the waves and pass into oblivion. Maybe this was the end. What had his life amounted to anyway? His crew was gone. He had no family. He envied Wilho his daughter. Toivo had always wanted a daughter, but now. . .

No! No. What was this crazy talk of dying? He was going to live, get another boat, find tuna like never before and retire one day back in Finland, back home. No, it was *not* his time to go ahead.

He pulled himself up so his mouth cleared the water. He coughed out the saltwater in his throat, and whistled. *"No. I do not wish to go ahead. I have many things to do."*

"Then we will still help you. Sometimes one knows it is time to go ahead and should not fight it. Since you do not feel ready, then your time has not come yet."

Toivo tried to say more but his grip failed him and he slipped back into the ocean. A rush of saltwater filled his mouth. He choked. His head went under. Poika pushed him up with his beak. Toivo spat out water, coughed, and gasped for air.

Poika shoved up with his back and dorsal fin and Toivo desperately rode out the storm, fighting for breath on the backs of the pair of dolphins. The hours wore on and Toivo lost count of the number of times huge waves tumbled him over and over like clothes in a washing machine. The blacker darkness of night came and was followed by the gray of a day with the sun hidden above an impenetrable cover of inky clouds. Rain lashed down, and though it stung his face, Toivo turned his mouth to the heavens and found life and hope in the raindrops that reached his eager tongue. Each time he thought his arms would give out, he willed them to have new strength and managed to cling to the dolphins.

#

Eventually the storm passed. The winds fell off to a soft breeze. Without the wind to push them, the waves quickly dropped to twenty-foot rolling swells. Somehow Toivo slept. Two dolphins sandwiched in on either side and curled around him so he lay in a living cradle.

Sometime near midday, Toivo awoke. The thirst was still there, but dulled by the rain he'd managed to drink during the storm. His stomach burned but Toivo ignored it, trying not to think of eating more raw, salty fish. He rolled over on his back and Poika held him up by putting his powerful flukes under the small of his back. Toivo slept again.

"*A boat is coming near.*"

The sound of Poika's whistle broke into Toivo's dream. The fisherman opened one eye and looked around. All he could see was the sky. He blinked, opened both eyes and tried to raise his head. His exhausted neck muscles struggled to respond, then failed. He couldn't see a boat, didn't even hear the propellers. He collapsed back into the water, submerging both ears. Yes, there was the hum of diesels, twin or quad diesels at that. Which way? Pain shot through him as he arched his back trying to get higher in the water. There! Way off to the north he saw a tiny black speck. It was miles away, a barely visible dot moving across the otherwise blue interface of water and sky. He slumped over, but the spark of hope burned brighter, giving him new strength.

"*Come, tow me over there.*"

Toivo tried to swim on his own. His arms barely able to move, he forced out a few shaky strokes separated by long pauses. He was determined to move toward the ship, though he knew it was hopeless. It was so far away and headed on a course that would take it a mile or more from him. "*Help me reach them before they pass by.*"

Poika swam around Toivo, stopping him. "*No,*" said the dolphin, "*the others have gone to see this ship. It is the vessel of killers-of-friends. You must swim away from it.*"

Killers-of-friends? The murderers! God, they were still out here. Maybe they were searching for him. No, think straight, Toivo. They couldn't possibly believe that you were still alive, especially after that storm. If they were still here they must be after more tuna. No, that tanker couldn't hold much tuna. What were they after? Whatever it was, it must mean there were other tuna boats around. Or maybe factory schools and the swimmers' rafts. Either way, there might be someone out here who would find him.

Toivo's arms refused to take another stroke. His thoughts blurred. He needed to think, but his mind was caught in a quagmire of exhaustion. Who could be in this part of the Pacific besides the mysterious tanker? Factory ships were more likely. There weren't many independents left anywhere, and most of them worked the inshore areas to conserve fuel. Factory schools meant shepherds, dolphins.

"Poika," he spoke the dolphin's name, then switched to their language of whistles and calls, *"are there other dolphins near?"*

"Not near. A half-day swim away there is a pod of those-who-are-men-who-are-fish. They are coming this way."

Those-who-are-men-who-are-fish meant shepherds. *"They are headed toward us? Then let us journey to meet them."*

"Are you strong enough to hold on while we swim?"

"Perhaps. I will have to be."

Poika called the others and the pod started off to the northwest. Toivo could barely hang on to the base of Poika's dorsal fin so they swam slowly. Still, the pod moved steadily through the rolling swells at a little over eight knots. Occasionally they stopped to let Toivo rest. His arms and shoulders burned with fatigue. He was beyond hungry and thirsty; instead he was consumed by a mirage of feasting, of platters heaped with pot roast smothered in gravy and stewed vegetables, of potatoes boiled with shredded beef, of white cake filled with layers of cloudberries. Despite his fantasies, the promise of rescue hardened his will and he clung stubbornly to his task. The sun passed overhead and they pressed onward.

#

The Sunrise Savior churned steadily toward the west. Poddington was glad the storm had finally blown itself out. Lately he'd been having nightmares and the sunshine was a welcome sight. The nightmares he'd had last night remained starkly vivid, the screaming swimmer woman, dead fishermen, the blood, the carnage. He'd lurched awake in a cold sweat.

Stop it, he told himself. Everything would work out. Soon they would be on the new plankton fields were he could begin filling the holding tanks below with microscopic gold. The submarine had left to deliver what PXC they had while he ran from the storm. It would be more than a week before the underwater craft would return. In the meantime, Poddington wanted to have the holds full again so the chemists could get busy. He was itchy to take his well-deserved vacation with Sleena in Singapore.

He closed his diary and leaned back from his desk, pulling his coffee cup toward him. He glanced up at the old fly rod hanging over his desk and thought of more peaceful times, of clear, mountain steams and how much he missed fishing in New Zealand. Maybe someday he'd get back there, buy his own stream.

He let his thoughts drift to Sleena. He remembered meeting her in a sleazy waterfront bar in Tripoli. They had both entered the same drinking contest and had eventually been the only two left still on their stools. She had been so much fun then. Lately she had turned sullen, not her usual self. He'd barely gotten any time with her at all. Whenever he tried to arrange a time and place she was too busy. Busy doing what, he wondered. When they did get together she was bitchy, quarrelsome, a general pain in the ass, and never in the mood. A trip away from the ship would do them both good; especially if he could get her sex drive rekindled.

Enough, he told himself, and rose from his chair, stretching his arms overhead as high as the ceiling would allow. He'd better get up to the wheelhouse and see how things were. It was still a few hours before they reached the new plankton beds and he was getting bored below decks. He would go up and get some air.

He pulled on his captain's cap, selected a movie disc at random, "Moby Dick," and put it in the player, flipped the switch so it would run on the viewer in the pilothouse and set the delay for five minutes so it wouldn't start before he got there. Then he left his cabin closing the steel bulkhead door quietly.

Poddington strode silently up the stairwell and entered the pilothouse through the aft hatch. Kong, another of Poddington's crew from his old trawler, had his back to the hatchway, intent on his job manning the wheel. He didn't see Captain Poddington enter. Deep was leaning halfway out the forward, portside window, glaring down at the main deck. In his tiny cubicle, the radio/radar watchman lounged in the leather chair, both feet propped up on the small glass-fronted case that held the manuals, code book and various crinkled charts. Nobody manned the sonar console.

Poddington set his fists to his hips, arms akimbo. "Isn't anyone going to announce that the captain is on the bridge?" he grumbled.

Deep's head snapped around. The radioman brought both feet down onto the deck with a crash. Kong glanced behind him then returned to watching the big, oil-filled compass.

"Captain's on the bridge," said Deep, half-heartedly. He returned to his business out the window.

Poddington stomped over the main chart table and fumbled with the compass and straightedge, as if he were interested. Except for the icon that represented the new plankton field, the chart was blank. He left the table and paced over to join Deep looking out the window.

"What ever happened to a little discipline?" he demanded.

Deep glared out the window, refusing to look up. "Pod, this isn't a warship and I ain't in the Navy."

"Aw, Deep, give the Cap'n a break," laughed Kong from his station at the wheel. "Things is too borin' for him here, or for me either, for that matter. Better we was chasin' tuna than suckin' up slime what's too small to see."

Deep shook his head. "Or lying in your bunk blasted out of your mind on pixie dust."

"Lay off Kong," said Poddington and slapped Deep on the back the way he used to when they were catching tuna on the old ship. "He's always done his job, stood his watch."

"He knows I'm just busting his 'nads," said Deep. "I think all this killing is getting to me."

"Don't worry. This is just temporary until we can get money enough to enjoy the rest of our lives. I'm not planning to run this barge forever."

"No," said Deep turning away. "I bet we all end up in jail somewhere and don't get to enjoy a damn minute of it."

"Are you still worried about that fisherman who went overboard? For God's sake man, nobody could have survived the storm that just tore through here. There's no one left knows anything about what we did. We're clean. Soon we'll have cash from the PXC load. And selling off the dolphins was pure genius. We've got it made. Nobody will be taking another ship away from us. Nobody."

For a fleeting moment, Deep let a smile cross his face. "I suppose you're right. But killing those fishermen still gives me nightmares."

"Me too," muttered Poddington to himself.

"Cap'n's right, Deep. Things ain't like they used to be. It's survival of the fittest. There ain't enough ocean for everybody anymore."

The door opened and Luis Jones swaggered into the wheelhouse. Poddington saw Deep's lips curl in disgust. Kong's smile faded and the wheelsman turned resolutely to watching the compass.

"Permission to leave the bridge?" asked Deep. "I'd like to go below to the mess hall."

"Yeah, go ahead."

Poddington turned to scan the surrounding ocean. There was still nothing like the view, horizon to horizon, glittering blue, devoid of flaws for as far as the eye could see. He loved the ocean, loved being in command of his own ship. Only this wasn't his ship. A drug cartel owned it and operated it under some false shipping company front. He just ran it while they were out to sea, or did he? He glanced at the dark-haired second mate, took in a deep breath and let it out. Instead of chasing and catching the noble tuna, he harvested and produced drugs to poison people in cities he'd never visited. He knew Deep didn't like it, and neither did most of the rest of his old crew. He couldn't help wondering if their loyalty to him was misplaced.

Chapter 9

Homestead floated listlessly on the light swells. Her motors were shut off while the dolphins rounded up the tuna shoal. A cool breeze swept across the ocean, all that was left of the storm. Ni sat on the cabin roof with Ici standing at the rail beside her. Olga leaned on the rail a little apart from them, her elbows resting on the top rail. The trio watched the efficient dolphins circle the darting tuna, always just ahead of the fish, forcing the school to maintain their heading. The gray mammals were like fleet shadows in the water next to the flashy yellow tuna.

Olga shaded her eyes and scanned the water to starboard, looking for stray tuna. "There's a couple more strays over there," she said, pointing to the swirls on the water that marked tuna feeding on baitfish.

Ici turned from the rail, put the binoculars to his eyes and looked in the direction Olga pointed. He saw the baitfish jumping clear of the water, trying to escape the hungry rush of the tuna. The shimmering gold sides identified them as factory fish, not wild tuna that had taken up with their herd, and more importantly, they were some of the bigger ones left after the harvest, too. He craned his neck to see back toward the bow where Pungee and several others worked to keep the school together. Ici started to raise his hand straight overhead to get Pungee's attention, but the big bottlenose dolphin was already turning and heading toward the strays at full speed.

"Pungee's after them," he said over his shoulder.

"Do you think that's the last of them?" asked Ni, lying back on the deck to get the full sun on her chest.

"No," replied Ici, "but I think it's the last we will find." He shook his head. "We probably lost fifteen thousand fish." He glared at Olga. "I don't know why in the hell I let you try that sonic call stuff while we were submerged. It not only stampeded the fish, it nearly spooked the dolphins away."

Olga's jaws tightened, the muscles making little knots. "The company wanted the tests run. They gave us the equipment and orders to check it out. I just do what I'm told."

"Next time do what I tell you. No more experiments. The company isn't going to pay for lost fish and they aren't paying us to run experiments."

"Fine. You tell them you won't do it."

Olga whirled and stormed down the ladder into the cabin in one continuous, fluid motion.

"Women," spat Ici.

Ni kicked him playfully on the thigh. "Don't give me that 'women' stuff. You screw up about as often as anybody."

Ici snapped his head around, a mock grimace on his face. "Me? I didn't do anything."

"Oh yeah? Who burned breakfast?"

Ici's grimace broke into a smile. "Okay, okay. But this is serious. It's bad enough that the harvest sucked. Now we try this stupid experiment and guarantee ourselves a lousy harvest next time, too. I'm so close to being free, I thought I might make it with the next one. Then the two of us could work on your share of the debt. We'd get rid of it in no time."

"I know," she said, standing up behind him. She wrapped her arms around him and pressed one cheek against his back. "I want to be free as much as you, but bitching at Olga isn't going to bring back the lost fish. They're around here somewhere. Most of them are too big to get eaten. We'll pick them up, a few here, a few there, and by the next harvest we'll have most of them back in the shoal."

"I hope you're right. There's too much riding on this." He turned and hugged her. "If the company wants somebody to run experiments, they should pay us for it. Or at least cover the losses if the experiment screws up."

He let go of her and leaned on the rail to watch Pungee, Sheriff, Slim and Kitty round up the strays and herd them back to the shoal. Ni stepped over next to him.

"I think we should swing a little farther south before we head back to the plankton fields."

"Okay, maybe we can pick up a few more stragglers. I wish I knew how to tell Pungee to go out on his own to round them up. It would save us a lot of time."

She pursed her lips, cocked her head to one side. "Yeah, but we don't know how. We'll have to do it ourselves. Only one swing south, though. Any longer and they'll be too dispersed to make it worthwhile. Besides, maybe some of them will end up back on the plankton beds anyway. I'll go below and set us to run south-southwest for a couple of hours, then curve back around again to a course charted for the fields."

"Go ahead. I'll be down in a few minutes. If you trust me, I'll make some lunch."

"Trust you? It's your duty today. You're not getting out of it that easy." She jabbed him in the ribs and threw herself down the ladder, laughing as she skipped down the hallway.

#

Ici and Ni sat at the galley table. He'd already cleared the dishes, racked them and hit the ultrasonic cleaning cycle. Olga had been moody and sullen through lunch and Ici was glad when she excused herself to get some sleep. He leaned forward to get closer to Ni.

He took her hand. "I would have been clear next harvest," he started but she cut him off.

"Forget it. If you want to be free, all you have to do is spend some of your cash reserve and cancel the rest of the debt."

"Yeah, but that won't leave anything to buy a house, investments to provide income. . .

"Buy a house? I told you I want to homestead in Pacifica. We aren't lubbers. What would we do with a house?"

"A house by the sea, our own beach. Safety, security. A real doctor for you and the baby. It's everything you deserve."

"Everything you want, you mean."

Ici let go of her hand. "Let's go topside. I need some air."

Ni nodded and bounced up from the table. She was out the door, down the hall, and up the ladder in a flash. Ici ran to keep up.

On the flat roof of the cabin they walked to the edge and leaned on the railing. From the sun's position, Ici knew they had already finished their south-southwest run and had started to swing due south. Their turn was gradual but constant, and would continue until they came back around to the north. The dolphin pod kept the tuna shoal tightly bunched, almost as if the dolphins were afraid to repeat the disaster they had been through during the storm. The underwater sonic herding experiment was supposed to give the Homestead crew a method of communicating with the dolphins while they were submerged. Instead, the noise from the underwater speakers had scared the dolphins half to death and scattered the tuna like dried leaves in a tornado. The more Ici thought about it, the more it burned in his gut. Damn it, they wouldn't do anything like that again.

The pontoon boat dipped lightly in the gentle seas, moving ahead at about fifteen knots. The steam generator was working at top efficiency again. With seven more hours of daylight, they should complete their southern swing and be headed north before the sun went down. At that point, they'd have to go back on battery power and reduced speed.

"From up here things always look better," he said and put his arm around her. "We'll work it out when the time comes."

She snuggled against his side. They rode that way for a while. Suddenly, Ici noticed Pungee break away from the herding pod and race off to the southeast.

"Where the hell is he going?" he asked, releasing Ni to step up on the first rail for a better look. "Get the binoculars, will you?"

Ni squinted after Pungee. "What do you think he's after?" she asked, pivoting and stepping toward the ladder.

"Probably more of our lost tuna."

Within a minute Ni had the binoculars and was back up on the roof. She stared through them off to the southeast. After only a quick look, she shoved the binoculars at Ici.

"Someone's in the water. Someone with dolphins. I'm changing course."

Ni scrambled down the ladder. Ici raised the binoculars. Pungee was almost a mile from Homestead where he'd joined a half dozen or so dolphins, swimming slowly, deliberately toward Homestead. Someone was cradled between the mammals but they were too far away to tell if it was a man or cowboy.

Ici looped the binocular straps over the rail and let the glasses hang. In three steps he went down the side rungs and dove into the sea. He caught the crest of a swell and knifed smoothly into the water, leaving almost no wake.

He swam with long, powerful strokes, angling away from the boat on a heading toward Pungee and the strange dolphin pod. Already he could hear the motors change pitch as Ni adjusted the computer course.

Periodically, he stretched his neck up for a better vantage point, looking for the strangers. The dolphins' calls echoed shrilly through the water, their whistles guiding him even though he couldn't see them. At last he crested a wave and saw the struggling group less than fifty meters away. With a burst of speed, he raced to them.

The survivor was definitely not a cowboy. He was nearly unconscious and hung like a rag over the dolphins. His face was cracked and salt crusted; his eyes sealed closed. His light brown hair was matted and caked to his scalp. He held the dorsal fin of the biggest dolphin in a death grip. Ici swam to the side of the dolphin and tried to release the man's fingers. It took all of Ici's strength to pry them from their hold. Even then, the fingers would not relax. The big dolphin whistled at Ici, then rolled away to make room as the Homestead eased up to them.

With one arm Ici grabbed the man under the armpits and swam to the side of the Homestead. Holding the half-drowned stranger's head out of the water with one arm, Ici fumbled with his free hand for a handhold on the wet deck. His hand slipped and he struggled to maintain his grip. Ni appeared around the corner of the cabin, running down the deck. When she reached them, she bent down and grabbed the man by both wrists. She pulled and Ici pushed and they managed to get him on deck. Ici vaulted up next to them.

"Who is he?" asked Ni, kneeling to wipe the salt and blood from around his eyes.

"I don't know. He's unconscious. He was clinging to one of the dolphins.

"He looks pretty bad. I'll get Olga up. You see that he doesn't roll back into the sea."

Ni didn't wait for an answer, and Ici watched her scamper down the deck, disappearing around the corner at the back of the cabin. As soon as she was out of sight, he leaned over the man, putting his ear next to the stranger's nose. The survivor was still breathing—barely. Ici felt for a pulse and was surprised to find it immediately. The heartbeat wasn't very fast, but it was strong.

Carefully he undid the buttons and slipped the wet shirt off over the man's arms. He flipped the soggy mess farther up the pontoon deck. The man's chest was wrinkled and puffy, and there were scattered sores where the salt had attacked his flesh.

Hearing footsteps behind him, Ici turned as Olga and Ni arrived.

"Holy shit," gasped Olga, staring at the stranger. She knelt reverently, fascinated to see a man aboard Homestead. Gently, she touched the sores, running her fingers over his shoulders, arms, chest. "You weren't kidding."

Ni wrinkled her nose in exasperation, but said nothing.

"Should we get him inside?" asked Ici, straightening from his spot beside the stranger. "We can put him in the extra crew quarters."

"Yes," said Olga, "but first I want to get his clothes off. I don't want to soak the sheets with saltwater."

The three of them loosened his belt, pulled off his sox, pants, and at Olga's insistence, even his underwear. Then Ici and Olga carried him while Ni guided them to make sure they didn't ram him into a bulkhead. They took the survivor to the forward crew's quarters, and laid him on the bunk.

"I'll have to sponge him off with fresh water," said Olga, starting for the shower room.

"No problem as long as the steam generator keeps working," said Ici, thinking of the extra water this would sap from their reserve. There was little enough, what with the generator only just being repaired before the storm. Most of the time since had been spent underwater where the generator couldn't produce any steam.

"Quit worrying about the steam generator," snapped Olga. "Make him some fish broth while I wash him. I think we better try to get some warm liquids in him before he slips any farther."

"Come on, Ici," said Ni, tugging on his arm. "Help me in the galley."

Reluctantly, Ici went with Ni. Using the microwave, they stewed fish and squid in a light broth, careful to keep the mixture bland to avoid upsetting the survivor's system. Ni combined several long, low power heating cycles with a final full power burst to bring the thin soup up to steaming hot. Ici poured off the broth and placed the solid pieces in a bowl. He headed back to the starboard crew's quarters with the soup while Ni brought the chunks in a cooking bowl.

By the time they returned, Olga had washed the newcomer, applied ointment to the sores, and tucked him under the crisp white sheets. The stranger's head lolled back against the pillows plumped up behind it. His mouth worked slowly as if chewing. Olga sat on a seat next to the bunk.

"Here," she said, reaching for the bowl of broth, "I'll feed him."

Ici handed the bowl to Olga. "I think you can handle this. I'm going to check out his clothes. Maybe I can find some identification."

Olga nodded. Ni followed Ici into the passageway. They went out through the starboard door, walked around the front of the cabin and crossed over to the port pontoon. The stranger's shirt and pants lay drying in the sun.

Ici picked up the pants and felt in each pocket. Nothing. Ni turned out the shirt pockets. There was nothing in them either.

"I guess we'll just have to wait until he comes to," said Ni, plopping down on the deck to dangle her feet in the wave tops.

"If he comes to," added Ici, sitting down next to her. He stared off into nothing for a long minute, and then said, "We'll have to radio the U.N." He was in no hurry, a few minutes one way or the other wouldn't matter. He couldn't help wondering how much time the bureaucracy was going to waste before they took the stranger and let Homestead get back to their business.

#

Things were finally looking better. Poddington sensed that Deep was calming down and most of the crew had lost their nervous edge. Sleena hinted about more amorous adventures, promising to have dinner in his cabin later. There were days when she seemed to disappear and Poddington wondered where she went, but today wasn't one of them.

The submarine would be back on duty before too long and they had reports of another possible plankton field, one that was supposed to have the new plankton, the good stuff, fresh from a drop by a factory ship. They'd also received a report that their last delivery had gotten through to the United States without a hitch. It had even arrived on time, despite some delays due to the storm. He had verified the cash deposit in his Swiss bank account and now even the crew had relaxed since the word got around their wages were waiting at the nearest landfall.

Poddington directed his attention back to the chart. He'd momentarily forgotten he was on the bridge, supposedly charting their course for this new suspected plankton bed a hundred kilometers north. Automatically he laid a line from their present position to the black "X" drawn a short distance away.

"We might as well get under way," he said to Deep who was at the forward window.

The first mate pushed open the window and yelled down orders to the deck crew to shut down the pumps and withdraw the siphon piping.

Poddington would have done it himself, just to watch Sleena's shapely body gliding across the deck, but he didn't need the distraction right now. Besides, he would have a better view later in his cabin.

Deep turned from the window, having finished passing on the instructions. "We cleaned this one out almost completely." He tossed his baseball cap on the chart table. "I don't get it. How did these drug lords figure out this tuna food was a good source for pixie dust. How'd they know it was any better than the regular stuff that's been floating around out here forever?"

Poddington looked up from the chart. Did it really matter how the drug people knew about the plankton, or how to convert it to PXC? He was about to brush off Deep's question but the look on his face convinced Poddington that for once Deep was taking an interest in his new line of work. Maybe the announced payday had soothed his conscience a bit.

"I don't know," replied Poddington. "Kong said he heard some big shot scientist in the States discovered the plankton and also discovered the side potential for producing PXC from it."

"How would Kong know?"

"Probably heard it the same place he used to buy his dope. Kong claims the new stuff comes out purer, less hazardous, and gives a better high than the stuff made from the natural plankton."

"He ought to know," interjected Deep.

Poddington continued. "I think it's the same guy that developed the swimmers—a Dr. Shikawa. Something like that. I'm not sure who this guy is, or why he would throw in with the druggies, but it doesn't matter. Originally I take it he worked for the fish factories. He couldn't be too smart working for those assholes."

"Yeah," said Deep, lighting a cigarette from a half-crushed pack rolled up in his T-shirt sleeve. "Speaking of Kong—did you know he's been sneaking a pinch or two of the PXC from the lab? Says why should he buy it from the dock scum when there's plenty for everyone right aboard?"

"Yeah, I know. Not that he's asked, but as long as his habit doesn't get in the way of his job, I'll look the other way. We've been shipmates too long to start riding him about his little snort now and again."

At that moment, the radioman stepped up to the chart table, his hand shaking slightly as he held out a crumpled note to Poddington. He stood by while the Captain read the scribbling.

It said, "Captain. Intercepted radio transmission between a swimmers' raft and the frigate Stockholm. Raft has picked up storm survivor. Requests aid to transfer to hospital."

A survivor? Poddington cranked the news into his brain. What ship had been reported lost during the storm? None that he was aware of. He handed the note to Deep. "What do you make of this?"

Deep's face went white. "It has to be that sonofabitch fisherman! There's nobody else around here, and I'm damn sure no other ships have been lost."

Poddington glared at the radioman. "What was this raft's name?"

"I didn't pick up the conversation early enough to get the name."

"Did they give their coordinates? A location?"

"Y-yes, sir, but the transmission was garbled and I couldn't make it out. I think they're close on to us, but I couldn't catch whether they are to the north or south."

"What about the frigate? When are they going to arrive?"

"Not very quickly. They asked if the swimmers could care for him for a bit as they are in pursuit of some whaling pirates. Since he is alive and mostly needs food, water and rest, the swimmers said they could handle it for the time being."

"Then you don't know when the frigate is going to be there to pick up this guy?"

"No, sir."

Poddington's brow furrowed. Just when things seemed to be going his way, there had to be a hitch. Always one more loose end. When would it be over? But at least for now, it seemed that neither the swimmers nor the U.N. knew who this half-drowned fisherman was and they were in no hurry to handle it. Like it or not, Poddington knew he would have to do something about it himself.

"If anybody else in the crew gets wind of this, you're a dead man. Now back to your post." Poddington waved him away with a single brush of his hand.

The radio operator shrank back a step then turned and dived back into his cubicle.

Deep crushed out his cigarette in the shell ashtray. "What are we going to do?"

"Goddamnit, I don't know. I suppose we'll have to hunt them down and kill them all." Poddington pulled off his captain's hat and rubbed his hand through his sparse, red hair. "It just keeps getting worse," he muttered to himself and plopped down in the chair next to the chart table. His eyes remained glassy, fixed on the holo-monitor without seeing what was showing.

#

After a pleasant, private dinner in the officers' mess, the day's troubles had evaporated in the food and too much wine. Now Poddington pushed open the watertight door to his cabin and flipped on the light. His mind raced with anticipation while the wine buzzed around in his head, releasing his pent-up desires. He felt Sleena squeeze against him as they slipped through the door together. Her hard body was already sweaty, the glistening droplets shimmering on her black skin.

As they stepped into his cabin, he grabbed her butt and felt the muscles tighten like concrete in his grasp.

She brushed his hand away. "No you don't," she growled, "tonight I'm calling the shots. You're going to get it the way I want it."

Poddington's imagination sent another pulse of blood rushing to the already growing pressure in his loins. Yes, he loved it her way. He would let her have him anyway she wanted.

Facing him, she grabbed him by the shoulders, her fingers like vises pinching him until it hurt. She backed up, pulling him toward the bed. He followed willingly. Next to his bunk she twisted him sharply, spilling them both onto the bed. She landed on top of him, pinning him in the soft, azure spread. For a long moment she eyed him lustily. Then her fingers found the buttons on his shirt and she undid them one by one. As the last one came open she pounced on him, kissing him hard on the lips, her long, warm tongue forcing its way into his mouth.

"You want me, don't you," she rasped, her breath coming hard like his. "But you can't have me until I'm ready."

Poddington nodded. Yes, when she was ready. He knew she would torment him, then explode on him like a fireball. "Yes, yes," he panted.

She ripped Poddington's shirt out of his trousers, peeling it back so it pinned his arms behind him. Then she turned him over and knotted the shirt so he would have to struggle to get his arms free. But he wouldn't. It would ruin the illusion.

Before going to work on his pants, Sleena rolled him over on his back. She scrambled up on him, sitting so she straddled his legs, and deftly yanked off his belt. Then slowly, seductively, she pulled down his zipper. Hunching over him, she teased him with her mouth. As he watched her lips come nearer and nearer, his excitement rose. Involuntarily, he swelled larger and larger. Before he knew it, he was so engorged that his shorts no longer covered him. Then she paused, stopping only an inch away. She let her tongue lick him lightly, one stroke, then another. Poddington felt like he would self-destruct any second.

She slid backwards off the side of the bed, pulling his pants off as she went. He arched his back, trying to reach her full lips, but she pushed on his chest to hold him down. Then she released him and stepped back from the bed. Deftly she unbuttoned her coveralls, letting them slide to the floor in a pile around her ankles. Poddington stared as the single garment dropped away to reveal her naked body. Her muscles were hard, chiseled in black granite. Her breasts were small, dark mounds that stuck out defiantly.

She stood there for a moment, making love to him with her eyes, visually fondling his bursting erection. Then she was on him like a panther. First she scrambled over him, slid off the other side of the bed, and stood looking down on him like an obsidian goddess, her loins barely an inch above Poddington's face. He could smell her sweat. It gave him new rushes of lust.

Yet he lay there, motionless, waiting to see what she would do, his arms still held by the shirt tied behind him.

Gently she reached down and took hold of his arms, pulling him headfirst off the bed until his shoulders touched the floor. His head rested flat against the gray carpet. His legs remained bent over the bed and Poddington felt like a side of meat hung on a hook. What would she do with him, he wondered, his mind full of desire and excitement.

She put her hands on his knees and stepped forward until she had one foot on either side of Poddington's head. He looked straight up into her, and then slowly, slowly she lowered herself down on him until she settled onto his face. At the same time her mouth engulfed him.

Poddington let his tongue caress her, gently at first, then as the fire in him built to an inferno, his tongue worked in and out, up and down, in a frenzy. He found himself fighting for air, yet at the same time lusting after more of her. Suddenly, in a towering rush, it was over for him. But Sleena didn't let him up, not for a long time.

Chapter 10

Toivo tried to open his eyes. They hurt. They were puffed up like marshmallows. He forced them open a crack but could barely see through the narrow slits. The room spun, everything was fuzzy and out of focus. Bright light from overhead, fluorescent tubes forced him to shut his eyes and wait. Slowly, he tried to open them again. A little better. He closed them once more, blinked, and then opened a slit to let in faint light.

Strange metal walls surrounded him. A woman—was it a woman?—sat in a chair that was bolted to the deck. She wore only a thin strip of cloth that must have been the bottom to a skimpy bikini. Her short blond hair barely covered the top of her head and exposed tiny ears that were molded tight against her temples. The gentle slope of her skull blended into her neck and tapered smoothly into broad shoulders in such a way that there was not a single sharp angle to her golden brown figure. Her chin rested against her chest above sculptured breasts that were streamlined into her torso. Yes, she was a woman—or at least mostly woman. Toivo guessed she was one of the shepherds that watched the factory tuna, one of the mutated people. Her eyes were closed.

What was she doing on Sisu? He looked around again. No, he wasn't aboard Sisu. Memories came flooding back. His crew—gone. The days at sea with Poika holding him afloat. Where was he now? And who was this woman?

He tried to roll over but his muscles had no strength and refused to respond. Total fatigue had overtaken every inch of his body. With a low grunt he managed to turn halfway, pulling the sheets off his chest as he did so. He was suddenly acutely aware that he was naked under the sheets. With a supreme effort he pulled the sheet back up to cover himself.

The shepherd's head snapped up. She rubbed her face and Toivo noticed the long thin fingers with full membrane webbing. Rolling her head to loosen the stiff muscles, she sighed. Under the crop of blond hair, the clear blue eyes were full of kindness and intelligence. Her high cheekbones blended smoothly into a dimpled chin. Her shoulders were streamlined, tapered into her neck and her skin was smooth and tanned. Though she had a flowing, fleshy appearance, the muscles below the skin were hard and strong and rippled as she moved. There was a strange alien beauty about her that intrigued Toivo.

"You are awake," she said in a whisper that carried the rasp left from sleep.

Toivo tried to speak but his tongue felt fuzzy. It refused to respond. He rolled his tongue around the inside of his mouth trying to wet it, trying to clear the dryness. "W-where am I?"

"On the Homestead," she said, reaching out, letting one hand lightly touch his shoulder.

Her hand was warm and soft and Toivo felt something human in her touch. It was comforting, reassuring, and it reminded him of his mother's touch at bedtime when he was young. Toivo let her hand stay on his shoulder.

"The Homestead?" he repeated. "Is this a factory raft?"

"Yes. There are three shepherds here. I'm Olga. The other two are Ici and Ni. We rescued you from the sea yesterday. You were in pretty bad shape, but nothing a little broth and some good T-L-C won't cure. You're safe. You'll be feeling fine before long." She leaned over and seemed to size up Toivo, her eyes barely an inch from his. "What's your name?"

His mind struggled with his new reality. These were shepherds. Had they sent the armed tanker after Sisu? Did they blame him for what the IFG had done to the Oyster Bay? What about Poika? Surely they wouldn't hurt a dolphin. "Poika. Is he all right?"

Her look saddened. "There was no one with you. Your shipmate must have lost his grip."

Toivo's mind stumbled. Shipmate? Then, realizing her mistake, he tried to chuckle. It stuck in his throat. "No, Poika is my dolphin. If you found me, Poika must have been with me."

"Your dolphin?" she asked, straightening with a quizzical look in her eyes. "People don't own dolphins. Only the factories can own a dolphin and then only under strictest humanitarian regulations."

"Of course I don't own Poika. He is my friend. Is he here? Is he alive?"

"If he is one of the dolphins we found with you, then he's fine." She paused, glanced away for a second, then added, "But what about you? Don't you have a name?"

"Of course I have a name. I'm Toivo. But what about Poika? Is he okay?"

"He's fine. Did he herd tuna for you?"

Thinking of tuna made Toivo think about Sisu. Sunk, maybe by agents of the factories. He remembered the Sunrise Savior—a research ship on a humanitarian mission. No, not the real Sunrise Savior but a ship disguised to look like the research ship. Then a black vision of the submarine's conning tower reminded him of the deadly accomplice. Only the factories had enough money to buy a submarine, even an old one; or to alter a ship to look that much like the Sunrise Savior.

They had taken his Sisu. And now that he thought of it, the insurance had lapsed last summer. Now what? How would he make a living? He looked at the shepherd. How did he know she was a shepherd? Maybe she was a pirate or working for the same people as the killers. He remembered the armed tanker, the one that had attacked Sisu; the one Poika had towed him away from. They could have killed Poika and taken him prisoner. Maybe Toivo was aboard that same tanker right now. He struggled to get out of bed.

"Easy, easy," she said both hands gently but firmly pushing Toivo back into bed. "Everything is fine." She stroked his cheek, letting her fingertips run down along his neck. "What happened to you? Did the storm sink your boat?"

"Storm?" Toivo remembered the towering waves. It was like a dream. Yes, there had been a storm. What should he tell her? Maybe they didn't know he was a survivor from the boat they had attacked. No, he would wait until he knew more about them, where he was, and who his captor or captors were. "Yeah," he said, "she broke up in the storm and went down like a rock. How did you find me?"

"Your dolphin towed you to us. Our D's heard them calling. They steered us to you. Lucky thing."

"Yeah," he said, and tried to slip farther under the sheets. "When can I see Poika? He's probably worried about me."

"He'll be okay. All the D's that were with you, even the ones without I-D tags, have taken it upon themselves to help herd our tuna." Here her eyes narrowed, her mouth went taut. "Where did you get factory D's to run with your own?"

A good question, Toivo thought. If he told her about the dead shepherds it would connect him to the murders or identify him to the killers, if that was what she was. No. Better to keep quiet. "Strays," he muttered. "Poika brought them along."

"Huh," she snorted, wrinkling her mouth. "You rest for now. I'll be back with some broth in a little while. Maybe tomorrow you will be strong enough to go up on deck and see your D's. They are fine. Good workers, too."

She turned, went out the bulkhead door and eased it closed. Toivo wondered if she was going to get the guards or if she was just a shepherd like she said. He was too tired to worry about it for long. He fell asleep.

#

Olga walked quickly to the galley. Ici sat on a stool drinking a cup of coffee. He looked up when she entered.

"He's awake," she said.

"Did he talk?"

"Yes. Well sort of. I think he's still delirious. He's says the untagged Ds are his. Says they're his friends."

"And where did he get those factory Ds?" Ici put down his coffee cup. "Maybe this fisherman had a hand in killing cowboys."

"I doubt that. More likely he's the one that radioed in finding the Oyster Bay. He says the factory Ds are strays that were led to him by his Ds."

"Sounds like lies, to me." Ici picked up his coffee cup again and took a sip.

"Could be. But the Ds towed him here and I've never heard of them doing that before, just as a random act of kindness."

"So you believe him."

"Not exactly. I think there's more than what he's telling, but I do believe he's one of the good guys."

Ici looked up, caught the smile on Olga's face. "Wouldn't be because you've taken to this castaway, would it?"

"No." She turned into the galley proper. "I'm taking him soup when he wakes up again."

"Good idea. We can't starve him," said Ici on his way out.

#

How much time had passed, Toivo wasn't sure. He had eaten more broth and Olga had come and gone more than once. In his waking moments he thought about his predicament. He decided Olga was a strange name for a shepherd, it sounded too Russian. He promised to be wary of what he told her. He knew better than to trust a Russian.

A couple of times she brought the other two shepherds. Toivo only remembered faint shadowy outlines. Now, sunlight streamed through the single porthole in the bulkhead. By the steep angle the rays made with the walls he could tell the sun must be high overhead. It was near midday. But which day?

He sat up, his arms providing shaky support, and managed to prop himself against the wall. He tried to rearrange the pillow so it supported his back, but that was too much to ask. His weary muscles refused to cooperate. Right now he needed the bathroom and he damn sure didn't want another bedpan. He looked around the small quarters, barely three by three meters. There was no door that might lead to a latrine.

"Hey," he yelled. "Can anybody hear me?"

There was a scurrying in the hall. The tall, blond shepherd-woman rushed into the room. As always she wore only the bottom of a swimming suit and it still unnerved Toivo to see her tanned breasts uncovered.

"What is it?

"I need to go to the bathroom. Right now."

"I'll bring the dishpan you've been using as a bedpan," and she started to bend to retrieve something from under the bed.

"No. No more bedpans. Get me some clothes and I'll use the latrine."

"I don't think you're able. . ."

"Don't stand there arguing with me. Get me something to wear and help me to the latrine before I wet myself."

"There isn't anything to wear, except one of Ici's suits. He's up topside right now. It'll take a few minutes to go ask if you can borrow something. Can you wait?"

"I doubt it."

"Then let me help you to the head."

Toivo swallowed hard. What kind of people thought it was okay to run around naked? "Forget the suit, just help me to the bathroom."

Her hands were soft and the bones delicate, almost fragile, but her strength gave Toivo a begrudging respect for the shepherd woman. Olga wrapped her arms around his shoulders and muscled him out of the bunk. He staggered to keep his feet, although with her firm grip there was no way he could fall. His nakedness left him feeling self-conscious, vulnerable. His skin tingled where it pressed tightly against hers while she dragged him upright down the hall. They went through a narrow door and around the partition wall to the latrine.

"Can you stand?" she asked, stopping before the lone urinal, "or do you want me to sit you down?

"I need to sit." He didn't want to sit but his knees wobbled so badly that he would have fallen if she had let go. He wasn't going to have her hold him while he peed standing up.

She turned him and lowered him to the stool. He noticed her eyes sweep over his body. She smiled. "Anything else?"

"Get out of here and let me go in peace," he snapped. In a few minutes it was mercifully over. She carried him back to bed. "I want to go on deck," he had insisted, but she refused. He fell asleep before he could debate the issue.

Olga waited a moment until she was sure Toivo slept, then she let herself out. She'd been sleeping in a chair in the hallway outside his room in case he'd needed something. Now she picked up the chair and moved it quietly into Toivo's room. She propped it against the bulkhead, leaned back in it and tried to go to sleep. Night watch would be longer than usual without sleep.

#

Sometime later Toivo awoke. The sun was still up, though it had sunken low in the sky. Olga sat in the chair next to his bed. He had grown accustomed to her alien physique, even found it pleasant. Still he constantly reminded himself that until proven otherwise, she was his enemy and most likely Russian as well. The minute he opened his eyes, she smiled and patted his leg through the sheet.

"Feel better?" She held out a bowl of broth that smelled delicious. "Here, drink this."

She started to spoon out of the bowl for Toivo. That was too much for him. He reached out and took the bowl and spoon from her. He felt stronger, more like himself. A lot of the stiffness seemed to be easing, although many of the worst sores still burned like fire when touched. It didn't matter; he wanted to go up on deck. He had to know before another day was done whether he was on a compassionate shepherd's raft or the armed tanker. Poika would tell him who these people were. *If* the dolphin was still around like she said he was.

He gulped down the broth and handed her the bowl.

"I want to go up on deck."

She started to shake her head no, but he stopped her. "I mean it. I want to talk to Poika now. Today. Now. Help me up on deck."

"Okay. First let me help you into these." She pulled a pair of blue stretch bikini trunks from her lap.

He looked at the tiny fragment of cloth. It would hardly qualify as clothing. Then again it was better than being naked.

"No," he said, "I'll put them on." He'd suffered enough indignity. He could at least dress himself.

He pushed off the sheet and wiggled to the edge of the bed. She handed him the suit. Toivo bent as far as he could, straining to raise one leg high enough to get a foot into the suit. He couldn't do it and felt his face redden. Struggle as hard as he could, he couldn't reach it. He leaned farther and farther. This was ridiculous. He would dress himself. He teetered on the edge of the bed. Without warning he pitched forward—right into her arms.

"Here," she said, gently straightening Toivo. "I'll help you."

He started to argue, but what was the use? If she didn't help him, he wouldn't get the suit on. He let her slip it up over his legs.

She pulled him to his feet, once more wrapping her arms around him. Her grip was strong, comforting, yet he stiffened with discomfort. She shuffled him to the door. "It's not far."

Out in the hallway, Toivo saw she wasn't kidding. To get to the latrine they had turned to the left, now they turned right and only fifteen meters away the doorway to the aft deck stood open to the Pacific. She half carried him down the hall, past an open doorway that led to some kind of control room. Toivo didn't bother to look into the darkened room. He had his eyes riveted on the rolling blue swells beckoning to him through the aft door.

They stepped out onto the deck that connected the two pontoons. In the middle was a funny dome-like contraption surrounded by small mirrors. They skirted the glass dome and went to the port pontoon where she sat him on the deck almost at the water's edge.

No doubt. This was a factory shepherd's floating home. He admired the compact construction, the solidly welded outer hull that he knew was built to survive the pressures of submersion. Toivo had seen a few of them in his fishing travels, but never up close. The boxy cabin wasn't much to look at but Toivo admired the vessel's practical design.

More important right now were the dolphins, especially Poika. He shaded his eyes and caught sight of the mammals off to port. They were between seventy and one hundred meters away, working a large school of tuna that milled around countless frightened baitfish. He tried to count the number of dolphins, but the irregular timing of the leaps that marked their breathing cycles made it impossible. He watched for minute, scanning the sparkling water. There, at the flank of the tuna shoal was Poika.

"Poika." he called. *"Come to Toivo."*

The big bottlenose rolled away from the working group and buried his flukes into the sea, making short work reaching the pontoon boat.

"Toivo. You have returned from your rest-that-heals."

"Yes. I am glad to see that you are finding work to keep you out of mischief."

"It is a pleasure to guide plump tuna such as they oversee. I like keeping busy as long as these men-who-are-fish help you."

"What of these men-who-are-fish? Are they part of the men-who-kill's pod? Are they only trying to learn how much I know about them before they kill me?"

Poika did a snap roll beside the boat, spraying water from his mouth when he surfaced. *"Toivo, you worry too much. If these men-who-are-fish wished to kill you they need only have left you to die. Can you not see that they are hard working and honest as you yourself. I have spoken with the members of their pod and they are worried and puzzled by those that kill. They are not part of it."*

"How can you be sure?"

Poika hesitated and Toivo swore that for a moment he saw a look of hurt in the big dolphin's eyes. *"We do not tell lies to each other."*

Shame held Toivo's fears in check. Instead of more questions the fisherman said," *Of course. They are taking good care of me and I will be better soon. We will be going fishing again."*

"Good. You rest now while I work. We'll talk more later."

Poika turned and dove back toward the other dolphins. In the distance Toivo saw Tyttö and the factory dolphins that he'd adopted from the Oyster Bay. Evidently they had all decided to go to work for these shepherds. It must be as Poika had said. These people were not the killers.

A strong hand gripped his upper arm and pulled him around to face the blond shepherd. "What the hell were you doing?"

"Talking to Poika. I didn't mean to be rude, but. . ."

"Rude!? You expect me to believe you were actually talking to a D?"

Toivo looked incredulously at the woman. Her eyes were ice, cold pinpoints of hard blue. She didn't believe him. "Y-yes," he stammered, remembering all the doubters who had harassed him when he was little. Even his father hadn't believed him. It had been so bad that he'd refused to discuss it for years—until he met Poika. "I talk to dolphins." Maybe he shouldn't have revealed his ability so quickly. The distrust crept back into his mind.

Her eyes narrowed. "Christ, how did you learn to talk to them?"

"Easy. I was too young to know I couldn't."

Olga gave Toivo a sharp look. "That's it?" The serious look twisted into a sad little half smile and she shook her head. "I think you're putting me on."

"Okay, I'm joking. I didn't just talk to Poika, I can't talk to dolphins and I've never had a conversation with any cetacean." It rolled off his tongue so easily, the denial that was built in after repeating it thousands of times to his father and his father's colleagues at the Kewalo Basin labs. If he hadn't found Poika drifting alongside his dead mother Toivo probably never would have spoken another word of dolphin as long as he lived.

"Oh Christ, can you talk to the D's or not? You sure were making a bunch of weird noises and that dolphin seemed to be listening. What did he tell you?"

Now she had that serious look again. Well, what did he have to lose? "He told me you weren't involved with the men who sank my boat and killed my crew that it was okay to tell you how I got scuttled and left to die."

Olga's eyebrows arched. "You were the one who sent the Mayday. Wait here. I've got to tell Ici and Ni."

She started back through the door.

"Where else would I go?" Toivo retorted. He'd told the Russian too much.

Chapter 11

Aboard the false Sunrise Savior the deck crew had knocked off for lunch and Poddington, Deep and Luis Jones sat in the officers' mess. Poddington was trying to enjoy the cabbage-and-ham dish the cook had served them hot from the galley. Lewis' presence put a pall on everything. Poddington had decided some time ago that the second mate wouldn't hesitate to kill him or Deep if it seemed expedient. Making a getaway at the next port had started looking better all the time.

There had been no sign of swimmers since they had arrived at the new plankton beds and down in the bowels of the ship their production of PXC was running ahead of schedule. Poddington had hopes that they would make the next shipment early. He still clung to dreams of getting Sleena off on a vacation, away from the ship, though lately she seemed irritable, argumentative. If he suggested planning a trip to Singapore, she preferred Australia, if he said okay, Australia, she wanted to go to Hong Kong. And money, always she talked about making more money.

Too bad they couldn't manage to take in a few more dolphins before they sent their cargo in. The submarine captain had mentioned that the demand for dolphin meat had created a much more lucrative market than either he or Poddington had imagined. It was cash straight into their pockets—no splits, no payroll.

Poddington's one nagging worry was that damn fisherman. If indeed, he was the one who had gone overboard when they sank the Sisu. Poddington didn't see how it could be, but then again, if it was true, there would be hell to pay. In some ways, he wished Jones would just give up the idea of killing the fisherman and they could scoop up the plankton and get out of the area.

Deep spooned in another mouthful of the greasy casserole. "Another good day's work and we can get off this bed with a full load," he said with a mouthful of mashed food.

"Yeah, and I'll be ready to see port," added Luis Jones. "Any port—that is, any port where there's women and good scotch."

"Another day or so at most and we'll be heading in," said Poddington. "This is one hell of a lot easier than fishing. And the pay is better."

Poddington liked reminding everyone how much better off financially they were since he'd made the deal to take over the Sunrise Savior. Maybe he was just trying to convince himself.

He eyed the second mate suspiciously. The man remained an enigma. He never said much except to remind everyone who they worked for. Despite attempts to get the man to open up, Poddington had failed to find out much about him. No one doubted that he was a plant by the ship's owners to keep things in line. Poddington had made sure to cut him in on the dolphin profits. So far it appeared to have softened the man's outlook, but it had not necessarily changed his loyalties. Everyone was looking after himself in the end.

There was a clatter of boots on the gangway and a young sailor ducked into the officers' mess. "Captain," he said stiffening as he stopped before the table. "We have radar and visual contact with a raft that surfaced a kilometer off our stern. I don't think they are aware that we are here. There has been no radio transmission and there's no one on deck."

"Can you see her name?"

"I think she's the Turtle."

Poddington rose from the table. "This could be the raft we're after. She had to be in these waters somewhere."

The others rose with him.

"Let's get up on the bridge. We may need to take immediate action."

Poddington strode around the table, his uneaten ham and cabbage forgotten. The others followed him up the stairwell to the wheelhouse.

Once on the bridge, Poddington took the binoculars from their case near the chart table and looked where the young sailor pointed. Sure enough, there was the low-slung, boxy, pontoon raft bobbing on the swells. The name painted on the bow was indeed "Turtle".

Over his shoulder he said, "You on the radio, if there is even a peep from that raft, jam it, and fast."

He turned back to the binoculars. Now that he had steadied them he could make out a pair of swimmers in the water along with a half dozen dolphins. As he watched, they dived beneath the surface. Poddington was amazed at how long the mutants remained underwater before they had to surface for air. They went back under after only a moment topside to catch their breaths.

"I think they're having some kind of trouble," he said to Deep who stood next to him watching with the spare set of binoculars.

"I'd say so too," said the first mate, "though I'm not sure whether it has anything to do with the raft or it's some damn thing with their tuna."

"It doesn't matter," said Poddington. "Signal the engine room for 'Ahead Slow'. We're going to ease our way over to them and find out who they are."

"Shall I ready the deck gun?" asked Luis Jones, suddenly intent on the raft. "I think we'll find a few dolphins with them so we might as well break out the small arms as well."

Poddington looked uneasily at the second mate. There was an animal look about the man's dark eyes. If Poddington didn't give the order, he had no doubts Jones would, and probably send Poddington below in irons. He hesitated a minute. What if this wasn't the raft with the fisherman on board?

"What are you waiting for, Captain?" snarled Jones.

"Do it," snapped Poddington. He prayed this was the raft that held the mysterious shipwreck survivor. If so, they might be able to wrap up all the loose ends and be done with the whole mess.

"What are you going to do?" asked Deep. "What if this isn't the raft that picked up the missing fisherman?"

"What difference does it make? They know too much by now to let them go. I just want to be sure before we sink her that we've put an end to this."

Poddington didn't like it but couldn't think of any way to change it. He felt pressured forward by the rush of something too big to stop. Whether this was the raft they were looking for or not, they would have to sink it and kill the crew. More killing. The nightmare visions returned to his mind. The same scenes replayed over and over, the screaming swimmer woman, dead fishermen, the blood, the carnage. He didn't want any new nightmares. This time he wasn't going aboard.

Glancing down at the Sunrise Savior's foredeck, he saw Sleena come up from below, an automatic rifle slung over her shoulder. She motioned for the other armed men to take up station along the rail, directing them to stay behind the bulkheads where they couldn't be seen. She was going to lead the boarding party. Poddington noticed almost absentmindedly that none of the men were crewmen from his old fishing vessel. It made him wonder who was in charge anyway?

Sleena glanced up at the wheelhouse, saw Poddington and yelled, "Are you coming?"

Poddington swallowed hard. "No, you take care of it."

"We will," said Jones, emerging from under the overhang.

For a long moment, Poddington watched Jones and Sleena as they prepared to go slaughter the swimmers aboard the raft. A queasiness came to his stomach and he turned away from the scene out the window. The holo-monitor was blank. He would have to go to his quarters and put in something to watch—anything to take his mind off this mess. Maybe he would write in his diary. That seemed to ease his feelings of guilt.

#

It wasn't long before it was over. The raft sunk, the swimmers dead, and what dolphins they could shoot were killed, hauled aboard and frozen. Poddington remained in a funk. He'd gone below, and written in his diary, but couldn't stay cooped up in his quarters. He'd trudged back up to the bridge in time to see the dolphin carcasses disappear down into cold storage. Sleena and Luis Jones came up the stairs and entered the wheelhouse.

"Only swimmers on board," spat Jones.

"Killed them all," said Sleena with a grin. "Ugly things they are."

Poddington scratched his thinning red hair. "Then we still haven't found the fisherman. What now?"

The Second Mate scowled at the Captain. "You know what. Track down every raft out here if necessary until we get him."

Poddington realized his vacation was a long way off. Tracking down little rafts in the middle of the Pacific would be nearly impossible.

"Why bother?" asked Deep. "Why not just finish siphoning the plankton until we've got a full load then get the hell out of here. There has to be other plankton fields far enough away that no one will make the connection."

"That's not the way we do things," said Jones flatly.

"Well, I'm the Captain," started Poddington but Jones cut him off.

"Yes, and you work for the company. So get busy figuring out where that sonofabitch is and take us there."

With that, the Second Mate jerked open the wheelhouse door and went out.

Poddington looked around. Deep stood stoically by the wheel. Sleena leaned against the aft bulkhead, her arms folded while the silence hung thick.

"So," said Poddington, "what do you think we should do? These rafts are scattered all over. They aren't going to be easy to find."

Sleena smiled slyly, walked to the door and said, "You figure it out. I've got better things to do," opened the door and went out on deck.

Deep stared after her. "What's with her?"

Poddington turned to look at the map. "I wish I knew. I hardly see her anymore," he said, a touch of regret evident in his voice.

#

Toivo leaned back against the thick metal exterior wall of the cabin, trying to get comfortable while he waited for Olga to return with the other two shepherds. He watched the ocean roll past, enjoying, as he always did, the feeling of wonder. Nothing compared to the thrill of being on the deck of a ship at sea. Now that Sisu was gone, he might not be able to put to sea again. He had a few dollars saved, though not nearly enough to buy even an old boat. Who would loan him money for fishing? Only the factories made money anymore. Maybe it was time to find a new line of work. Even as he sat there thinking about being forced to find a regular job, the sea whispered in his ear, calling as it always did. And what about Poika? And Tyttö? Where would the dolphins go if Toivo didn't fish anymore?

"You look much better."

The masculine voice startled Toivo and he turned to see Ici squatting down on the aft deck near him. Behind the dark-haired man with oriental features, Olga and Ni were just coming out through the doorway. Ni, who was even shorter than Ici and had the same Asian eyes, squatted next to her mate. Olga remained standing, arms folded across her chest.

Ici's eyes went to the tuna herd first, checking as if by habit. Then he looked back to Toivo. "You look a lot better than you did a couple of days ago. When we picked you up you were hanging on by willpower alone. Olga worked a miracle." He motioned with a nod at the taller woman but she remained expressionless. "Olga says you talk to the dolphins."

"She told you that, did she?" Toivo wondered what was next. Accusations? Pointed questions to prove he was a fake?

"More important," broke in Ici, "you have a story to tell. Olga says that it was you who sent the mayday we picked up a few days ago. That you found Lisa, Vern and Wing. Did you send the message about them? What happened?"

Toivo told his story starting with the dead shepherds and finishing with the killing of his crew. Despite his best efforts to control them, tears trickled down his cheeks and he had to stop his story twice to regain his composure. Thinking about Wilho, Helmar and Gunnar, seeing their faces, it hurt, really hurt.

Ici patted Toivo on the shoulder. "It's okay, I understand. The loss hurts us all." An awkward silence followed until Ici asked how he had managed to survive the storm. Toivo told them how the dolphins had kept him afloat. Ici sat back, looking off toward the tuna herd, a blank glaze on his face.

"Ici, you don't understand," shot Olga, "he talks to the dolphins."

"So do I," snapped Ici.

"No, not like that. I mean Toivo speaks the dolphins' language."

Ici's head snapped around to look at the blond shepherd woman. Then he looked at Toivo. "Show me."

Toivo grumbled. Was he a trained seal? But these people had rescued him so he would show them. He stood up, tottered, and Olga caught him, steadied him.

"*Poika*," he called. "*Bring me a fish. I am hungry.*"

"What did that mean?" asked Ici.

"Bring me a fish. I am hungry."

A few minutes went by. Ici stood up and looked across toward the tuna school. "So, what's supposed to happen?"

At that moment, Poika leaped high out of the water right next to Homestead. In his mouth he held a small bonito. As he fell back into the sea, Toivo reached out unsteadily and took the fish from the dolphin's mouth. Olga held on to keep him from falling overboard.

"Thank you."

"You are welcome. Do you need anything else?"

"No. Return to your friends."

The dolphin turned away from the boat and swam back to the tuna shoal. Ici stood scratching his head.

"I can't believe it. How can you talk to the D's?"

Toivo retold the story of his youth at the Marine Mammal Laboratory and about how years later he had found Poika swimming next to his dead mother.

Before he could finish, Olga cut him short. "He's too tired to stay up here. Let's go in the cabin. Can you sit for a while? I'll make you some broth."

"Yes," said Toivo. "I'll try sitting but I don't know for how long." His knees were shaking so badly he wasn't sure he could make it back inside.

Olga helped him into the dining area and lowered him into a chair. Toivo rested his arms on the table, using them to support his tired body.

"What I don't understand," said Ici, once all four of them were in the dining room, "is why someone wants to kill shepherds. Or your crew. We've seen rustlers from time to time, but they only sneak in, net some of our tuna and run as fast as they can. They never shoot at anyone."

"And who pays for the tanker, the men and all the guns?" asked Ni. "These cannot be fisherman, any kind of fishermen."

Toivo shook his head. "I don't know. It all happened so fast. It seems like a dream. And, even stranger, I saw the name of the tanker. It said 'Sunrise Savior' but it wasn't the real Sunrise Savior. I've seen the environmental vessel and that wasn't it. Who could afford to make a ship look like something it wasn't? And why?"

Ici's mouth opened, but Toivo continued. "There's more. Along with the Sunrise Savior there was a submarine. Granted it was an old model, a collector's item out of some museum, but it was a submarine, nonetheless. And capable of firing torpedoes as well."

Olga stood in the doorway connecting the galley and the mess hall. She had soup on the stove already and was watching it while she tried to stay abreast of the conversation. "The Sunrise Savior? She was doing research on oceanic pollution. A good cover to be almost anywhere you want."

"Yes, I'm sure that's why the name. But what are they doing?"

"And what's the connection with us?" asked Ni.

Ici scratched his head. "I think you're having delusions. Or worse, you screwed up and let your ship sink in the storm and now you're trying to cover up your own mistake." His dark eyes were hard, gauging Toivo.

Toivo fought to control his rising anger. "It happened exactly like I told you. Poika saw it all."

Ici rolled his eyes. "Yeah, your D will tell us all about it."

"Lay off," snarled Olga, stepping into the dining room. "He's been through enough."

"Of course you would stand up for him. You're so hung up on him you couldn't tell if he was lying or not."

Ni held up her hands just as Toivo was about to unleash his own broadside. "This isn't getting us anywhere. If he's making it all up, why did we receive that mayday before the storm? And why is that U.N. frigate, the Stockholm, snooping around?"

"Right," added Olga, "and you heard him talk to his D."

Ici folded his arms across his deep brown chest. "Maybe you are telling the truth—maybe not. If you are, who is behind it?"

"I told you I haven't got a clue," said Toivo, shaking his head.

"You must have heard some of the other fishermen talking about the Sunrise Savior in port," said Olga still glaring at Ici.

"Nothing. Nobody gives a damn about research vessels unless they put more fish in their hold. The only talk in port is about the factory ships taking all of the prime fishing areas and now the wild fish are too hard to catch. There are a lot of angry people, but I don't think murder is a fisherman's game."

"It is someone's," said Ici, his forehead furrowed. "Do you think we should radio the Stockholm? Maybe if I told them about Toivo's dolphinese I could get a finder's fee."

"We could radio the frigate, ask for help," suggested Ni.

"What good would that do? They already know we picked up a shipwreck survivor." Olga retorted. "Why aren't they here?"

Ici stalked toward the door. "Someone else must know what's going on. Maybe one of the other cowboys has seen or heard something. I think I'll radio Michael. The last time I talked to him their raft was only about a hundred kilometers north of us."

"Who is Michael?" blurted Toivo.

"He was my first partner. We both were initially assigned to the Homestead. We worked it for a couple of years together until Star-Kist reassigned him to his own raft, Turtle, with Joshua and Sandy. We talk to each other pretty regularly. One of these days we're going to buy property next to each other and retire."

Toivo saw Ni's mouth wrinkle in disgust but she kept quiet.

"Maybe you know some people ashore," suggested Olga. "You could radio them and find out what's going on."

Toivo chuckled. "Not really. The only friends I have are halfway around the world. Right now I would just as soon not broadcast my whereabouts. The killers probably assume there are no witnesses and I'd like it to stay that way."

Olga's cheeks flushed. Her mouth twitched involuntarily and she strained to get out words she didn't want to have to say. "I'm sorry. We already radioed both the Stockholm and our factory ship, the Martin B., that we had picked up a fisherman."

"Even if they did overhear your radio messages, it doesn't mean the killers know who I am or what I've seen; but if they figure it out they'll be looking for us."

"Maybe they already are," said Ici. "In which case radioing the U.N. frigate can't hurt."

"If they are looking, at least they don't know exactly where we are. They'll still have a hard time finding us," said Toivo, rubbing his eyes. He just wanted to go to sleep. He was too tired to think.

"Maybe not as hard as you think," said Ni, "we radioed our position."

Ici stood up. "Then our only hope is that they didn't pick up our transmissions. I'm calling Michael." Ici walked out of the dining room and crossed the hall to the control room.

With both doors open, Toivo could hear every word.

"Homestead calling Turtle," he heard Ici's voice. A pause, then the same call repeated.

Another pause, then an answering voice. "This is Turtle. Is that you, Ici?"

"Roger, Michael. Ever hear of anyone who can talk to D's? Sounds impossible, but it isn't. We need to get together and have a talk."

Static. "No, . ." Static. "—do you want?"

"What is your current position? Can we set a rendezvous?"

A long silence filled only by the buzz of radio static.

"Michael, are you reading me?"

"Roger, your transmission is loud and clear—and very strong." There was an unnecessary emphasis on the word strong. "We are experiencing—pause—extreme difficulties, will be submerged for some time. Stay away!"

The radio spewed static and though Ici asked them several times to repeat the transmission, there was no further communication.

Ici returned to the dining room. "What the hell was Michael talking about? Difficulties, must submerge, stay away. He's in trouble."

"No shit," snapped Olga. "He's trying to tell us he is in big trouble. He doesn't want to endanger us. Maybe he thinks they'll leave us alone if we don't know anything."

"How could he be so stupid? We're going up there." Ici slammed his fist on the table.

Ni put one hand on his shoulder. "Take the whole herd a hundred kilometers or more off our feeding zones just to see what might be going on?"

"Or stay here and wait for whoever is out there to come looking for us," said Toivo, biting off the words. Frustration and fear made his insides churn.

A buzzer sounded. Ni sprang from the table, crossed the hall and ducked into the control room. "Unidentified vessel on radar," she yelled back.

There was a scurry as the other shepherds rushed to the control room. Toivo was left sitting at the table. He had thoughts of joining them, but his legs wouldn't hold him. Footsteps pattered through the corridors as the shepherds ran for the deck to get a look. The fading light that filtered through the portal told him the sun was almost below the horizon. Total darkness would be on them in an instant.

"There it is," he heard Olga say. "They're going for the tuna."

"Ni," ordered Ici, "bring us to full power. Bring her around twenty-five degrees to port."

Racing footsteps, then Ni's voice giving commands to a computer. Toivo strained to hear. What if it was the killers? He could see the black, long-barreled cannon traversing to take aim at the Homestead. They would all be killed. He had to warn them. Toivo tried to stand. His legs wobbled and he fell, barely breaking his fall with both hands. Weakness flooded every muscle.

He crawled toward the door. Hand over hand he pulled himself up and over the lip of the watertight hatchway. Like a fish he flopped into the hallway.

"No," he yelled. "If it's the Sunrise Savior they'll kill us all."

Olga stuck her head inside the aft door. "What the hell do you think you're doing?"

She dashed to him, scooped him up in both arms and carried him out on deck. "There," she said, pointing to the dark silhouette, running without lights. "It is not the Sunrise Savior. Do you still think it is the killers?"

Toivo took one look. He could see the main net boom highlighted against the fading glow on the horizon. It was a fishing trawler, and an old boat at that. Not very big for being so far from land. These were desperate fisherman, he thought, but they were not the men who had killed his crew. "No."

"Rustlers," snapped Ici. "They are already pulling up their nets. They'll outrun us, but I don't think they got many of our tuna."

"They'll be back," said Olga. "But probably not tonight."

As they watched, the fishing boat turned and ran. In the gathering darkness, Toivo could see the shapes of the men on deck pulling the tuna out of the nets even as they started to make speed. They were heading away, the nets still partially in the water, men stowing them as the winches reeled them in. Men trying to eke out a living from the sea, much as he had done only a few days ago. In a way, he envied them. They had their own ship, were in charge of their destiny. Would he ever be able to do so again?

"I wish we had a gun," snarled Olga.

"We'll have to take turns on the radar bench tonight," said Ici. He ducked through the door into the cabin.

Olga's eyes followed Ici inside, then turned to meet Toivo's. "Are you ready for bed?"

"Yes," muttered Toivo. He had no strength left.

She carried him to his quarters and gently laid him on his bunk. Sitting beside him on the edge of the bed, she massaged his tired legs. She rubbed them gently with short vigorous strokes of her fingertips. Toivo felt the blood rush through his exhausted muscles. It felt good.

"You are a handsome fisherman," she said, letting her hand slide a little higher on Toivo's thigh.

Toivo winced. He thought he knew what she wanted and seeing her bare breasts almost thrust in his face, knew he wanted it too. Physically he was unable, which was good. He wasn't sure he could have forgiven himself for making love to a Russian. He tried to smile, to avoid thinking about her hands on his body. "You have been at sea too long," he joked.

Nevertheless, the blood rushed through his cheeks. He couldn't fight his thoughts. For an instant, wild desires burned in his mind. It had been so long since he had been with a woman and he wanted her. Olga's gentle touch fueled his emotions. No, he thought, he couldn't let this happen; and though his desire faded, his mind remained full of guilt. She's Russian, he kept telling himself, remember that, she's Russian.

Flashes of Anja flickered through his mind, of the summer they'd been in love and how it had ended. He'd never had another love. What's the use, he thought, it hadn't worked twenty years ago, it wouldn't work now. Toivo rolled to face the bulkhead.

"What is wrong?" she asked, her fingertips trailing off the back of Toivo's legs.

What could he tell her? Certainly not that he hated Russians. Instead he said, "You are young enough to be my daughter."

"But the massage is good for you. It will help the muscles heal."

"Right now, I'm too tired for this nonsense, just let me sleep."

Behind his back, Olga bit her lip. Quietly, she slipped out the door, closing it softly as she left. Tears welled up at the corners of her eyes as she shuffled back to her quarters mumbling to herself. At that moment she hated being a freak.

Toivo felt the solitude of the small room, the same loneliness he had known for a long time. He was very slow to fall asleep.

Chapter 12

It had been a long night for Toivo. As tired as he was he couldn't sleep. The constant chatter between the shepherds woke him repeatedly. The fishing boat did come back and the shepherds shouted orders to each other as they chased it away from their flock. When the first rays of sunshine finally filtered through the small porthole over his bed, Toivo lay in a tangle of sheets. His eyes burned from lack of sleep and every muscle ached from fatigue. Slowly sunlight brightened the seascape visible through Toivo's porthole and he knew they'd changed course and were headed north. Probably to find Ici's friend Michael.

The door opened a crack, Olga peeked in and then seeing Toivo, she knocked lightly to get his attention.

"Are you awake?" she asked.

Toivo pulled the sheet up to cover his chest. "Yes, I'm up."

She pushed the door open. "Do you want some breakfast? We have a few eggs."

Toivo eyed her appreciatively, the blond hair, the blue eyes, the supple lightness of her figure, the ripple of muscle below the skin. Exotically striking, but still Russian. "No," he grumbled, "I'll fix my own breakfast when I get up." He rolled over to face the bulkhead.

The door slammed. Toivo stared a long moment at the blank steel wall, his anger rising. He was angry about being kept up all night and now angry with himself for acting so callously. He got out of bed and slipped on the bathing suit. He still wasn't used to wearing such a skimpy piece of cloth. The revealing bulge was too obvious but the small suit would have to do, and it was better than nothing. He opened the door and peered out into the hallway. He saw only the shadowy gloom from the dimmed ship's lights that were turned down for night running.

Gingerly, he stepped out, pulling the door shut behind him. Testing his legs, he found them stronger than they had been yesterday, despite his fitful night. He stood for a moment, measuring his balance, then hurried to the bathroom where he washed his face and hands. Someone's razor lay on the side of the basin and he used it to shave the ugly brown stubble from his face.

Ah, that felt better. He dried his face with a square of cloth that passed as a towel and headed for the galley, enticed by the smell of frying eggs.

At the galley door he hesitated, wondering who was on the other side. Probably Olga. He really didn't want to face her. He wasn't in the habit of being rude to attractive young women. Then again, he wasn't in the habit of having young girls press him for his attention. It gnawed at him that she was Russian.

Getting involved with her was something he couldn't allow. Forget it, he decided, and pulled the door open.

Olga stood at the stove, her back to him. Through the opening that led into the mess hall next door, he could see Ni sitting at the table eating eggs and toast.

"Smells good. Can I change my mind?" he asked, slipping past Olga through the interconnecting doorway between galley and mess hall.

She turned, her eyes narrowing and stared sharply at him. She started to say something then smiled instead. The smile faded, losing its usual natural appeal. "Of course. Sit down. I'll bring them in. How do you like your eggs?"

"Scrambled, thanks."

He ducked through the watertight doorway. Ici sat at the table across from Ni. He was forking in the last mouthfuls of eggs mired with chunks of bread.

"Did you change course during the night?" asked Toivo, settling onto the bench at the table.

Ici raised his eyebrows, looking up from his plate. "Yes. I decided to find out what's wrong with Michael."

"Are you herding the tuna with us?"

"Yes. The dolphins can herd the tuna faster than we can move anyway. I don't want to lose this harvest."

"He'll finally be out of debt," said Ni, hardly looking up from her plate. "Then our debt reduction will double up on my portion."

"What do you mean, your debt?"

"What we owe the company."

"Owe the company? For what?"

"It's a complicated system. First the ovum and sperm are selected, usually from Oriental or Russian parents, since the rest of the world has been pretty much against us even before we were born. At fertilization we are biologically re-engineered to what you see now."

"Or the fetus is taken in the first trimester," interjected Olga from the galley. "Not all of us were produced from a clinically isolated egg and sperm."

Ici glared at Olga for a long moment. Then his eyes softened and he went on. "True enough. Anyway, for most of us, after nine months in an artificial womb, we are born and shipped off to one of the Schools of Fisheries. Star-Kist paid for everything, including the school, room and board plus expenses while we are growing up. The total is our indebtedness. We are obligated to pay off the factory before we can go off on our own."

Toivo gulped back his surprise. "Are you kidding? That sounds like slavery."

"In a way it is," came Olga's voice from the galley. There was a hint of bitterness. "But we don't have much choice. On the other hand, we are guaranteed a job. In addition to the allowance that is deducted from our indebtedness, we get a cash stipend each harvest that we can spend or leave to accumulate. It could be worse. Eventually we pay off the debt and end up with a tidy sum in our account."

Toivo thought of the years he had made payments on his ship Sisu. It wasn't much different except he alone had decided how much debt he could afford. The shepherds were born into debt. "What do you do after you pay off the debt?" He had remained a fisherman even though he'd paid off the boat over five years ago. Then again he'd chosen to be a fisherman in the first place.

"Retire. Buy a nice piece of property and settle down as a lubber raising fish in pens," said Ici.

"Or homestead a piece of the ocean," snapped Ni, her eyes glowing like coals.

"Or keep working for the factory," added Olga, bringing Toivo's scrambled eggs. She dropped them on the table in front of the Finn so the plastic plate bounced, clattered and threatened to land in his lap.

He pushed the plate back with one thumb. "I was thinking of contracting out to one of the big factories," he said, picking up the fork and stirring the soft yellow egg mass. "What's it like? I mean, working for someone else?"

"It's okay," said Ici. "Not really that bad. It's a job, and they pay on time."

Toivo shook his head sadly. "It doesn't matter now. I don't have a boat to contract out."

Olga slid into the seat next to him. "But you can talk to the D's. Any factory would pay big bucks for the chance to clean up on wild tuna."

"Maybe so, if I could clean up. But one look at my records and they'd know I don't find fish much more often than any of the other independents."

Toivo sampled the eggs. Very tasty. Soft, fluffy, and yet not watery or dried out. "Good scrambled eggs."

Olga nodded. "I'm sure you can get money to buy another boat. The market is there for fish, factory or otherwise."

Toivo scooped up the eggs. It didn't matter. Right now he was stuck in the middle of the Pacific and didn't know how he was going to get home. Worrying about a new boat was a waste of time. He dipped up the last of the eggs, stuffed the remaining bite of toast in his mouth and chewed contentedly. What the hell, he could have drowned.

"Thanks," he said and got up from the table. "I want to sit on deck and talk to Poika. I don't want him to think I've forgotten him."

He strolled out of the dining room, heading down the hallway through the aft door and out onto the stern deck. The ocean was running in low, rounded waves. It rose and fell in endless turquoise undulations. He would never tire of being at sea; the ocean held a power over him. She called him back again and again, whether he could make a living or not. She was in his blood. Somehow he'd get another boat. Maybe he would contract out with one of the factories.

"*Poika*," he called, lowering himself gingerly to a seated position on the starboard pontoon with his back braced up against the cabin wall.

He looked across the swells, trying to see the tuna school. Off to starboard he saw several dolphins break, blow and plunge back into the sea. Then a couple more rolled their heads out, rode gently through the waves, then dove under again. The tuna were running six to eight meters under the surface. Their yellow sides flashed through the clear water and Toivo could almost count them. The school turned as one and dozens of golden reflections shimmered in unison.

As he watched, one dolphin broke from the school, swimming toward the boat. From the dolphin's shape, the peculiar bob of his head as his tail thrust him forward, and the coloration, Toivo recognized Poika. A second dolphin, only a little shorter than Poika and thicker through the midsection, followed. Her dorsal fin was shorter and more rounded and Toivo knew immediately it was Tyttö. Like twin underwater missiles the two dolphins streaked for the boat and were soon alongside.

"*Hello, man-who-speaks-dolphin,*" said Poika, holding his head out of water and still keeping pace with the boat.

"*Hello, Poika. Is the food plentiful?*"

Poika nodded his head yes. "*Tyttö and I enjoy working with the people-who-are-like-fish and the dolphins who accompany them. You are looking much better than when we brought you here.*"

"*I am much better thanks to you and the other dolphins. Please accept my appreciation. You saved my life.*"

"*We only helped you continue on the path to death so that you could go ahead at your chosen time. There is much in life that you have not had time to contemplate and we hope you will slow down long enough to think about the course of the universe.*"

"*I know you always think we humans spend too much time worrying about material things instead of the vast realm of the mind but I would settle for a new boat right now.*"

"*As we knew you would. You will get a new boat when the time is right. For now conserve your energy and use this natural lull in activity to contemplate the glorious riches that nature has set before you.*"

"What's he saying?" Olga's voice was practically in Toivo's ear and startled him.

"*Voi, voi, voi,* you scared me."

"I'm sorry," she said, her mouth turning down into a weak frown. "I wanted to talk to you, but hearing the sounds you make with the dolphins captivated me. Do you think I could learn to talk to them?"

"If I could, I'm sure you could. It's not so much that it's hard, it's more that they don't use single words put together like we do to form an idea. Each sound carries multiple messages all wrapped in the subtleties of the carrier frequency. It is so complex that it took me three years to understand any of it. Once the basic pattern became familiar, the rest fell into place."

"How do you say his name?"

"*Poika*," he sang. "You must be careful, since it is easy to mispronounce the name into a multitude of other ideas."

She whistled long and low, trying to imitate Toivo, but it wasn't right and Toivo broke out laughing. Poika shook his head back and forth in an exaggerated series of arcs, then rolled into the next swell and swan a circle back to the side of the boat.

"What did I say?"

"You asked him if the night's moonlight held more fish than the sea. He actually took it as a philosophical question, but then realized that humans don't think about such things. He was laughing at himself for taking you seriously at first."

"Oh. Maybe you can teach me later."

"*Your new mate is amusing to you. We, however, must return to our duties. We will talk at a better time for both of us.*"

Poika and Tyttö turned away from the boat. Toivo swiveled around to look into Olga's blue eyes. They waited expectantly for him to speak.

"They think you are my new mate." He leaned back against the slope of the cabin. "I'm not sure how they came to that conclusion." Especially since you're Russian, he thought.

"Are you embarrassed to be thought of as my mate? Does my physical appearance repulse you?"

He looked carefully at her feminine shape. Sculptured breasts that were distinctly female with enticing nipples faintly outlined a darker brown. Her hair, though short, accented her delicate facial features. He was ashamed for looking, for in that moment, there was something both alien and appealing about her. A burning desire built in Toivo. He fought down his impulse and answered her question. "No."

She put one hand on his shoulder. "I never had anyone care about me." Her voice was low, almost lost in the soft breeze.

"I never knew my parents—never knew who they were until I was about to ship out for this boat. Now Star-Kist will pay for me to visit them on my first R&R if I want. While I was growing up at the St. Croix School of Fisheries, the island boys called me a freak. My only friends were those few shepherds in school."

"But I thought you were Russian," blurted Toivo.

123

"Technically, I guess I am. Both of my parents live in St. Petersburg. I've never seen them, nor they me. Like Ici was explaining, we were developed from an ovum and sperm, or in my case from a fertilized egg robbed from a mother who didn't care. We were all born in a laboratory not a hospital. Nowadays most people won't even talk about how we came about. There was such a religious backlash that the U.N. has outlawed the bioengineering of our kind. All the information regarding our development is classified. We are the ultimate racial minority, and there won't be any more of us unless we procreate. In my case that seems unlikely."

Toivo found himself fumbling for words. He wanted to believe her but the ingrained distrust told him not to. "M-maybe we can be friends," he mumbled and felt his cheeks flush as he thought about what kind of friendship they might have. He turned away from her, feigning attention to the sea.

Suddenly, out near the tuna school, a series of tall black and white fins sliced up out of the water. One of the largest jumped, blew, and thundered back into the sea. Killer whales! Probably after the tuna—or the dolphins. Toivo was on his feet.

"Get Ici and Ni. Bring the gun."

"We don't have a gun."

"Well get Ici and Ni anyway."

Olga looked up. Her eyes followed Toivo's line of sight. They grew big and round. "Shit," she spat and dashed around the corner and into the cabin. Toivo heard her yelling for the others as she ran.

To his horror, Toivo saw the biggest black and white dorsal fin turn sharply toward Poika. There was a rush in the water that left behind a swirling crest of foam. Poika jumped away, and the huge body of the killer whale leaped after him.

"*Poika. Tyttö. Come quickly. To the boat.*"

He saw Poika dodge left, then swing back toward Homestead. The ominous black torpedo bore down on him from behind. Almost immediately, Ici, Ni and Olga were on deck.

"Killer whales," snarled Ici as soon as he could see the tuna school. "They'll wipe us out."

"Or kill Poika," snapped Toivo kneeling down so he was almost falling into the water. "*Poika, lead the dolphin-that-eats-everything over here.*"

Poika leapt again, shaking his head. "*Dolphin-that-eats-everything is gaining. I fear it is my time to go ahead.*"

"*No, you helped me now I will help you. Tell him I will shoot him if he does not leave you alone. He must know humans can kill if we wish to.*"

"*I will tell him.*"

"What's going on?" asked Ici.

"I told Poika to lead the killer whale over to Homestead and I will shoot it."

"But we don't have a gun."

"The killer whale doesn't know that. We'll have to fake it. Think of something."

Meanwhile, Poika ran full speed toward the boat, the massive black and white terror right behind him. "*Dolphin-that-eats-everything doesn't see your flash-and-bang stick. Only if you shoot at him will he leave me alone. Dolphin is his favorite food.*"

"They want to see the gun," said Toivo, turning to the others. "Quick, think of something."

"How about a piece of pipe, a broomstick, something that looks like a gun," suggested Olga. "Their eyesight isn't very good."

"Yes," said Ni, scrambling back into the cabin. "I know just the thing."

The whale had nearly caught Poika, the round white teeth nipping at his flukes. Poika put on a last desperate burst of speed, the horrible tall fin slicing behind him, ever nearer.

"*Toivo, you will have to do something quick. I can not stay ahead of him much longer.*"

"Here," said Ni, handing Toivo a meter-long piece of metal conduit.

Toivo took the piece of pipe and brandished it like a gun. As the huge bull whale poked his head up out of the water to get a look at his fleeing prey, Toivo aimed it menacingly at the killer.

"*I don't want to hurt you or your pod,*" he whistled in dolphin, "*but you must leave my friend alone.*"

The killer whale slowed for an instant, rising slightly higher in the water until almost two meters of his bulk was suspended above the surface. "*I cannot tell if it is a weapon-of-noise-and-pain or not. Let me hear it thunder.*"

Toivo lowered the metal pipe. Now what? At least for the moment Poika was gaining ground and would soon pass under or over Homestead.

"What did he say?" asked Olga, crowding next to Toivo.

"He wants me to shoot the gun so he can hear it."

"Stall him," said Ici and ran inside.

Toivo stared down at the onrushing killer whale. How did he stall a whale? He cleared his throat. "*I don't want to shoot you.*"

The whale slowed, again, seemingly puzzled. Before he could resume the chase, Ici stepped up behind Toivo and inserted a lit firecracker into the back of the pipe.

"Don't stand behind the opening," Ici whispered in Toivo's ear as he moved off to Toivo's right.

Toivo raised the metal tube, pretending to sight down the barrel off to the whale's left. The firecracker exploded with a boom that rang the pipe like a cheap bell. A puff of white smoke rolled out the end of the pipe forming a little smoke ring that quickly faded in the breeze.

The bull whale flinched back from Homestead. "*The next shot will be at you,*" whistled Toivo in what he hoped was a serious expression that the killer whale would understand.

The killer whale backed up grudgingly, keeping a wary eye on Toivo. "*We cannot fight your weapon-of-noise-and-pain. You may keep your friend.*"

A grating groan sounded underwater and the killer whales submerged in unison, swimming just far enough beneath the raft for their fins to scrape Homestead's bottom.

"Whew," said Ici, and sat down on the deck. "That could have been a disaster."

"But it wasn't, thanks to Toivo," snapped Olga. For an instant she glared at Ici, then turned on the ball of her foot and went below.

"Thanks, Toivo," said Ni, as she sat down next to Ici.

"We'll have to watch out for killer whales in the future," said Ici, gulping down unnamed fears. "Not only do they eat D's, they could gobble up a lot of tuna."

"Don't worry, Ici," Ni reassured him, "we will have a good harvest."

He put one arm around Ni. "I know but I want to be free of the factory. I can't help thinking about just how close we came to losing our herd then. I don't want to wait for another harvest."

"Be happy you're alive," said Toivo and went below.

Chapter 13

The shepherd's vessel plowed steadily through the calm seas, heading on a northwest course. The cowboys had tried repeatedly to raise Michael's raft on the radio, but got no answer. Ici took it to mean the worst. He muttered about losing his friend. Toivo hated to agree but he suspected the same. The gloom aboard Homestead grew as they neared Turtle's last known location.

Toivo was getting around much better now and walked up and down the deck, short as it was, for exercise. Olga joined him from time to time, her smile missing. In the anguish over Turtle's fate, Toivo forgot his concerns about befriending a Russian. Not that they got to spend much time together since Ici made sure she remembered that duty came first.

It was mid-afternoon and Toivo sat alone atop the cabin roof sunning himself. He stared across the sea, scanning the horizon. The tuna school swam several hundred meters ahead of the raft, herded constantly from side to side across Homestead's path so the fast-swimming fish would not outdistance the raft.

Having time alone was almost a curse. Toivo's mind ran a continual string of internal dialogue. There were so many things wrong, so many problems. Wilho, and Gunnar, and his crew remained in his thoughts. He worried about Wilho's daughter. By now she would know something was wrong; they should have been in Hawaii days ago. He wished he could be there, wished Wilho was still alive to hold his daughter again. Tears forced their way into the corners of his eyes. He wiped them away, gritting his teeth against the pain. Finns don't cry. We're a tough lot. The thought brought a bitter laugh to his lips.

Why did this happen to such good men? They had been fishermen, simple fishermen. They weren't soldiers or thugs armed for war. What was so important that his entire crew had paid for it with their lives? Life could be so ugly. For all man's potential, he was still God's most terrifying creation.

"We should be able to see them by now." Ici's voice, thin with worry, drifted up through the open hatch in the cabin roof. "Not a trace on radar."

"Are you sure the radar is working?" asked Ni.

"I'm sure."

"Maybe they're still submerged. They said something about going under."

"For three days? Why would they do that? There's no storm, no danger. Maybe they moved."

"Do you want me to try the radio again?"

"Yeah. I'll go topside and check once more with the binoculars."

Toivo heard the soft footsteps of bare feet on the ladder rungs. Ici's black cap of hair rose through the hatch. A pair of large, black binoculars hung from a strap around his neck. His round face was tight, the jaw muscles little knots. His serious dark eyes burned intensely.

"Good morning," said Toivo, nodding to the swimmer. "No sign of your friend?"

"Nope."

At the railing, Ici kneeled, braced his elbows on the top rail and raised the binoculars. Slowly he swept back and forth across the horizon. Toivo watched for a minute then turned his attention back to the dolphins and the tuna school. Suddenly, Poika and Tyttö swam sharply away from the school, heading off to the east. What were they doing? It was not like them to leave their station, and in a hurry, too. Both dolphins drove ahead with all the power they could muster. Toivo could see they were in a hurry to get somewhere, but where? He stood up to get a better view to see what might have caught the dolphins' attention. Blue water stretched out to the horizon with no sign of anything worth such a fast swim.

Toivo sat back down. "Look to the east."

Ici looked down at him, frowning, then turned his binoculars east. For a long minute he scanned the sea. There was something there! A dolphin. Ici pointed toward it and shouted down the hatch, "Hard to starboard. There's a dolphin in trouble."

Toivo leaped to his feet. Was it Poika or Tyttö? No, he could see both of them leaping through the waves on their original course. "Are you sure it's a dolphin?"

"Well, we'll find out in a minute."

Homestead began to turn. Ici cupped his hands and yelled directions down the hatch to Ni, who guided the boat. It wasn't long before Toivo could make out the dolphin Ici had spotted. Poika and Tyttö had reached it and were circling cautiously, warding off a lone shark. The new dolphin swam sluggishly through the swells. Its body was turned half on one side, one pectoral fin flailing uselessly in the air. As Homestead neared the dolphins, Toivo saw a wide stain of red that trailed off behind the mammal.

The raft eased alongside the dolphin. "Cut the engines," yelled Ici and dove off the roof.

"Olga," yelled Toivo, "there's an injured dolphin." Toivo saw the flash of the metal tag at the base of the dorsal. "A factory dolphin. Come help."

Ici reached the dolphin at the same time Olga and Ni came running out on deck. They took one look and dove over the side to join him. Within minutes the three swimmers guided the dolphin to the side of the boat.

"Gunshot," said Olga. "We'll have to get the bullet out."

"Listen," said Ici, "rig a sling with a sheet between the pontoons to cradle him. Then we can hold him still while Olga removes the bullet."

Toivo slid down the ladder into the hallway below. He ran to his room, pulled the sheet off his bed and went out the aft door to the rear deck. At the very stern of the pontoons he stretched the sheet between the tube-like floats and tied it off like a hammock. It hung just to the surface of the water. The three swimmers worked the wounded dolphin around to the sheet and gently lifted it into the makeshift cradle.

Olga bounced up on deck and went inside. She came out a minute later with a medical bag.

"How bad is it?" asked Toivo, leaning over the side to get a better look.

"I'm not sure," said Ici, stroking the mammal on the back. "There are three wounds. One is high through the dorsal. That's not bad. The other two are in the back. They don't look so good. We'll have to see what Olga thinks."

Olga set the medical bag on deck and lowered herself over the side. A wave rushed between the pontoons, pushing the dolphin up in the sling. Olga came up and motioned for Toivo to hand her down the bag.

"You two hold him steady. This will hurt, but we can't leave the bullets in him," she said, opening the bag and setting it on the upper edge of the sheet.

"Are you sure you know what you're doing?" asked Toivo, realizing as Olga pulled out the scalpel that she meant to cut the bullets out.

"Oh Christ, shut up. I know what I'm doing, or didn't you think the freak woman could do anything right?"

The bitterness stung Toivo. "Okay, okay," he said, then turned to the dolphin. "*You will feel pain. This must be done. The bits of metal lodged in your body must be removed*." Toivo tried to touch the dolphin as he spoke, but his body was still too stiff to reach down far enough. A sharp pain in his back pulled him up short and he settled back on the deck, acutely aware of his lost flexibility.

"*I can forget the pain, man-who-speaks-with-us*," said the dolphin. His muscles relaxed and a glazed look covered his eyes.

Toivo stood up and noticed Poika and Tyttö waiting just on the other side of the pontoon. *Poika. Tyttö. Your friend will be all right. Who shot him? Why?*

"*The same men who sent the others ahead*," said Poika.

Toivo scratched his chin. 'The others? Was he talking about the men that killed Toivo's crew? "*The men who killed Wilho?*"

"*That I do not know. These men killed the swimmers that were with this dolphin and the rest of his pod*."

"*Where's the raft?*"

"*Sunk*."

"*They killed all the swimmers and the dolphins?*"

"*Yes. As the dolphins came to the side of the boat to see what was happening, men shot them. Only he got away. It is the same way they killed many of the dolphins-who-swim-with-men-who-are-fish from the other raft of dead men-who-are-fish*."

Toivo felt his knees go weak. He could still see the dead shepherds inside the first raft, the one that had become their steel coffin. "*Why didn't you tell me before that the killers slaughtered your brothers?*"

"*It is hardly important. The others have gone ahead. Nothing will change that*."

"*Not important? How can you say that? It is murder*."

"*Murder as you define it. All creatures eventually go to the plane beyond the doors of death. Once it has happened the only thing left to do is rejoice at their passing and continue the long process of contemplation. We must understand the meaning of life on this lower plane of existence*."

"*Not now*," said Toivo. "*We can talk philosophy later*."

Right now they needed to figure out what these dangerous men were doing. Toivo hunched over, thinking, trying to make sense of it all. He drew in a long breath, and then let it out slowly. What pieces of the puzzle did he have? Who were these men who killed other men and dolphins, and maybe took the tuna. It was murder—and for what? Toivo felt the adrenaline rush, the anger, the outrage. He wanted to do something—revenge the dead. He was powerless, and the questions remained. Why? What were they after? And why had they killed his crew? Or the helpless crews of the two rafts?

"Did you hear that?" he asked the three swimmers busy around the wounded dolphin.

"Hear what?" snapped Ici. "You jabbering to that dolphin?"

"They killed this dolphin's swimmers and sank their raft," said Toivo. "Is this one of Michael's dolphins?"

Olga fingered the metal tag on the dolphin's back. "Yes," she said. "He was with Turtle."

"Then Michael is dead and Turtle has been sunk." Toivo hated being so blunt, but there were no words to soften the truth.

"What the hell are you talking about?" screamed Ici. An eerie silence fell. Ici's face went white, his eyes rolling back in his head until only the whites showed. Then his face flushed red and he shook his head. His eyes cleared and he scrambled up on deck. "They killed Michael?" His hands clenched into fists, the knuckles whitened. "They can't have killed Michael."

"I'm afraid they have."

Ici breathed in, exhaled through teeth clamped tight. "That can't be it." He shook his head, tears running down his cheeks.

Ni was beside him now, her arms wrapped around his waist. "It'll be all right," she whispered, "it'll be all right."

Ici unwrapped Ni's hands from around him. He screamed from deep in his guts and hurtled himself into the water. A hundred meters from the boat he surfaced and swam toward the horizon, his powerful strokes pushed him ahead faster and faster. Ni started to go after him.

"Let him go," said Olga. "He'll come back when the pain burns out. Right now I need help."

Ni stood transfixed, watching Ici disappear toward the distant vault of the sky. Then, as if making up her mind, she jumped back into the water next to Olga, careful not to splash the injured dolphin.

Toivo watched the two women work. Already they had removed the first bullet. Now Olga dug at the second while Ni held the dolphin with both her arms wrapped around its midsection as best her short arms would manage. The dolphin lay unmoving in the makeshift sling.

"Got it," said Olga and let the deadly piece of metal plop into the ocean. "I wish they made waterproof pads," she muttered and returned the scalpel to her bag. She pulled out a tube and squeezed some white cream onto the wounds. "If we can keep him turned on one side for a while, this should stop any infection."

Both of the women climbed up on deck beside Toivo.

"Do you think these killers are nearby?" asked Ni, staring at the distant form of her husband, still swimming away from Homestead.

"They can't be too far away," said Toivo, glumly. "They seem to be working this general area and I doubt they'll leave until they have whatever it is they're after. They could be a couple of hundred miles away or just over the horizon."

"Could they have come from Guam or one of the other islands?" Ni sat, legs folded, her eyes fixed on the distant spot that was Ici. "I think he's coming back." She pointed, a smile trying to force up the corners of her mouth.

Toivo looked out to where Ici swan, a tiny black dot, appearing and disappearing with each wave. As Toivo watched, the dot grew ever so slowly. "Yes, he's coming back. He must have known Michael very well."

Ni stood up, shading her eyes. "Ici and Michael worked together on Homestead until Michael got his own raft. They were like brothers."

Olga stood beside her. "Out here people become friends fast. The bonds grow so strong that we are all like family to each other. The family we never had ashore."

Toivo stood up, too, bracing himself against the cabin. "We had better call the U. N. If these men are near, they will not stop until we are dead too. Somebody better watch the radar. They may be coming up on us even now."

Olga turned to look at Toivo, hardness in her eyes. "And maybe the radio will bring the killers instead."

"It's a chance we'll have to take," said Ni, turning on the balls of her feet and disappearing into the cabin.

Chapter 14

Ni sat down at the radio cabinet, pulled the doors open and punched the digital tuner until she had the desired setting. Toivo and Olga squeezed into the cramped control room and watched from over her shoulder. Within the close confines of the cubicle, Toivo felt the warm skin of Olga's bare back pressing against his side. Surging desires flushed his face. He fought them and concentrated on Ni. She pulled the microphone over and keyed the talk button.

"Calling United Nations frigate Stockholm. This is Homestead." She released the talk button. They all held their breath. Ni repeated her message.

Her third transmission brought an answer crackling over the radio. "Homestead, this is the United Nations frigate Stockholm. What is your position?"

Toivo felt something comforting about the stranger's voice. They weren't alone. There were friendly forces out on the vast Pacific.

"Stockholm, this is Homestead." Ni's voice quivered just a bit as she read their position. "We are at 15 degrees 37 minutes north, 156 degrees 12 minutes east. We have rescued a lone dolphin suffering a gunshot wound. The dolphin has indicated that his pod, as well as the shepherd Michael and his crewmates, Sandy and Joshua, have been murdered. We require immediate assistance. We believe whoever is responsible is still in the area. What is your earliest arrival?"

There was a long pause. "He's working out the distance," said Toivo as they waited.

"Homestead. We are approximately 1200 kilometers from you, but are low on fuel. Refueling to be completed tomorrow. Earliest rendezvous is three days. We will send search aircraft to scout vicinity. Satellite surface surveillance shows no suspect craft in your area."

"Three days," hissed Olga. "We could all be dead by then."

Ni stabbed the microphone button. "Send the airplane and keep your eyes on your satellite scanner. We are unarmed and cannot, I repeat, cannot, defend ourselves."

"Understood, Homestead. We will watch for unknowns." The speaker cleared his throat. "We'll watch out for you, don't worry."

"Don't worry," mocked Olga. "Asshole."

"Now what?" asked Ni, turning from the radio set.

"Watch and wait," said Toivo. "Especially our own radar. I don't trust the U. N. to be overly alert on our behalf."

#

On the bridge, Poddington, Deep, and Jones stood still, trying to catch every word coming over the intercom. The radioman had switched the radio traffic between the raft Homestead and the U. N. frigate to the intercom and everyone listened intently. The conversation ended and the radio fell silent.

"This is going to get ugly," shot Poddington, again wishing he'd never taken the job on this cursed ship.

"Why are you worried?" asked Luis Jones, a thin smile twisting his lips. "The frigate won't be here for three days. Can't we beat them to the raft?"

"Sure," said Poddington. "But will we get this over with and be gone before the frigate arrives?"

"You better be," said Jones, a false sweetness in his tone.

Deep slid in behind Poddington. "What about the aircraft? What are we going to do about that?"

"We're just the Sunrise Savior out here monitoring ocean currents," said Jones, as if that answered the question. "Quit being so negative and let's get on with it."

Poddington glared at the Second Mate. "If you're so damn smart, you figure out where they are and get us over to them. Every time I turn around you're giving me orders on my own ship."

A hard glint came to Jones' eyes, his hand went to the gun Poddington knew Jones carried in a holster under his shirt but he didn't pull it out. "This sounds like mutiny," Jones said.

"No," said Deep, pushing his way in front of his Captain. "This is no mutiny. But it gets frustrating when you give orders that go against the safe operation of this vessel. Come on, Jones, you have to admit you don't know shit about running this ship. Pod'll get the job done. Just give him a chance."

Jones' hand dropped slowly to his side. "Okay, then get on with it. I'll stay out of the way, for now."

"I've got an idea," said Deep, "what if we called this raft and pretended to be their factory ship. Tell them we'll come stand by them until the frigate arrives."

"What would that gain us?" asked Poddington.

"For one, they won't think twice when they see our radar blip. They'll think it's help."

"Hmm," Poddington thought about it. Couldn't hurt, he decided. "Figure out how to do it and get it done."

#

Ni glanced at the radar screen. The thin sweep line circled the scope leaving a flawless green afterglow. "Nothing within a hundred kilometers," she said, standing. "I'm going topside to make sure Ici makes it back okay. I worry when he goes so far. Olga, watch the radar screen. I'll relieve you as soon as I know Ici is aboard."

Olga backed through the doorway and into the corridor to let Ni past. The radio squawked. "Homestead, Homestead, come in Homestead. This is the Martin B."

Ni was already down the hall out of hearing range. Olga sat in the chair facing the set.

"Martin B., this is Homestead."

"Homestead, stay put. We will rendezvous tomorrow. No sign of the killers at this time. We will escort you until frigate arrives."

"Roger, Martin B. Homestead out."

Olga clicked the microphone off. "Lucky they aren't too far away. At least we won't be out here alone for long."

Toivo took one last look at the empty radar screen. Tomorrow, he thought, the Martin B. would be here and surely he would be off-loaded to the factory ship. Then probably they would take him back to Hawaii. To what? He would have to face the prospect of being without a ship, without a job and nearly broke. And what about Poika and Tyttö? How would they find him? Somehow, he supposed, like lost dogs finding their way home.

Then there was Olga. The thought of leaving her twisted his stomach like a wrung out washcloth. He felt empty, but at the same time, his wariness of her Russian heritage told him he should be happy to be rid of her. Still, the moments they had shared were a glimpse into life without loneliness, a life he had never thought possible.

His stomach rumbled as he turned and started for the galley. In all the excitement he had forgotten to eat. "I'm going to get a sandwich," he said over his shoulder. "Do you want me to bring you something?"

"No. I'll be over as soon as Ni comes back."

Toivo crossed the hall and slipped into the galley. He pulled open the refrigerator and grimaced at the sight of the few fillets left from yesterday. Ugh, more fish. He pulled a couple out and popped them into the microwave. While they heated, he got the bread from the cupboard. A bit of lettuce, tartar sauce and he had a fish sandwich. It seemed like his millionth fish sandwich since he'd been rescued. Rescued, he reminded himself, was the key word. His mind flashed with vague memories, blurry scenes of mountainous waves and screaming winds. It hardly seemed real anymore.

After making himself a glass of powdered milk, he put the sandwich on a plate and went in to sit down at the table. He had just started to eat when he heard Ici and Ni come in through the aft cabin door. Their voices grew as they came down the hall toward the galley. Politely, Toivo tried to ignore them, but the conversation was too loud. She was scolding him for being so stupid, for swimming so far from the boat. He reminded her that he had been engineered for just such things.

". . . think I should be happy they killed Michael? I can't help it. He was my only friend," said Ici, as the two of them entered the mess hall.

Ni glared at him. "Not your only friend."

Ici sat down. He nodded to Toivo. "Nobody understands," he said, shaking his head.

"Yes, I do," said Toivo, his tongue thick and dry. He swallowed but his mouth felt like it was coated with cement dust. "Wilho was my only real friend."

Ni had followed stride for stride behind Ici and stood behind him where he sat, rubbing his back with both hands. "I'll get you a sandwich. Or would you rather have some fruit?"

Ici stared glumly at the bulkhead, his eyes red and dark. "Nothing," he said.

Ni frowned. "You've got to eat something."

"Okay," he mumbled. "Fruit then."

Ni stormed into the galley, her teeth clenched to check her rising anger. Toivo put his half eaten sandwich down on the plate. "I know how you feel." He thought about Wilho, about his crew. "But feeling sorry for them won't help, and feeling sorry for yourself only makes it worse. The thing to do is to be thankful that they have gone on to a better existence and thank God we are still alive."

Ici bit his lip. "Bullshit," he snarled. "They killed him, killed them all. For no reason. I'd kill them all if I could, kill every one of them."

"You think I wouldn't? You think I haven't wished for that very same chance?" Toivo felt his anger rising, his face flush, but he also knew that thinking like that would get them nowhere. He picked up his sandwich, took a bite and chewed it slowly. "We need to figure out what we can do if they find us before the factory ship gets here. I still can't understand why they are killing shepherds and dolphins, but they are, and we need to be ready for them."

Ici looked up through red, bloodshot eyes. His mouth was a grim slash across his face. "What does it matter, why? I only wish we could pay the bastards back."

Toivo's right fist clenched involuntarily as his anger sent an adrenaline rush coursing through him. "No more than I do, but it won't save us if they catch us. We need a plan."

Ni rushed in with an apple sectioned on a plate and plunked it down in front of Ici. "We need to do something," she snapped. "Maybe we should call the other shepherds. See how many of us are left. Find out if anyone knows what is going on."

Ici bit into the apple. "Good idea. If nothing else, we can warn them about the killers. Maybe prevent them from suffering the same fate."

"Finish your apple," said Ni, heading for the galley door. "I'll get the directory from our cabin. Jason and Sarah will be glad to hear from us anyway."

Toivo watched her duck out of the galley. "How many swimmers are there?"

A dark scowl swept over Ici's face. "We're not swimmers!"

Toivo's face went crimson. "I meant shepherds. Sorry."

Ici gritted his teeth, the jaw muscles knotting up, then let it go and his face relaxed, the tension draining away. "About fifty. Only about twenty are in this area of the Pacific, though there are another dozen between Wake Island and Hawaii. Originally there were seven rafts in this sector. With Oyster Bay and Turtle gone that leaves five. The other four, Tranquility, Tiger, Sting Ray, and Squatter, are herding tuna farther north. Jason and Sarah are on Squatter. They're the only ones we have kept up with on a regular basis. Of the others, Mark, Chrissy and Helicia were all in the Guam school while I was there, and Luke and Beth were at St. Croix with Olga. Tiger has Luke, Beth, Victor and Chrissy. Sting Ray has Charlie, Petre and Wathan, and Tranquility has Mark, Helicia, Aaron and Rebecca. It's all in the log."

"Let's hope they are still around to answer."

Toivo tried to finish his sandwich while they waited for Ni to return.

An instant later, she reappeared with a small, leather-bound ledger tucked under one arm. Poking her head into the mess hall, she said, "Let's go," then ducked out.

Toivo heard her scurry across the hall into the radio room. Ici jumped up and followed her.

As Toivo finished his sandwich and stood up, Olga entered the galley. "I thought you were bringing me a sandwich?"

"I was but Ici and Ni came in and decided to call the other rafts to see if anyone knows what's going on. Do you want me to make you a sandwich now?"

"Nope. I'll make my own—to go. I want to listen in when they call the other rafts. Why don't you go ahead? I'll be right there."

"Okay," he said, swallowing the last bite of his fish sandwich.

He rinsed his dishes, put them into the mini-dishwasher and crossed the hall to the radio room.

Ici stood squeezed between Ni at the console and the far bulkhead. Ni had the radio dialed in and was already speaking into the microphone.

"Squatter, this is Homestead." She repeated it several times, then waited. Long moments ticked by without an answer. Toivo saw her tears start to form. Ici's face hardened and he patted Ni's back gently.

"Maybe they are all off the raft," Toivo suggested.

"For what?" asked Ici.

Olga squeezed in behind Toivo. She had a fish sandwich in one hand and a glass of powdered milk in the other. "Did you get a hold of anyone?"

The radio sputtered. "Homestead, this is Tranquility. Come in, Homestead."

Ni keyed the microphone. "This is Homestead. Come in Tranquility. Is that you, Rebecca?"

"Yes, this is Rebecca. How are things on Homestead? Is Ici okay? Did he clear debt?"

"No, not yet. Have you seen or heard from Squatter?"

"Yes, that's why I'm calling. I talked to Sarah this morning. They are pulling roe—probably be in the water all day. You might try them after sundown."

Toivo chuckled. Even this little relief felt good. "I told you," he said to Ni's back. She didn't pay any attention.

"How's Aaron and the baby?"

"Aaron's fine, and Ruth is doing wonderfully. She's swimming already, and the dolphins love her. They treat her as if she were one of their own children. I never have to worry as long as they're around. How about you?"

"Well, we've had some trouble," started Ni. She paused to wipe the tears from her eyes. "We found one of Michael's dolphins, shot three times. It looks like Michael, Sandy and Josh are dead and their raft sunk. And they're not the only ones. We don't know why, or who, but someone has been killing cowboys and it isn't rustlers. A U. N. frigate is on the way. They say there's no sign of a suspicious vessel. Have you seen anything? Heard anything from anyone?"

"Christ Almighty, are you kidding?"

"I wish I were. I'm telling you someone is killing us off."

"Who? Why? Could it be one of those fanatical, anti-shepherds religious groups?"

"Doubtful. Or why would they be killing the dolphins along with the cowboys?"

There was a long, deep sigh over the radio. "What should we do?"

"We don't know. Have you seen anything suspicious? Anything at all?"

"No. Not really. Though we haven't been looking for anything either. In fact, except for an occasional conversation with Jason and Sarah, we've been too busy taking care of Ruthie to pay much attention to the rest of the world. The herd is almost ready for harvest and we've had our hands full."

Ici leaned in toward the microphone. "If you hear anything let us know. Watch out for strange ships; especially be careful if you see one that looks like the Sunrise Savior. If you see anything strange, anything that shouldn't be out here, get under first and ask questions later. They don't give second chances."

"You know, I almost forgot. Aaron talked to someone on the radio last week about buying the new plankton we just got from the Martin B. Aaron thought they were crazy. We thought about reporting it to the U. N. but didn't bother. The vessel name they used was reported sunk a couple of weeks ago. I think they were on the Shisu, or something like that."

"That's my ship! Their using Sisu's name," snapped Toivo. "Scum!"

"It's just the name," said Olga. "Sisu is gone."

"And another thing," said Rebecca, "a while ago Wing reported seeing a tanker siphoning off plankton. He said they were going to investigate. That's the last we heard from them."

"Well don't you go investigating anything strange," said Olga. "There's few enough of us left as it is."

Toivo slumped against the doorsill, his mind tuning out the rest of the conversation. His chest was heavy with the sorrow of too many things he loved that were gone. He took a deep breath; let it out slowly, reminding himself that he was still alive. Collecting his resolve he thought about their chances. Maybe if they had a plan, were prepared, they would all get out of this alive. He felt Olga's breath on his shoulder, turned and looked into her blue eyes. Pretty eyes, he thought, but hard. Such a young girl shouldn't have hard eyes.

She touched his shoulder with the very tips of her fingers and smiled. "All we can do now is wait. Soon you will be on your way home." Her eyes saddened. "I will be sorry to see you go."

Her openness surprised him and Toivo felt a rising heat. The thought of never seeing Olga again burned in him like fire. His eyes could not avoid the rise of her smooth breasts. Lust roared in his ears, but with Ici and Ni there, he turned it aside. Why the hell did she have to be Russian? And a young Russian, at that. He studied her flawless face, no wrinkles to mar her delicate skin, not even at the corners of her eyes. In many ways she was more like a daughter might have been. He tried to pay attention to Ni's radio conversation, but his desire kept buzzing around his mind and fantasies of Olga's warm body pushed their way into his consciousness despite his attempts to put such thoughts aside.

Toivo turned, stepped out of the radio room. "I'm going on the roof."

He didn't wait for an answer, just bolted for the ladder and scurried topside.

Her footsteps were light, tentative, as if she were apologizing for following him, but Toivo knew Olga was right behind him. Fighting his own confusion, the lust, the guilt, he refused to turn, refused to look at her. He strode to the cabin roof rail and grabbed the top metal bar with both hands, gripping it hard. "Why did you follow me?"

"Don't you want me here?" She stepped up close behind him, but didn't touch him. "Do you think I'm a freak, a monster?"

"Of course not, I'm just tired." He stared resolutely ahead, concentrating on the waves slapping at the twin bows. "You are very attractive. You'll find someone."

"Out here?"

She turned and Toivo heard her patter across the metal roof to the stairs, then the quiet squeak of her bare feet on the iron rungs. The Homestead rose and fell gently. Toivo stayed on the roof for a long time. He watched the waves, the dolphins herd the tuna, and the horizon for signs of any other ship. He couldn't get the image of Olga's soft blue eyes out of his mind.

Olga slid gently down the ladder and went straight to her quarters, intent on sleeping while she was still off watch. Instead, the sting of Toivo's words burned at her heart. Why was she so attracted to him? Did he care or not? Why did he hint at feelings that seemed to evaporate every time they were alone? She didn't sleep.

Chapter 15

Poika and Tyttö swam easily side by side, their flukes undulating in perfect synchronization. Though he could see well enough in the sunlit water, Poika tracked things better with the three-dimensional image his echoing gave him. Each tuna, each dolphin and their internal organs, reflected specific echoes that produced a three dimensional representation in Poika's mind. If he concentrated hard enough on the details of an individual's reflected pulses, he could tell which fish were healthy and which suffered any of a number of ailments. He and Tyttö examined each other regularly to ward off little ills.

Today they worked the tuna, herding them as Toivo and the men-who-are-fish wanted. Mindless work, good work. It gave Poika time to think about important things, life, death, and the beyond. He had a long time before he would go ahead, but the complexity of life was enormous. He needed the time to understand it.

Tyttö nudged him out of his thoughts. "*Many-arms is below. Let's eat while we can.*"

"*Good idea*" he agreed and called to the others, "*Time to feed.*"

They peeled away from their station on the tuna school's flank and dove deep looking for many-arms. Away from the tuna and in the underwater blackness, his sonar made the things that swam in the depths more clearly visible than if there had been sunlight. Many-arms were easy to catch. Ah, the flavor, a delicious meal. Surface, blow, breathe, blow, breathe, dive, eat. Surface, blow, breathe. He was a long way from the tuna now but distance mattered little since the underwater speech carried far and he could easily call to the pod. Tyttö was trailing him by some distance and they talked about the great delicacy, the goodness of the provider.

He dove again. Suddenly, he slammed headfirst into a crisscross of strange grasping threads. As he twisted away, his right pectoral fin snagged in the folds. He thrashed and pulled. His flukes tangled in the clutching weave. What was this nightmare? His sonar said clear water. He fought harder and only managed to tighten the lines around himself. A net! Just like the one his mother had died in, one that some fisherman had set and forgotten. Now he saw the puffy bodies of half-decayed fish hanging lifeless like washed clothing from the line. Fish that had been strangled by the net. Now he too was trapped and unlikely to get out.

"*Tyttö*," he screeched. "*Help. Bring Toivo.*"

Poika hung wrapped in the drifting net. He tried not to struggle, holding his oxygen reserves for as long as he could. Tyttö might bring help in time—if not Poika would experience the beyond before he was ready.

#

Toivo sat on the port pontoon, dangling his feet in the warm salt water of each passing wave crest. It was another beautiful day, sunshine, a balmy friendly breeze.

Tyttö shot to the surface nearly between his feet. "*Toivo, Poika is caught in fish-catcher. Follow me*," and she turned away from Homestead, stopping to look back like an expectant puppy.

Toivo was on his feet. "Olga! Ici! Steer west-southwest. Hurry. Poika is caught."

"Caught? How?" asked Ici as Homestead swung on the new course.

"I don't know, probably some kind of drift net," answered Toivo, thinking of the net that had killed Poika's mother.

As Olga dashed down the deck toward the sheet that held the wounded dolphin, she yelled, "Don't give her full ahead until I can cinch up the dolphin. Otherwise, we might lose him."

Ahead, Tyttö circled impatiently.

"Okay, okay," shouted Olga from the aft deck, and Toivo felt Homestead surge ahead.

At full power they followed Tyttö. She quickly outdistanced them and circled back, urging them on. It took almost fifteen minutes before they reached the spot. Tyttö dived and Ici, Olga, and Ni went in after her, each armed with a razor sharp diver's knife. The bubbles vanished on the water where the three of them had submerged and Toivo wished he could follow. He stared into the water, trying to see anything that would serve as a clue.

Beneath the surface, Olga swam as fast as she could, knife clenched in her right hand. Passing Ici and Ni, she arrived at the net first. Poika was wrapped head and tail in the unforgiving strands, tangled worse from his thrashing. Olga pulled the section of the net around Poika's head tight to take out the slack and hacked at it with her knife. Sharp as the diver's knife was, the net was tough and Olga had to saw at the strands to cut through. Ici and Ni were working on the tough fibers that held Poika's tail now, all three of them cutting frantically at the stubborn net. How much longer could Poika hold his breath, she wondered, and the worry made her cut faster.

On board the Homestead, Toivo stood helplessly at the bow of the port pontoon. His heart hammered in his chest and sweat ran from his palms and armpits. The waves rose and fell, Homestead bobbed up and down and Toivo waited through an eternity. As much as he wanted to help, there was nothing he could do. He felt like excess baggage left behind. He wondered how long Poika's air would hold out. Why didn't they come back? If Poika died—he tried not to think about it. The shepherds had been underwater for a long time. They would have to come back to the surface soon. He prayed they would bring Poika with them. The minutes crept by, each clock tick a lifetime, and still there was no sign of them. He leaned over, shaded his eyes and peered into the blue-green water, but the shepherds were too deep to see.

Poika's head bobbed to the surface. The dolphin blew hard sending an explosive spout of moisture high in the air. He gasped, blew again and was surrounded by the three shepherds. "*Thank you, men-who-are-fish*," he said between gulps of air.

"Thank God," whispered Toivo, his hands relaxing. Kneeling, he leaned over and stroked Poika's head. "*It is good to see you.*" He nodded to Ici. "Poika says thanks. What happened down there?"

"He was caught in a ghost net. One of the outlawed gill nets. Who knows how long that damn thing has been drifting around. Fortunately we were able to cut through it quickly enough."

"We'll have to find something to weigh it down and sink it permanently," said Olga, climbing back aboard.

"The spare anchor should do," said Ici, pulling himself up on deck.

"Thanks again," said Toivo, resting his hand on Poika's back. To Poika he said, "*Are you going to be okay?*"

"Yes, my friend, I will not go ahead today." With that the big dolphin rolled and leisurely swam back to where the rest of the pod was herding the tuna.

#

Toivo went up on the cabin roof and watched Poika and Tyttö until the sun dropped behind the horizon. As he went down the ladder the last faint rays fanned up and out from behind a line of clouds. Below decks the stark white of the fluorescent lights made him blink. He paused at Olga's door. Maybe he should knock, say something, maybe thank her for helping save Poika. Or maybe apologize for being such a jerk? He listened but there wasn't a sound. No, he thought, rationalizing his cowardice, she was probably sleeping. He went on to the radio room.

Ni sat behind the console, her head resting in the palm of her left hand. She looked bored, but had her eyes glued on the soft green sweep of the radar screen.

"Anything?" asked Toivo, though he could see the screen was empty.

"Nope."

"Where's Ici?"

"Sleeping. Same as Olga. You should do the same."

"I've slept too much lately. Do you want me to watch the screen for a while?"

"For a few minutes, yeah, thanks."

She hopped up and slid out the door, headed for the forward section of the cabin where the latrine was. Toivo tried to sit at the console but, as he lowered himself into the chair, he kept going down, down without finding the seat, his knees folding nearly double. He straightened, realizing the chair was adjusted too short. Bending over, he looked for a height adjustment, but couldn't find one. Finally he managed to contort himself sufficiently to sit down. The radar sweep line circled endlessly around the screen. Not a sign of anything. He examined the other equipment in the small room. There was the radio and a host of computer equipment. He read the plastic labels attached below each dial and switch. Evidently the entire boat was controlled from this one little room.

Toivo continued to watch the hypnotic sweep of the radar screen. He caught himself dozing and shook his head to clear the sleep away. The radar sweep line circled the screen leaving only an empty swath behind. This wasn't hard, decided Toivo, but it sure was boring.

Ni edged in behind him, chuckling, "Kinda cramped in here for you, isn't it?"

She backed up enough for Toivo to worm his way out of his position at the console and then slid back into her seat.

Toivo leaned against the bulkhead. "Is everything computerized?"

"Just about. There is a manual wheel up in the forward compartment for emergencies but we've never used it. This equipment works pretty well."

"Makes Sisu look like a toy."

Silence. Then Ni swung the chair around. "You know it's not my place, but Olga is a woman in every sense of the word."

Toivo blinked. "What?" he asked, stumbling, caught off guard. Of course Olga was a woman. Was Ni accusing him of eyeing her too closely? "Of course she is. A very attractive young woman who deserves a handsome young man to sweep her off her feet."

Ni shook her head. "You don't get it do you? Whether you realize it or not, she's completely taken by you. She's had a hard time of it and you treat her like she was poison. At least show her a little courtesy once in a while."

"I don't want her to get the wrong idea. I'm not some horny old sailor looking to shack up with a kid."

"Of course not, but you are a man and I think she's attracted to you. Lighten up. Forget her age. She's a lot more mature than women who are forty. She's been through a lot more than most people and she's lonely."

Toivo crossed his arms on his chest, his mind racing. This wasn't her business. The situation was hard enough to deal with by himself without Ni trying to make up his mind for him. Of course, she didn't know his real hang up.

"You do understand that I'm Finnish."

"Yeah, so?"

He cut her off. "Do you know what the Russians did to the farmers near our border? I was there; I saw it." The memories made his blood boil and now he found himself shouting.

Ni's eyes widened in surprise and her mouth dropped open. "I can't believe what I'm hearing. You're blaming Olga for something that happened before she was born?"

"Not her. Russians!"

Ni put her hands on her hips, shook her head and sighed. "Just how Russian do you think she is? The girl has never even set foot on Russian soil. Her parental stock may be of Russian origin, but she's no more Russian than Poika."

"But she's going to Russia to see her parents."

"So what? Do you think she even looks the slightest bit like they do? And what about her upbringing? She spent every minute of her life in St. Croix. My memory fails me on that one—I can't remember which part of Russia St. Croix is in."

Toivo wilted under the barrage. "Okay, okay. Maybe she's not Russian." He couldn't find any more words. It seemed the firm ground he'd built his foundation on had suddenly become quicksand. "But her parents are Russian," he added lamely.

"Yes," snapped Ni, "I guess you win that one on a technicality. But you damn sure aren't being fair to Olga. Bad enough we've got to take guff about being mutants, but you have to give her crap about being Russian."

"Okay, okay. Maybe she's not so Russian." Toivo's head was spinning. Russian, not Russian. It was hard to know what he thought. He'd had enough. "If you need a rest, I'll be sitting on the aft deck."

He walked out onto the aft deck. The wounded dolphin still swung in the makeshift hammock, low enough for the wave crests to wash over him and keep him wet. He didn't move as Toivo stepped out on deck. Toivo walked over and sat down on the edge where the sea rolled past at his feet.

"Crazy women," he said to no one. "She is Russian—she isn't Russian. Hell, I don't know. She's still young enough to be my daughter. What kind of relationship could we have? Her a shepherd out here at sea all the time and me a 'lubber' and fishing for a living." He spit into his hands and rubbed the palms together. "That's if I get another boat."

Almost at his feet, Poika surged up out of a wave, sprayed a mouthful of seawater at Toivo, then sank back below the surface. A moment later, the always-smiling face bobbed up again.

"*Talking to one's self is good for the soul. What troubles you, old friend?*"

"*Olga. The blond woman. I think I like her.*"

"*Why is that a problem? You need a mate.*"

Toivo laughed, letting his head roll back. The sound fluttered out across the open ocean. "*You are on her side, too.*"

"*On her side? Since when did the sharing of each other's fortunes take sides? Do you care for her or not?*"

"*It isn't that simple. She's Russian—or I think she's Russian. And she is much younger than I. She needs someone her own age to share life with. And she is half fish. What would she do with a lubber?*"

"*These are just excuses. She will make a better mate than most women. And you are wasting time you do not have. Only the young can afford to waste time avoiding their feelings. We should get on with the living and sharing before our time is gone.*"

Toivo pulled his knees up against his stomach and wrapped his arms around them. The moon rose slowly above the horizon, a big round golden disk that sent shimmering lights dancing across the ripples of the wave tops. It was beautiful, like Olga. But Toivo carried other images with him, ugly images of death and murder.

"*Why do these men kill your people?*" he asked Poika.

"*I don't know. Maybe they feel superior by the act of their killing. Men have such strange desires. It is impossible to understand why they do anything.*"

"*You must be wrong,*" said Toivo, feeling accused as a man, but he knew men well enough to know that many of them would relish the killing—killing anything.

"*It does not matter the why of it. The shame is in the lost knowledge of the beyond and all the spirits whose exit from this life we have missed. Men need to spend less time snatching at the material and seek to understand the true nature of life.*"

"*Nonetheless, it is murder. It must be stopped. There are laws against killing your people.*"

"*As, I am sure, there are laws against men killing men. Perhaps not all men abide by the laws as you do.*"

SHEPHERDS

"Of course not," said Toivo, rubbing his chin with thumb and forefinger. The killing of dolphins or men revolted him. For a moment his stomach rolled and he nearly retched. *"Yet the question remains, why do they kill?"*

"It is not important in the grand scheme of things. It is the grand scheme that you should spend more time thinking about instead of the petty hardships of daily life. Some day you will go ahead and for that day you should prepare. It is very bad to go ahead without preparing. That is the only reason we suffer through this plane of existence."

Toivo stood up, stretched his back, and looked down at the dolphin swimming alongside. *"I don't understand how you can think about going ahead when I'm trying to think about living."*

"That perspective is also bad. You are so busy concentrating on the here-and-now that you never stop to realize that death is the doorway into a superior existence. It is toward that end that you should aim. Instead you collect 'wealth' which is lost on Passing. What you should be saving is the warm thoughts of loved ones, the well-wishes of those you have met and your own thoughts about the beauty you have seen so that you may take some of that beauty with you to the beyond.

"You have become so enchanted with the collection of things that you no longer have time for all the wonders our Creator put here. And because of it you have become so poor as to become lesser beings for it. If only you could see the true meaning of life. If only we could show you."

Poika fell silent for a moment, and Toivo ran the dolphin's words around in his mind. A lot of it did make sense but was there no worth to man's accomplishments? Toivo turned to Poika. *"What about all the things we've built, all the things we've done that we could never have seen or accomplished or experienced without our technology? How can you say it isn't important?"*

Poika dove under the next wave, surfaced, and rolled over on his back. *"Because none of it matters once you've passed through the doorway into death. That doorway leads to an elevated level of life, one where you can travel the universe in a moment, see and feel all that happens for eons, begin to understand the Creator's design. This is only the tiny beginning for our souls to blossom into the vastness of life. It is our preparation for the next life. It is only the means to a far more important end, not an end in itself."*

"Sounds like dolphin religion isn't much different than ours. Except that you probably practice your religion and generally speaking, we don't. But what is important?"

"To learn to perceive all that surrounds you, to receive the sensations that are available, all of them, and to sing our song for those we leave behind. It is our song that we pass on. The song is all that we are able to leave. The song guides those who follow so we may all remember to concentrate on that which really matters."

"But that is what we do. We leave the legacy for our descendents."

"What legacy? The things you have collected during a lifetime? These things only trap the next generation into the illogical thinking of your kind? You have built a web that is very hard to break. We have a system where all have equal opportunities for food, for survival, for thought. We cannot accumulate things, let alone this money you are always talking about and our hearts are glad for it. We share love, respect and the struggles that the world places before us. We do not fear death because we have prepared for it. We accept it and though we do not rush into death, we do not become fanatical in our struggle to prolong that which is inevitable. It is a fine line we walk but the songs of those who have come before guide our way into enlightened life."

"You make humans sound hopeless. Why do you bother with us?"

"There's hope for you. Especially since you have begun to revert to the sea. The men-who-are-fish, the ones who can swim, like Olga, are an example. Someday maybe your kind will join us in the ocean and sing your own songs to add to our understanding of the Creator's purpose."

Toivo braced both hands at his lower back and arched to stretch the stiff muscles. Dolphin philosophy, he thought, wasn't all that different than humans' but other than some orders of monks, man didn't live up to the ideals very well. It certainly wasn't easy to do, given the structure of society. This was true, man did have his heart where his money was, and most never thought about dying except for how to avoid it. Maybe it was because we haven't lived up to our responsibilities.

"The sea would never support us all," Toivo finally said.

"And the land will?"

Poika turned a lazy circle in the water. Now Toivo squatted, then sat with his feet dangling over the side. A wave nipped at his feet. *"There's a lot of truth in what you say. There have been many holy men who have preached the same message though we haven't always been listening. On the other hand, it seems such a shame to scrap all our technology. Why can't we find a compromise?"*

"That is a question for men to answer. We answered it long ago when dolphins returned to the sea."

"Returned to the sea?"

"Ancient songs tell of the time when dolphins walked on land. We had a life not too different from yours. We realized the error and returned to the sea, much as you have started to do."

"Then why doesn't any record of your accomplishments exist?"

"It does. There are landing strips in South America, stone idols in the tropics, and paintings of my ancestors in the caves of your ancestors. They looked upon us as gods, superior beings, and though we tried to explain the error, we could not. A series of catastrophes finally led us to realize the error of our own ways. The Creator has ways of making the truth known. We changed and returned to the sea where the bounty that we needed was at hand. Now we can survive in comfort and prepare for transition into the beyond. You should join us."

Toivo was still a product of his society, his technology. His values were ingrained. Poika's philosophy sounded familiar, but it felt foreign. Toivo hadn't studied religion since childhood Sunday school, and fatigue was setting in. His mind refused to wrestle with the subject. He stood up. *"I think we should continue this later. I'm too tired to think clearly. Maybe tomorrow."*

"Maybe. In the meantime, remember what I said about the young woman-who-is-fish. Stop wasting time you don't have."

"It is the principle that bothers me. It won't go away, and as long at it feels wrong. I'll avoid her company."

"As you wish, but I think you are missing the point. She is one of the new people, and she likes you. I think maybe you are afraid of having someone depend on you."

"Voi, voi, voi," snapped Toivo in Finnish, then reverted to dolphin. *"Just leave me alone. When I'm ready to take a mate I will."*

"Sorry," said Poika. *"I will leave you alone. I should probably rejoin the herd now and do my share of the work."*

"Peace until our paths meet again," said Toivo, and watched Poika turn and swim to the tuna school. There was a lot to think about but right now

he didn't feel up to it. He stood up, ran his fingers through his hair, and strolled towards the bow. The moon was higher now. Its pale white light cast a beautiful, shimmering highway to the horizon. He stood on the fore deck, wishing the breeze could scrub away his troubles, while, the dancing, hypnotic lights soothed his mind.

Chapter 16

Poddington entered the bridge using the stairs from his quarters like he usually did, quietly so as not to alert the watch that he was coming. As he stepped lightly into the wheelhouse, he was surprised to find Deep at the wheel.

"Where's Kong?"

"Didn't show up for his watch yet," said Deep, looking at his watch. "He's only half an hour late. Happens all the time."

"Why haven't I heard about this?"

"Never seemed important."

Poddington wondered if it was important but let it go, as he had other things on his mind. "How much longer until we rendezvous with that swimmer's raft?" he asked.

"Tomorrow."

"This better be the right raft."

A loud bang carried across the deck from the fantail, followed by a second, then a third.

"What the hell was that?" asked Deep, turning to glance aft.

"Sounded like gunshots," said Poddington, hurrying to the door.

He jerked it open, leaned out and stared aft down the deck. A skinny, boyish deckhand ran forward, Luis Jones stalking behind him with Sleena at Jones' shoulder.

Poddington noticed further aft, two burly crewmen were struggling to pitch a body overboard, a body that looked surprisingly like Kong. He could see dark stains on the wheelsman's bulky chest. As Poddington watched the crewmen lifted the body over the rail, and with a concerted effort, heaved it into the ocean.

Poddington's first instinct was to dash aft to find out what was happening, but before he could move, hard footsteps rang on the steel steps that led up to the wheelhouse. The thin deckhand who had been running up the deck, appeared, panting to catch his breath. Poddington retreated into the wheelhouse and the crewman entered.

"What is it?" asked Poddington.

"Captain," said the deckhand, gasping for breath, "the Second Mate just shot Kong."

"What?"

More heavy steps thudded up the stairs to the wheelhouse and Luis Jones stormed in, a heavy scowl on his face, righteous fire in his eyes, and an ugly automatic pistol that smelled of gun smoke clutched in his right hand. "You're short one wheelsman," he said matter-of-factly. "He was stealing drugs from the company. I shot him."

The glower on the man's face dared Poddington to do something about it, almost as if he looked forward to a confrontation.

Sleena slipped in behind Jones, a pistol in her hand.

"Goddamnit," shouted Poddington, "you don't shoot people for taking a snort now and again. Hell, you'd shoot half the crew."

"I'm not talking about doing drugs," shot back Jones, "I'm talking about stealing from the company. There are no second chances."

As Poddington took a step toward Jones, the barrel of the Second Mate's automatic pistol tilted upward toward Poddington. The Captain froze, torn between a fierce thirst for revenge and the logic that he'd probably die for the attempt.

Behind Poddington, Deep stepped away from the wheel, leaving the ship on its own. As he moved to flank Jones, Poddington snarled out of the side of his mouth, "There's three of us. If we rush him, we can take away that gun and get out of here, no more harm done."

Sleena took a step nearer Jones, her gun pointing at Deep. "I think you better recount. As I see it, it's two against two."

Poddington's eyes widened. "So, that's how it is."

"That's how it is," she said, a coquettish smile on her face, grinding away at Poddington's guts. "I stick with the one holding all the cards."

"Okay, okay," said Poddington, stepping back and flinging one arm across Deep's chest moving him back at the same time. "You've made your point. What's next?"

Jones put his gun back in the holster hidden under his shirt and stated flatly, "Find the swimmers, kill the fisherman, and clear out. That's your job. Do it well, and things will be fine. Screw up, and. . ."

Poddington nodded agreement and waited silently. Jones motioned for Sleena to follow and the two of them left the bridge.

"We should have killed them both," said Deep once the bridge was clear.

"How? They'd have likely killed us. And maybe they still will. Have we got any loyal crewmen left?"

"Only a couple. Most of the rest are men hired by the company. Jones' men, for sure. And they're all armed."

Poddington took a deep breath. He should have seen this coming. In the future, he reminded himself, he'd better think ahead or he'd end up a dead man.

Deep cleared his throat.

Poddington, one eyebrow raised, turned to catch a glimpse of the First Mate. "Have you got something to say?" he asked.

"Yeah, I guess I have. But I don't want you getting pissed about it."

"What do you mean by that?"

"I mean the bitch is sleeping with Jones. I should have told you."

For a moment the silence was electric. Poddington's jaw muscles tightened, his mind burning with the reality of Sleena's betrayal. How could he be so stupid?

"Yes, you should have told me. How long have you known?"

"She's been hanging out with that bastard ever since they went on board Turtle and killed the swimmers without you."

Poddington pretended to study the map, the radar, anything, but he was thinking only about what a mess he'd put himself in and how the hell he was going to get out of it. Definitely he and Deep were skipping out the minute they hit shore.

"My guess is we'd better think of something, or we're going to join Kong. At least for now, Jones needs us. He's short one wheelsman and none of the dock rats he hired know shit about running this ship. Maybe we'll still be alive when we reach port but we'd better have a plan to disappear as soon as we tie up."

#

While Toivo stood on the deck, thrilling to the natural beauty of the sea at night, Olga remained entrenched in his thoughts. The blond shepherd had an alien beauty that attracted him in ways he really didn't want to think about. It made Toivo smile. Why did she have to be Russian? And practically a kid at that. At the same time, the curve of her thighs brought other thoughts to mind.

He heard the light footfalls of bare feet behind him. By the long stride and the softness of the step, he knew it was Olga. As he turned to face her, the moon cast soft shadows across her face and for a moment he was stunned by her ethereal beauty, barely able to breathe.

"Hi," she said, stepping past him to stand at the very bow, her back to him. He noticed the way she bent her legs, like every good sailor, to absorb the rise and fall. "What are you doing on deck?"

He studied the delicate outline of her head, the short blond hair combed back and down. Her bikini bottoms barely covered her sensuous behind. For an instant he had the urge to grab her, to touch her firm flesh, but he didn't. His mind still wrestled with his prejudice.

"I was watching the moon on the waves," he said. "I thought you were standing watch."

"I am. That doesn't mean I have to stay chained to the control room. Some nights I leave Homestead on autopilot and come up here to look at the stars. It helps me think. Tonight is one of those nights."

"Oh." Toivo started to put his hand on her shoulder, but caught himself and let it swing back to his side. "What are you thinking about tonight?"

She turned to face him, her eyes asking him questions. "Do you really want to know?"

"Of course," he said, wondering if she was thinking about him.

She bit her lip. Then, as if making up her mind, she started in. "I've been alone most of my life. At the St. Croix School of Fisheries we were surrounded by 'professional' people who were good at teaching us the textbook things we needed. Most of them didn't really care, they were just doing their job."

Toivo felt foolish. Of course she wasn't thinking about him. He said, "Tell me more about this school."

"All of us cowboys went to either Guam or St. Croix. They were schools dedicated to our development, learning, rearing, the whole works. Originally they were sponsored, along with the Shikawa labs where we were created, by the World Health Organization. That is until they came under fire from just about every holier-than-thou religious group you could think of. With that kind of pressure, WHO dropped us like a hot potato, but they couldn't kill us and nobody would adopt us. We were in limbo until Star-Kist saw a chance to monopolize the fish farming industry and bought up everything, under the table. About the same time as WHO ditched the project, the General Assembly passed a moratorium on bio-engineered people. After that, officially, we ceased to exist. Star-Kist kept things quiet until we were old enough to put to work and the schools closed."

"But what about the schools? They sound like glorified orphanages."

"I suppose so. I've never been to a regular orphanage. St. Croix was a cold, emotionally sterile place. I couldn't wait to leave. Not only were the housemothers not mothers, but also we had no friends outside the other cowboys. When we went beyond the confines of the school grounds, the native kids thought we were freaks, weirdos, monsters. They were cruel little bastards."

She pursed her lips, took a breath and continued. "For the longest time I blamed God for allowing this to happen to me. I cursed the day I was born. It never occurred to me that I might be somebody worthwhile; I hated being me."

Softness tugged at Toivo's heart. She was pouring her guts out, venting feelings that she'd harbored for years, and it was he, a poor Finnish fisherman, that she chose to be open with. "And now?" he asked gently.

"I feel better about myself here. I belong. They made me for the sea and I love the mistress I serve. But more than that, I found out recently that I have parents—of a sort. At least I know who was the source for my genetic material though I never existed within a mother's womb. The people at Star-Kist gave me their names, addresses, pictures. They told me I could go to see them on my first R&R."

"Did you go?"

"Not yet. My first R&R won't be for another eight months. Even if it were tomorrow, I don't know if I could go."

"Why not? They are your parents."

"Yes, biologically they are my parents. Emotionally they are strangers. I've built up so much resentment. In many ways they aren't my parents at all, yet they are my flesh and blood. It's kind of like having been given up for adoption before I was even born. Do I want to know my parents? Do they want to know me? I'm afraid I won't like the answers. I just want to belong somewhere."

Toivo rubbed his chin with his first two fingers and noticed a little stubble; he should have shaved. "They must be very good people to have produced such a wonderful woman as you. If you go, at least you'll have your questions answered, one way or the other and you can get on with your life. The worst thing is not knowing and worrying about it."

She sighed, shook her head ever so slightly. "I tell myself the same thing, but it's hard to make the decision, to get the wheels in motion for taking that step. Still, I ask myself, could I handle the rejection if they just don't want to see me?"

"Of course they'll want to see you. Now you're making up reasons to avoid reaching out to them. At least give them a chance. I know it's a huge emotional risk but think of the potential reward. How could they be anything short of terrific with a daughter like you?" Standing there in the moonlight, his eyes feasting on her marvelous body, Toivo meant what he said.

She stared at him, a fierce glare that penetrated to his soul. "I'm not even very much like them. Look at me!" She held up both hands, the fingers spread open to show the thin, strong webbing stretched between the delicate fingers. "I'm a 'swimmer.'" She spat it like poison. "A product of the best bio-engineering the world could manage. I'm a freak."

"Hardly." Toivo clasped his hands behind his back to prevent himself from putting his arms around her. "You have never stopped to see the beauty," he said through clenched teeth. "The blond hair and figure of a goddess and you think yourself a freak? Maybe the rest of us are the freaks, only a shadow of what we might be." He was embarrassed. The look in her eye told him she was reading more into it than he meant—then again just what did he mean? He turned to walk back to the cabin.

"Don't go," she whispered. "It's been so lonely. Can't we talk a while longer?"

"What about your shift at the radar?"

"The alarm will sound if anything shows up. Tell me about you. We found you barely alive, and though I know they sank your boat and your crew was killed, I don't know anything else about you."

"There's not much to tell. I was born in Oulu, Finland, and spent most of my life there. When I was seven, my father took a job with the Kewalo Basin Marine Mammal Laboratory in Hawaii. We spent five years there while he tried to work out the computer algorithms to understand dolphin speech. While he was busy with his computers I spent more time with the dolphins than with my family. That's when I learned to speak dolphinese, or whatever you want to call it.

"When I was twelve we moved back to Finland. My mother died from pneumonia, in the winter a year later. For the next three years I lived a miserable life. My father had no time for anything except his work and especially not for a son who only wanted to talk about the sea. When I was sixteen I ran off to go fishing with my uncle on a Norwegian deep-water ship.

"I spent about six months at sea, came home, argued with my father about everything, finished high school, worked for a while at a dairy and served my term in the Finnish Army. As soon as I had saved up enough, I went back to fishing. When my father died, about ten years later, I sold everything he had and bought Sisu. I didn't do badly for a while, but as the factory schools spread and took more and more of the open ocean, the tuna became harder to catch, unless you stole it from the factory shoals."

"You didn't do that, did you?"

"Of course not. Poika and Tyttö always managed to lead me to enough fish to keep me from going bankrupt."

"And how did you meet Poika?"

"It was in the summer, a couple of years after my father died. I found him circling a ghost drift net—he was barely weaned—and his mother was a cold corpse caught in that damn net. Poika wouldn't leave her side until I spoke to him. It's surprising how quickly the language came back to me then, considering that I hadn't spoken to a dolphin in sixteen years."

"It must be wonderful to run your own life, to decide what contribution you will make to the world. Better than having the choice made for you."

"Maybe, maybe not. It's the people like you who have filled the bellies of millions who would have starved. You have kept fish a plentiful and cheap source of food. If it were up to men like me, we would have fished the seas empty of tuna by now and the world would be a hungrier place."

"You don't know that."

"Of course I do. History shows men repeat the same patterns. We become so efficient we wipe out entire species, and as their numbers shrink, we don't go off to find other prey, we just hunt more and more until they are gone. No, despite all my complaining, the seas are better for all of us because of the factory farms. Even I've taken a few factory tuna that wandered away from your schools." He closed his eyes and thought of catching tuna again and a great sadness filled him, without a boat, without a crew, would such a life ever be possible again? His hands trembled with the thought. "I pray that there will be fish for men to catch for a long time to come."

"Then you would like to go on fishing. Did you have insurance?"

"Insurance, no, but I still have a little cash in the bank. It certainly isn't as much as I had hoped I would have by now."

"Can you buy another boat?"

Toivo thought about the Sisu. It was going to be hard to replace her. They didn't make boats like her anymore, at least not for what he'd paid when he bought Sisu. Nothing would ever really replace her, but there were other boats, and men desperate to sell. "I suppose I'll get something."

"You'll need a crew. Maybe you could find a place for someone like me. That is, once I pay off my debt."

He thought of Wilho and the others. Visions of gunfire rattled around in his mind. He could see the blood, hear the shots, the screams. God, he wished he could have saved them. He was alive and they were dead, but how could he have saved them? How?

She smiled. It was warm, genuine. "What are you thinking?"

He couldn't tell her. "Nothing. Really nothing."

"You don't want me on your boat."

"Of course I want you on the boat." How could he refuse? He chuckled softly, almost to himself. It was a trap but he didn't care. "But I have to warn you, the pay isn't very good."

"That doesn't matter. I'd be with someone who wants me around, not people who have to put up with me. Even Ici and Ni are too interested in each other to have time for me. I do my job; they do theirs. We don't socialize."

She looked away for a moment, her head turned toward the horizon. When she turned back, Toivo saw a lost, sad look in her eyes, maybe a tear. "I'm lonely. I need someone."

Toivo felt a sudden rush of warmth welling up inside his chest. It surged through his neck and temples, filling his brain with a euphoric drug-like hypnosis. Loneliness he knew. All the years at sea. Yes, he'd had Poika and Tyttö but human companionship had never been there. Most of his crew went home to their families between fishing trips. He had never had a real home. Sometimes when the urge overpowered him, he went to a hotel and talked to cheap women, pretending they were someone special. Or he went to his cabin up the coast and spent the days watching the sea, talking with Poika and Tyttö, or listening to Sibelius. The cabin had never been a home. There was no love there.

He remembered the times Wilho, his wife and Enni had visited him at his cabin. They had brought food, eaten and laughed, and always, when they left he wondered if Wilho knew how lucky he was. Now Wilho was dead, and Toivo knew what lonely was. His heart felt bound to this woman.

"I've been lonely, too," was all he could say.

"I knew you had," she said, touching him lightly on the cheek with the tips of her fingers.

He thought about the way he'd treated her. Was being Russian such a terrible thing? Right now it didn't seem to matter. She was a beautiful young woman—as real and vulnerable as anyone. He couldn't continue to treat her as if she were the enemy. He couldn't hide his own feelings. "I'm sorry about the way I've treated you," he said, letting the words escape as if someone else spoke them.

He drank in her image now, seeing her without prejudice. The moonlight cast a golden glow on her high cheekbones and made the moisture on her lips sparkle. He took her face in both hands, delicately cradling her head.

"You are beautiful," he whispered. "I think I've been too harsh on both of us. My own stoic morality. More likely, a fool."

"Not a fool." She threw her arms around him and hugged him tight.

He hugged her, feeling her warm athletic body pressing against him. Flames engulfed him, raging through his mind. He wanted her, needed her, his pent up passion exploding.

And then, just as the moment felt perfect, Ni's voice intruded, "Oh, I didn't know anyone was out here." A knowing smirk flirted with her lips. She stepped out of the starboard hatch and rounded the cabin. "Shouldn't you be in the control room?" she asked looking at Olga and winked.

Toivo loosened his arms from their encircling grasp, letting them slide ever so slowly to his sides. A frown stole his smile, his passion died, and he felt foolish, like a schoolboy caught sneaking kisses from the prettiest girl three grades his junior.

Olga untangled herself. "The autopilot and radar alarm are on. I just came out for a moment."

"Yeah," Ni said, her eyes twinkled with intrigue, revealing what she really thought was going on. "Sorry to interrupt but I wanted a breath of fresh air."

"Yeah, I suppose I should get back to the control room." Olga put her head on Toivo's shoulder and whispered in his ear, "Christ, as much screwing around as she and Ici do, you'd think she could give us a few minutes." Olga hugged him hungrily.

Toivo hugged her, then released and stepped back his embarrassment still flush on him. He folded his arms on his chest. He knew exactly what Olga was thinking, what he'd been thinking, too. He tried to remember how the conversation had taken them there. Maybe fate had saved him from making a bigger fool of himself.

"I guess I have to go. There'll be lots of time later." She winked at him, kissed him a peck on the cheek, and skipped toward the starboard cabin door. "See you later," she said over her shoulder, half turning her head to look at him as she went along the deck.

She had such a glowing smile that Toivo wondered how he was going to keep from letting her down when later came. Then again, as he watched the gentle sway of her behind, he asked himself why he was denying himself such a treasure. Didn't anything come easy?

Chapter 17

Toivo trudged slowly along the deck toward the aft cabin door. He ducked inside the doorway and as he shuffled down the corridor past the control room, he caught a glimpse of the back of Olga's head. She sat at the control console, oblivious to everything else. Toivo let the air escape from his lungs in a rush. She was beautiful.

Olga turned around at the sound. "Toivo, what was that for?"

"Er, nothing. Just tired," he said, wishing she hadn't noticed him.

He hurried on toward his room. He wanted to talk to her, but his insides churned with the thought of it. He rationalized it away by remembering that she was on duty and shouldn't be interrupted. He was feeling tired anyway and the thought of sleep was warm and comforting.

Behind him, Olga peeked out of the control room, started to speak, then let him go without a word.

He hurried to his room, grabbed a towel and retraced his steps forward to the showers. He let the steamy water relax his muscles, bringing on a mild euphoria. He toweled off and hurried back to his room. Within minutes of lying down, he was fast asleep.

#

Somebody was yelling. Toivo bolted upright in his bunk. Sunshine blazed through the porthole forming an almost solid cylinder of golden light. He rubbed his face, blinking to fight the glare. Who had yelled? Where had it come from? Had he been dreaming? No, there, from the dining room.

He heard Ici's voice screaming, ". .. too late already."

Sobs. It sounded like Ni.

Ici again. "I deserve to have a child. You are my wife. You should want to have my child. What the hell is wrong with you?"

"With me? Can't you see I want a child? But not until we can provide a decent life."

"Oh Christ. Always wait until later, until we're both free, until we have money. Bullshit. I may not be able to father a child tomorrow and you want to wait two or three years. I can't wait that long!"

"Then find someone else."

Toivo rolled out of bed. He pulled on his trunks, opened the door and stepped out into the corridor. In the dining hall he could see Ici leaning over, both hands flat on the tabletop. Ni was out of sight behind the bulkhead.

Toivo strolled into the mess hall, trying to appear like he hadn't overheard a thing. As he entered, Ici straightened and stopped talking. From behind the table, Ni looked up at Toivo, her eyes red, tears still glistening on her cheeks. Ici turned and started into the galley.

"Something wrong?" asked Toivo, trying to cover a yawn. He went to the coffeepot, poured a cup and sat down at the table across from Ni. "You two should be a little quieter when people are sleeping."

"Sorry," said Ni, turning away, her eyes brimming over with her hurt.

Ici turned in the galley doorway, folded his arms across his chest and leaned against the doorsill. "I think you should mind your own business. This is a private conversation."

Toivo took a sip of the black brew. It burned the tip of his tongue – hot—just the way he liked it. He set the cup down and rubbed the sleep out of his eyes. He examined the two shepherds. Ni still stared at the corner of the room and Ici glared back at Toivo. Toivo stood up, holding his coffee cup. "If it's so private, why shout so loud?" He started toward the door, then stopped. "With all the trouble we're in, I would think you could find something more important to discuss. Before anyone is going to have a baby, we have to get out of this alive. Try to think about how we are going to do that."

Ici straightened up. "The Martin B. will be here soon. Then we'll be safe."

Toivo pursed his lips and shook his head. If only things were as simple as kids always thought they were. "Do you think you'll be safe just because the Martin B. is here? Maybe the killers won't attack while the factory boat is around, and maybe they'll just sink the Martin B. along with us. They sure won't attack the U.N. frigate, but will we still be here when it arrives, and how long do you think they will be able to hang around to protect us? There are four other rafts out here and neither ship can protect everyone at once.

Sooner or later they'll leave, and then you'll be just as vulnerable as ever. You won't be safe until the murderers are captured or killed."

Ni glared at Ici. "All the more reason not to have kids right now."

"All the more reason to have kids right now," said Ici. "Just in case I'm killed."

"Stop," insisted Toivo. "This won't get us anywhere."

Olga stepped into the room.

"What do you want?" asked Ici, glaring at the tall blond woman. "You're supposed to be on duty."

"I am on duty. I came to report a message from the Martin B." She waited, as if expecting some other comment. None came. "They say they are still quite a way off, but right now I have another blip on the radar scope. If it's not the Martin B., who is it?"

Ici raised an eyebrow. "It can't be the frigate. It's got to be the false Sunrise Savior."

"Don't jump to conclusions. It could be anyone. How big is the blip?"

"Big, it could be the Savior. It's damn sure not a supertanker." Olga scowled. "I tried to raise them on the radio but only got silence. I thought I'd better tell everyone right away."

"How far away is the Martin B.?" asked Ni.

"Too far to do us any good."

Ici started for the door. "Whoever it is, the only way to find out is to look her over. I'm going topside with the binoculars and check it out. You keep your eyes on the scope."

"Maybe we should just submerge," suggested Ni.

"Not without knowing who it is," said Ici, the forcefulness still in his voice. "We can't stay under forever and I'm not about to waste our batteries if it's not necessary."

"Okay, I'll be in the control room," said Olga as she turned and went back across the hall.

Ni headed topside with Ici. Toivo sat back down, staring into his half empty cup of coffee. What was he going to do? Knowing a mysterious ship was closing in on them brought images of armed men, gunfire and horrors that he couldn't stand to think about. If it was the killers, what defense did they have?

He didn't even have a shark rifle here. He took a sip of hot coffee. Sitting there doing nothing gave him butterflies, yet there wasn't a single thing he could do. Another sip of coffee. Maybe he couldn't, but maybe the dolphins could. Some of them knew these men. They could conduct reconnaissance. If the ship was the Sunrise Savior, they could send the alarm. Sound travels a long way underwater and Poika could stay near the Homestead to pick up any alarm. It would be an interference-free transmission and, the more warning they had, the better.

He jumped up, splashed his coffee into the sink, and set the cup down. He dashed down the hallway. As he passed the control room, Toivo stuck his head in. Olga sat at the console. "How far away are they?"

"Closing to twenty kilometers," she said, keeping her eye on the scope. "We should be able to see them soon."

He went out on the aft deck. The sun was already halfway up the sky. The warmth felt good but Toivo didn't have time to notice. He whistled for Poika. Almost immediately the dolphin turned from the tuna school and dashed for Homestead. Once Poika was alongside, it only took a moment to explain the plan. Poika listened, nodded, and was off, whistling instructions to Sheriff, Slim, Gunslinger and the other members of the expanded pod. Toivo saw several of the dolphins leave their tuna herding duties, fan out and head for the horizon. Poika circled back to take up station alongside Homestead, ready to act as the receiver. Whoever was coming, they would be identified long before they could harm anyone on Homestead.

\#

Captain Poddington stood scowling out the bridge's forward window. He knew now they had the fisherman and the swimmers who had rescued him. As much as he hated killing fishermen, Poddington could see no other way out of the mess. The last link between the Sunrise Savior and the killings on the Oyster Bay was within his grasp, and in any case, Luis Jones wasn't going to let it drop. The tiny raft wasn't visible yet, but it would be soon.

"What's her bearing now?" he asked the radar watchman.

"Three-five-eight degrees," was the instant reply.

"What's her speed?"

"About three knots, Captain."

Deep stepped up behind Poddington. "We'll be visible to them long before they're visible to us. They sit so damn low in the water. What'll we do if they submerge?"

"Have the deck gun ready. I don't think they'll be able to identify us until we can put a shot or two on them. With a little luck, they won't be able to submerge."

Even as he waited, his mind was filled with thoughts of how much easier life had been when he and Deep were fishermen. Fondly, he remembered the days when he and Deep first started fishing the coastal waters around New Zealand. Just the two of them. Deep had been George then. That was before he'd run them aground calling "deep water" right up to the moment they hit the shallows. They had just a small boat then, but the catches had been enough for them to move up quickly to a larger one. It had been so uncomplicated; like a distant dream. Now chaos had taken over his life.

"It'll be good to have this cleared up, finally," he whispered to Deep, always aware that Luis Jones hovered only a few feet away.

"I still hate killing a fellow fisherman," spat Deep under his breath. "The longer I stay involved with this dirty business, the less I like it."

Poddington raised an eyebrow in the direction of the second mate. "Don't let him hear you say that. As far as he's concerned, this is lifetime employment. The end of the job means the end of your life. You saw what he did to Kong."

"Maybe so, out here. But when we hit port I'm jumping ship. They'll never see me again." Poddington saw the resolve in Deep's gray eyes.

Luis Jones stepped closer. Being a head shorter than Poddington or Deep, he was on tiptoes looking for the raft. "Don't you see them yet?" he demanded. "They should be right in front of us."

"Range?" snapped Poddington.

"Twelve kilometers," was the reply.

Right in front of us, my ass, thought Poddington. He looked down and saw the deck gun had already been raised out of the hold to the firing position. The crew stood by. As soon as they had a sighting they would fire off a round. Still, the raft was a small target and likely they wouldn't get it on the first shot.

He turned to the radio operator. "Be ready to jam any signal that comes from the swimmers."

The longer they waited, the tighter the knot grew in Poddington's stomach. If he could just get through the day, then it would be over. They would be more careful from now on. There didn't have to be any more killing. The more he thought about it, slipping away with Deep the minute they hit port seemed like the best choice left open to him. He needed a plan, all the cash he could scrape together, somewhere safe to go. In the meantime, he knew he had to play along with Jones and the thugs that served as the crew.

Poddington turned from the window and went to his charts. Plainly marked in red was the last known location of the U.N. frigate. He hoped they were still a long way off. He did not want to tangle with them.

#

The wait seemed to drag on interminably. Ici reached the cabin roof and immediately scanned the horizon with the binoculars. Toivo prayed it was not them, yet at the same time he tried to think of a way to stop the killers, if it was. The only plan that made sense was to submerge. They could not fight guns.

He stood near the stern on the port pontoon. Poika swam in the wake, hardly working to keep up with the slow moving Homestead.

"There she is," said Ici from the cabin roof. He leaned on the rail, the binoculars glued to his eyes.

Toivo stared off in the same direction but was too low to see it. The bow rose on a wave and he caught a glimpse of the black shape just before Homestead's nose dipped into the trough.

"*Any word*?" he asked Poika.

The dolphin dove into a wave, surfaced and rolled to look at Toivo. He kept pace with the ship even on his back. "*They are bad men. They are the ones who sent Wilho ahead.*"

Toivo gritted his teeth. If only he could get his hands on them, choke them to death. He had never hated like this. At the moment, there wasn't anything he could do.

"It's them," he shouted to Ici. "The dolphins recognize them."

"Get below," yelled Ici, and he and Ni turned from the rail, dropped through the hatch and slid down the ladder in one motion.

Before heading for the aft door, Toivo stooped over at the stern. The wounded dolphin still swung in the makeshift sling between the two pontoons. Toivo knelt and touched the mammal.

"*I hope you're ready to swim,*" he said and reached down to loosen the knots that held the sheet stretched between the pontoons.

Toivo pulled on the fabric but the knots held tight. The knots had been tightened beyond his ability to pull an end free. He tried to get a hold in the wet sheet with his fingernails, but only succeeded in breaking the nails. He tugged again, but still they wouldn't come loose. He grabbed the sheet below the knot and jerked hard, trying to tear the cloth. Nothing. Another fierce tug and the sheet tore below the knot. Toivo twisted, yanked, and the cloth ripped completely in two. The makeshift sling fell.

The dolphin swung down and dropped the short distance into the ocean. He rolled once, blew hard, and turned to swim away. "*Thank you,*" he said and dove.

"Come on," yelled Ni hanging halfway out the door, her right hand firmly on the dogging wheel. "We're going under before they get any closer."

Toivo glanced up toward the ship. It loomed larger now and he could make out the distinct forms of the men on deck, the ugly, black silhouettes of guns hanging from shoulder slings plainly visible. Images filled his mind and he replayed the slaughter of his crew again. Toivo wanted to do something, stop them, revenge his crew. Adrenaline surged through his veins and his hands shook.

Ni grabbed him by the arm. "Come on."

She dragged him inside, slammed the door shut and spun the hand wheel to latch it watertight. "Clear," she hollered.

"Going down," shouted Olga from the control room.

Toivo stepped around Ni so he could see into the control room. Olga fingered the buttons and controls with a light touch that reminded Toivo of her fingertips caressing his legs. He felt the deck incline as Homestead slipped under the Pacific. For a moment the raft lurched as she absorbed the energy of the waves against the flat sides of the cabin, then she submerged completely. There was a moment of eerie silence and almost weightless lack of motion. The sensation of quiet isolation, of being cut off from the world made him forget his interest in Olga's touch.

"We're under," whispered Olga.

Toivo saw the digital depth meter over her shoulder. He watched it register the meters of water that covered them. Now what, he wondered.

Ici shoved his way into the control room, leaned over Olga, and with one hand flipped the switches on the radio. With the other he keyed the talk button on the microphone.

"Martin B., Martin B.," he repeated. "This is Homestead. The renegade tanker has overtaken us. We are submerging. Need help fast."

He released the talk button. A rush of static filled the speaker. He tried again. More static, white noise that pushed his feeble signal off the air.

"We're being jammed." Ici peered at the meters above the radio panel. "The U.N. frigate won't be able to hear us, or if they do, they won't be able to understand what we are saying. The tanker is using a white noise pattern generated by their computer. Maybe the Martin B. is close enough to receive some of our transmission through it, but I doubt it."

The radio crackled. "Homestead, Homestead. Come in Homestead. Do you read me?"

Ici reached for the talk button.

"Homestead, Homestead, this is the Martin B. Come in, Homestead."

A sharp burst of static.

"The antenna just went under water," said Olga. "We can't send or receive anymore."

"Why wasn't their signal cut off by the jamming?" asked Toivo, leaning into the control room.

"Good question," said Olga. "They surely have a stronger radio than we do, but it wouldn't make that much difference. Their call came through loud and clear. I don't think it was the Martin B. I didn't recognize the voice."

"Me either," said Ni, frowning. "If it was our factory ship, why would the static stop only while they were transmitting?"

"Who knows?" asked Olga, swiveling a half turn on the stool to face the others. "Now what?"

"Sit tight for the moment," replied Ici and no one seemed to have a better idea.

Ni turned for the galley. "Anyone want some fresh coffee?"

They all nodded yes. Ici squeezed past Toivo and went to help Ni.

Toivo stepped up behind Olga. He let his right hand come to rest gently on her shoulder. "I don't like it."

Olga put her hand on Toivo's. "Me either. At least we're safe for now and the Stockholm will be here in another day and a half. I don't think they would give up the search now, even if we don't show up on their radar when they get here. We'll just have to surface while the U. N. is still here."

"Can we stay submerged that long?"

"We can manage three or four days if we go easy on the batteries. The trick will be to know when the frigate is up there. I think I'll be able to recognize a warship on the hydrophones."

"That would be good. In the meantime we need to think of a way to make contact with the frigate. Maybe we could ride near the surface and let the antenna poke out enough to catch the radio traffic."

Olga shook her head. "It might work, but the antenna isn't very long and we'd be dangerously close to the surface. They would probably be able to see us."

"I doubt they'll attack with the frigate standing by. Maybe they won't hang around once the U.N. ship gets close."

"I'm not going to count on it."

Toivo watched the depth meter continue to rise. "How deep are you taking us?"

"About a hundred meters. We'll be safe there."

"A hundred meters. Yes, we'll be safe, but what about Poika, Tyttö, and the other dolphins? They have to come up for air. They might be surfacing in the face of men who want them dead." His insides crawled. If there was only something he could do. Again he was helpless. He let his breath out in a loud, frustrated rush.

"They'll be all right," said Olga, craning her neck to look at Toivo. "They were born at sea and the D's won't fall for any tricks this time. Nobody will be able to get them."

"You're right," said Toivo, remembering how the other dolphins had gotten close enough to get shot. Poika would never let that happen, and neither would the others.

"Coffee's ready," said Ni from the galley.

"I'll bring you a cup," said Toivo. "Keep this thing under control."

Toivo returned a few minutes later with two cups of steaming coffee. He stayed while they drained the cups, talking little. Olga kept constant watch on the meters, dials and digital display. She made minor adjustments a few times, but mostly it was only her attention that the Homestead required. Toivo's mind was preoccupied by worries of surfacing to blazing guns and trying to figure out how to avoid it.

He wondered what kind of sonar equipment the Sunrise Savior had aboard and what, if any, antisubmarine weaponry. He doubted they would have depth charges or anything sophisticated, but the tanker might use deep nets to snag the Homestead. First they would have to locate the raft. Which brought him back to what kind of sonar they might have. Finally, as the coffee wore off, Toivo had to fight to keep from yawning.

Olga turned and for a moment her tight-lipped expression was replaced by a wry smile. "Why don't you go to sleep? I'll come keep you warm as soon as I'm off watch."

Toivo was about to say no, but the thought of her warm body snuggled up against him was too much. "Okay," he said. He picked up both empty cups and headed for his room.

Chapter 18

Toivo awakened to the sound of his door opening. A shaft of yellow light wedged its way into his room. Olga's blond head peeked in.

"Are you awake?" she whispered.

Toivo rolled over to face her. The hallway lights behind her clearly accentuated her silhouette so that Toivo could see every detail of her sensuous outline. It brought his desires burning to the surface.

"Yes. Come in."

She slipped in, closing the door softly behind her.

"Where are you? I can't see in the dark."

Toivo hesitated. He'd invited her. Now what? She must be expecting him to make love to her. Could he? He thought of her beautiful body, young, desirable. His face flushed. Could he actually go through with it? Of course he could, he was a man and the rising pressure in his loins said he wanted to have her.

"I'm right here," he whispered. He sat up and patted the mattress loud enough to guide her.

He felt her weight settle on the edge of the bed next to him. "It's scary, just waiting for something to happen."

"What can happen while we are submerged?" asked Toivo, reaching to put his arm around her.

She snuggled into his arms, then stiffened. "We don't have to make love if it bothers you."

At the same time she rubbed his thigh with one hand, slowly working her way up his leg. The warmth grew. He leaned over to kiss her on the cheek.

"I want to make love to you," he heard himself say. "I've been foolish for too long. It's time we forgot all that has been said and begin fresh from this moment."

She turned to him, wrapping her arms around him, kissing him hard, her tongue tickling his lips. She pushed him back, pressing down on him. His objections were lost in the sea of sensual fire that consumed him. His lust overwhelmed the last tiny kernel of illogical prejudice that was left.

He ran both hands up the backs of her thighs until he held her hard buttocks. He kissed her, letting his tongue search the inside of her mouth. Now he squeezed her buttocks, feeling her muscles tighten in his hands. He slid down, moving his mouth along her throat until he was kissing her breasts. Already her breathing was throaty, harsh, rushing in gasps. He worked his hands up between her legs, teasing, caressing, thrilling to her moans.

From there, Toivo slowed. He took his time, working in concert with her. She stroked him and he touched her. She kissed, he kissed back, their tongues working back and forth, teasing and thrilling. Their passion rose in concert until they reached a tumultuous, simultaneous climax. Afterward they lay arm-in-arm, kissing lightly, hugging, enjoying utter contentment.

"Have you known many women?" she asked after a long while.

"A few," he said, "not many."

She squeezed him tight. "You are my first."

Toivo winced. Not only was he robbing the cradle, he had taken her virginity. God forgive him.

She hugged him tighter. "You must be happy or you will spoil it for me. I wanted you from the first day we plucked you from the Pacific. I am a woman, capable of making my own choices. I chose you. Don't make me feel cheap."

"You are not cheap, Olga. I feel luckier than any man has a right to be. I never dreamed I'd find someone like you. You understand me and you understand the lure of the sea. Besides, Poika likes you." He grinned.

She kissed his right ear. "You make me very happy."

He encircled her with his arms. She felt so comfortable resting against him. This was part of the life he had always dreamed of but never had. Before he knew what happened, they both were asleep.

#

The bridge on the imposter Sunrise Savior was quiet. Only hours before the air had been charged with anticipation. Now the mood was heavy, weighted down by the drag of time spent in fruitless searching. Poddington scratched at his unshaven face. For the umpteenth time he scanned the charts, looked at the sonar scope, checked the radar for any signs of the impending arrival of the U.N. frigate, and generally cursed his misfortune. It was taking too long. He felt like naked prey waiting for the hunter to arrive.

"Where the hell are they?" He slammed the chart table with both fists. "Why can't we pick them up on sonar?"

Deep raised up from his position hunched over the sonar scope. He put both hands in the small of his back and stretched out the stiffness. "I think we are seeing them," he said, reaching for his cup of coffee that had long since gotten cold.

"What do you mean?" asked Poddington, stepping away from the chart table to return once again to the sonar. "There's so many echoes on the screen. How can you tell which one they are?"

Immediately, Luis Jones was at their shoulders, his eyes keenly examining the sonar screen. "If we are seeing them, what are you waiting for?"

Poddington felt like telling him to get the hell off the bridge, but knew he wouldn't go. Nonetheless, Poddington was the Captain. "If you're so smart, you tell us which echo is the right one."

Luis scowled. "Get on with your business."

Poddington locked eyes with the second mate. For a long moment it seemed they might come to blows. Instead, Poddington turned back to Deep and motioned for the First Mate to go on with his explanation.

"Right here," explained Deep. "See the big echoes here and here. One of them is the school of tuna and one of them has to be their raft."

"What about this echo, and this one? Aren't they big enough to be the raft?" Poddington pointed to the other bright green dots.

"Yeah, they could be," agreed Deep, "but watch them for a couple of minutes steady." He paused, giving Poddington time to concentrate on the two echoes. "See how they fade in and out. More like ghost echoes. I don't think they're real echoes at all. I think he has those damn dolphins giving us false signals somehow. It probably takes a couple of them to produce a strong enough echo to show up as if it were the metal hull of a ship. Maybe the fade in and out is caused by a lack of synchronization."

Poddington thought about it for a minute. This Finnish fisherman was supposed to be able to talk to dolphins. Poddington had heard that scuttlebutt around the fishing ports more than once, fishermen carping about the Finn catching fish when no one else was and blaming it on his ability to talk to dolphins. Maybe it was true. If so, maybe the Finn could get them to send phony sonar signals. And if he could do that, what else could he do with them? Locate sunken treasure? If nothing else, he could always call dolphins for easy killing and the Oriental market was crying for dolphin meat. It might be hard to convince him to call his friends to slaughter but then again, a few human hostages might change his mind. And it might be a way to keep from killing any more people. That is, if the Finn could really talk to the dolphins. There would be time to check that out later. Right now they needed to know where the swimmers' raft was.

"How could they be on our sonar frequency?" Poddington asked, half absorbed in the conversation and half in his own thoughts.

"How do I know? I'm just telling you what I think."

"Couldn't they be tuna schools?" Another idea was forming in Poddington's mind. Time was running out; they had to get them soon. He had to end this game of cat-and-mouse.

"Maybe," said Deep. He pointed to one of the brighter echoes. "I think this is the tuna school. See how it wavers slightly, then changes direction all of a sudden, like a school of fish turning together. Now watch the last blip. It stays steady. The course stays steady, only turning gradually. That has to be their ship."

"Then get them," snapped the second mate. He turned and stalked away from the sonar screen.

"He's right," said Poddington. "We've got to get them, and I think I know how, now that you've figured out which one of the blips they are."

Poddington tapped the sonar operator on the shoulder. "Don't take your eye off this blip." He pointed to the steady echo. "No matter what happens, I want to know where they go."

"Aye, sir."

Poddington led Deep to the windows overlooking the main deck. "Remember when we were fishermen?"

Deep nodded.

"We're going fishing again. I know we haven't used the nets or winches on this ship yet, and most of the crew aren't trained for it, but we're going to haul us up a heavy catch."

For the first time in a long time, a smile brightened Deep's leathery face. "I'll take personal control of the nets. We'll get this done and get the hell out of here."

Deep took a step toward the door to the bridge. Then he turned and grabbed Poddington's left arm, pulling the captain near enough to whisper in his ear. "Just promise me that we'll make port as soon as we can steam there. I'm still jumping ship."

Poddington nodded and Deep was on his way. Jumping ship sounded like a better idea all the time – but it would have to be done so he couldn't be traced by Luis Jones, or someone like him. Time to think about that later, right now his thoughts returned to the problem at hand. Soon it would be finished.

#

They slept on and off. Toivo, half awake, would kiss her cheek, squeeze her gently, then fall back to sleep. He didn't know how much time had passed and he didn't really care. The Homestead hummed gently in the background, a constant, rhythmic vibration of machinery. The warmth they shared temporarily masked their plight, but eventually they woke. Toivo got up, turned the lights on and motioned for her to get up.

"Why get up?" she asked, and waved for him to get back into bed.

"I'm hungry." He pulled on his bikini bottoms and came back to the bed. "I could bring you something to eat."

She rolled over and dropped on to the floor. "No. I'll go to the mess hall with you. It will be my watch again soon anyway."

She hugged him fiercely once before they went to the kitchen. There was something in her hug that made Toivo determined to survive. Maybe he wasn't too old to have a family or a future with a woman.

In the galley, he pulled out eggs and scrambled up a plateful for each of them. While they were eating, Ici wandered in.

"I don't like it," he said as soon as he saw the two of them. "They are up to something. The dolphins have been making all kinds of noise. I wish we were closer to the surface, close enough to see what is happening. The U. N. ship may have been convinced that everything is okay and they aren't needed at all."

Toivo studied Ici as he eased into the mess hall's bright fluorescent lights. The shepherd had dark circles under his eyes and there was tension in his shoulders. His hands clenched and unclenched as he stood next to the table. He licked his lips twice in quick succession.

"What noises have the dolphins been making?" asked Toivo. "I haven't heard anything."

"You can't hear it through the hull. We're picking it up on the hydrophones that were part of the experimental underwater communications equipment that was supposed to allow us to talk to the dolphins during storms. So far we haven't been able to talk to them but we can hear them at quite a distance. The speaker is in the control room."

"Are they talking now?"

"They were a minute ago."

Toivo pushed his plate back and got up. "I'll be right back," he said to Olga and dashed across the hall to the control room. As soon as he opened the door he heard Poika calling.

"*Toivo, Toivo. They are lowering deep-water fish-catchers. They will foul your ship. If you are not ready to go ahead you will have to do something to prevent this. We cannot stop them. So far they do not seem to know where you are.*" The message started over again.

"They are lowering deep nets," said Toivo. "They are going to try to snag Homestead and haul us to the surface. I wasn't sure if that Sunrise Savior would have nets aboard or not."

"Can they haul us up if they snare us?" asked Ni, turning from the console to stare at Toivo.

"Probably." He took a deep breath. Why did he feel so helpless? He hated it. The Homestead was still on the defensive. And it looked as if submerging, by itself, wasn't going to work. His stomach churned like hard surf. There must be something he could do.

"They must not know where we are or they would have snared us by now. The dolphins have been yelling out there for a couple of hours." Ici sat down at the one empty chair in the control room. "I wonder what kind of sonar that ship has. It must have limited lateral resolution."

Toivo's mind whirled. He needed to talk to Poika. If the underwater phones picked up the dolphin, could they send as well? "Can I talk to the dolphins somehow?"

Ni handed Toivo a microphone. "You can try to talk to them. I'm not sure how clear the underwater reproduction is."

"What choice do we have?"

Toivo took the microphone from Ni and thumbed the talk button. *"Poika. It is Toivo. Where is the ship with fish-catcher now?"*

A moment went by. The dolphins continued to whistle over the speaker. Then the sounds changed. *"Toivo. It is good that you hear us. We have tricked the evil men with false sonar-sight but they no longer are fooled. Fish-catcher is not far. From Toivo fish-catcher is toward where the sun falls into the water. They are sweeping toward you on a steady back-and-forth course that will soon intercept you. Turn and run with the flow of the force that surrounds the world."*

Toivo translated Poika's message. "The trawler is west of us. Poika says to turn north."

Ni spun the controls and Toivo could feel the ship gently swing away to the north. "How long can we keep running underwater?"

"About a day at any kind of speed," said Ici. "The batteries were made to keep us at station during a storm, not play hide and seek with a trawler."

"We're not going to last that long," said Ni. "We've only got fifty percent capacity left." She tapped a digital display as she spoke.

"We can't just sit here and wait until they catch us," said Toivo. "Either way, we can't hold out until the Stockholm gets here. We surface and get caught, or hide down here until we get caught."

Ni nudged Ici. "What about the fireworks you have left?"

Ici ran one hand through his short black hair. "They're not accurate enough to do much damage, and they really aren't all that powerful."

"Could we tie some of them together?" asked Toivo.

A look of hope came into Ici's eyes. "We could make a bomb with the powder. We'll have to unload the firecrackers and pack the powder into a pipe. To ignite it we'll use some of the fuses from the M-80's. We can connect a couple of the them together somehow."

Ni turned around in her swivel chair. "Would it be powerful enough to blow a hole in their ship?"

"I don't know. But it should be strong enough to blow the propeller shaft apart."

Toivo felt a hand softly against the small of his back. Glancing over his shoulder, he saw the twinkle in Olga's eye.

"What is going on?" she asked, patting Toivo on the back.

"The Sunrise Savior is trying to catch us with deep nets," said Ni. "We can't stay under without running away from their sonar and that will drain the batteries too fast."

"The only problem," said Ici, "is how do we get the bomb under their ship? Even we can't swim fast enough to put it there."

Olga stepped into the control room. "And what's going to hold it next to the prop shaft?"

"Tape it to the shaft," said Ici. "We've got lots of tape. A couple of loops around the shaft will hold it long enough."

"Tape won't work," said Toivo. "The dolphins can get the bomb to their ship, but the prop wash would suck them into the propeller. There has to be another way."

"We can tie the bomb to a rope and let the rope catch in the prop. It'll wind the bomb right up."

"Better yet," said Ni, "use lengths of light chain."

"That would do it," said Toivo. "Do you have a way to get out of Homestead underwater? And we'll need two bombs. On a ship the size of the Savior, they'll have twin screws, for sure."

"Okay," said Ici, "two pipe bombs it is."

"We can get the bombs to the dolphins without a problem," said Olga. "There's a pressure lock in the port side of the shower room."

Toivo stepped backward into the hall. "Time's wasting. Where are your fireworks? The sooner we make a bomb, the sooner we can go on the offensive."

Ici got up. "Keep us on course," he said to Ni. "If the dolphins start making noise, come and get Toivo right away."

They went down to the double room Ici and Ni shared. From his closet he pulled a huge cardboard box. As they started for the galley, the lid flipped open enough for Toivo to get a look inside. The box was packed with firecrackers, rockets, and silver-tubed explosives.

"What were you going to do with all this?" he asked Ici as they reached the mess hall.

"Fight a war," said Ici and winked.

He put the box down on the table. "Get a couple of knives and cut the ends off the firecrackers. Then you can dump the powder into a bowl. Don't worry about the firecracker fuses because they won't burn underwater anyway. The M-80's and M-1000's, save the fuses. And be careful, one spark and it won't matter. I'm going to get a couple of pieces of pipe from the ship's stores."

Olga and Toivo set about cutting open the fireworks, pouring the powder into a bowl. At first they didn't seem to be getting anywhere, but slowly the bowl filled with the gray explosive. Toivo's hands worked swiftly. It was so like cleaning fish that soon he had an efficient routine. He noticed that Olga was right there with him, cutting, shaking, tossing aside the empty husks. Before Ici came back, they had almost a half a bowl full of powder.

"Shit," said Ici, finally returning. "I got the pipe, though I had to cut off a couple of sections. I threaded the ends, got pipe caps, and drilled a fuse hole in each of them. How the hell are we going to seal the fuse holes?"

"Wax," said Olga. "I've got candles in my room. That is if you don't mind vanilla smelling seals."

They laughed, not a deep laugh, but it broke the tension. Toivo felt the weight leave his shoulders. They were doing something; they had a way to fight back. For now they worked with a frenzy, cutting open the containers, pouring the powder into the bowl. Ici carefully took the powder and packed it into the first pipe bomb.

Olga got her candles and put them on the table ready to seal the fuses in place. Before long, Ni ducked in and reminded Olga that her watch had started. Olga left and Ni took her place at the table.

It was going to be a long night, but Toivo didn't mind. The work pushed his muscles to a weariness that felt good after the long layoff. Later he knew he was going to sleep well—if he was still alive.

Chapter 19

Three bombs lay on the table, dark and ugly. Toivo looked at them, three pieces of black pipe, capped at both ends, about a meter long, packed solid with gunpowder. Each had a hole drilled in the middle where a silvery fuse was waxed in place.

Toivo was glad they were done building the bombs. His back ached, his shoulders were sore, and his fingers were cramped in knots from the hours of tedious work. He rubbed his hands together, forcing blood back into the joints. Fatigue had dulled his mind to the point he could hardly think, but the work was worth it. Now they had a means to get back at the men who had killed his crew. If they could blow the props off the Sunrise Savior, then the killer vessel would be stuck here until the frigate arrived. Right now, he could use some sleep.

"How soon can we put these bombs to use?" asked Olga, her short blond hair a disarray of spikes.

"Right away," snapped Ici, scowling, his arms folded across his chest. "The longer we wait, the more chance for something to go wrong."

Toivo stood up. He towered over the two, seated swimmers. "No. We're all too tired. We need to get some rest before we start this project. We'll need to think clearly and right now I can barely think at all. For the time being, as long as we stay clear of their nets, we should be safe."

Olga raised one eyebrow to look up at him. He thought he saw a hint of longing but he shrugged it off as his own imagination, "I agree with Toivo." Her head slumped to the table, resting comfortably on her arm. "Someone help me to bed."

Ici jumped up, his face reddening. "We've got to get this over with right now."

"We're hardly in a position to get anything over with. These bombs will stop the Sunrise Savior dead in the water, but it isn't going to disarm the men on board or their cannons."

Olga stood up, one hand on Toivo. "What are you going to fight guns with?"

Ni leaned into the room. "The trawler is turning the other way. I don't think they have any idea where we are. What now?" She looked at Toivo.

"Get some rest," said Toivo. He felt drunk with fatigue. He put his arm around Olga. He wanted to hold her, to be near her. In some ways it seemed a dream and even in the middle of this nightmare, she was a part of it that he didn't want to end. To Olga he whispered, "Will you spend the night with me?"

"Beautiful thought, fisherman, but I'm going to sleep. I want to be fresh when we blast these assholes."

Toivo stepped back away from her in mock surprise. "I meant to go to sleep. I had no other intention."

She smiled. "I knew that.

They went to his quarters leaving Ici grumbling. Before they closed the door, he heard Ici lamenting the stupidity of waiting. Ni begged him to shut up and go to sleep or stay up and stand watch, but either way just be quiet. Toivo closed the door and within minutes, he and Olga were asleep in each other's arms.

#

There was a solid rap on the metal door. "Toivo, wake up." It was Ni's voice. "Toivo, quick. The dolphins are calling again."

Toivo sprang out of bed, almost dumping Olga on the floor. "I'm coming," he mumbled, fuzzy-headed. He staggered to get the door open. "When did this start?" The light caught him full in the face and he threw his hands up to avoid the glare.

"A few minutes ago."

"Where is the Sunrise Savior?"

"I don't know. She shut off her engines a while ago. The last I heard she was a mile south of us. Soon after the tanker went dead I heard a small motor start up. I think they put over a launch."

"Where is the launch now?"

Olga climbed out of bed, pulled her swimsuit bottoms on and stood behind Toivo at the door.

"Zigzagging back and forth. Sort of headed our way without being headed in any specific direction. It's been doing that for a couple of hours."

"Come on, let's see what Poika wants."

Olga followed Toivo who followed Ni as she hurried around the corner to the control room. The eerie calls of the dolphins filled the hydrophones. Several different voices were evident and Toivo took a moment to sort out Poika's familiar calls.

"*Toivo, they are coming for you. You must move out of the way.*"

He turned to the woman. "He says they are coming for us."

Ni put on the headphones. She shook her head. "I only hear the launch. It's almost overhead. The Sunrise Savior is still silent. Wait! There's another set of screws, below us, behind us."

The black conning tower resurfaced in Toivo's memory. "Their submarine," he shot and picked up the microphone. "*Poika, what do you mean? Who is coming for us?*"

The dolphin noises ceased. Then, loud and clear. "*Little boat pulls big boat. Big boat drags fish-catcher. They will catch you soon.*"

"Voi, voi, voi. They are on to us. The launch is towing the Sunrise Savior and her nets, while the submarine stands by for the kill if we escape the nets. How close is the launch?"

"Just went overhead."

"Hard to starboard," snapped Toivo. He felt inadequate in the control room of a ship he could not run. He didn't understand any of the computerized controls. "Turn her, turn her."

Ni touched the console. Her nimble fingers danced over the controls and Homestead healed over. There was a sharp scraping. Homestead lurched, fought to right herself, then was thrown sideways by the force of the nets. Toivo slammed into Olga and they both toppled into the bulkhead. He managed to brace himself with one forearm while Olga grabbed onto the doorsill. Ni flew off the control stool and tumbled to the deck.

"Damn it, they've caught us," snarled Olga, pulling herself upright.

Ni bounded back to her chair. "The tanker's engines have started."

There was a surge as the false research ship's powerful diesels hauled on the net, towing the Homestead through the water. The shepherd's raft spun sideways, slammed against the nets again and was held crossways in the huge web. Fortunately Homestead remained upright.

"How fast are we going?" asked Toivo, looking for a knot meter he could understand.

"I can't be sure," replied Ni. "We are being towed beam on to the direction they're going and none of the instruments register lateral travel. I'd say we are making about ten or twelve knots."

"We've got to get free." Olga started across the hall. "I'm going outside and cut the net."

Ni jumped up from the console. "It'll take all three of us to cut a hole big enough. Toivo, you take the controls."

"How can I?" The console looked like an alien spacecraft. The instrumentation was so foreign. What was he going to do?

"There's nothing to do right now." She reached over and hit a red button marked "EMERGENCY STOP." "I've shut down the motors to save the batteries. As soon as you feel us come free, turn on the motors. Here." She pointed to a green button marked "ON." "The directional control is the joy stick," and she pointed to a miniature stick that reminded Toivo of an arcade game. "The diving controls are here." She pointed to a large black knob. "Keep her level and don't drop any deeper. If possible, come up to about fifty meters. The depth indicator is the digital readout here." She tapped the glass front that read 103.

With that, the shepherds were gone. Ni ran to her room to get Ici, while Olga rummaged around for the diver's knives. Within minutes Toivo heard the forward escape chamber clang shut and an eerie silence descended over Homestead's interior.

He sat down in the swivel chair in front of the console. In his mind he ran over what he was supposed to do. First, wait until the ship was out of the netting. He looked at the depth indicator. It read 81 meters. The men above were reeling them in. Then it hit him, how could the swimmers go out into the ocean at that depth? Ordinary human beings would have been crushed. Obviously they were not ordinary. Thank God for that.

He waited, time crawling by. What if the three shepherds had been swept off by the slipstream? They couldn't swim fast enough to catch up. Maybe they couldn't cut the net. He waited, itching to do something, his armpits growing droplets of sweat.

The silence brought no answers. What was going on? Nervously, he tapped his fingers on the console, careful not to hit any of the controls. He brushed the microphone, seeing it for the first time. What was wrong with him? The dolphins could tell him exactly what was happening.

"Poika, what is going on?"

Almost immediately the shrill whistle answered. *"Men-who-are-fish are caught in fish-catcher. They have cutting blades. They are cutting holes into fish-catcher. You will be free-swimming soon."*

"What are men-killers doing?"

"Little boat chases dolphins with noise-sticks. Little boat is too fast for dolphins to outrun so we dive and turn away where boat is not. Big boat pulls fish-catcher, but does not bother dolphins.

"Poika stay away from big boat too. How soon before men-who-are-fish cut my boat free from fish-catcher?"

"Almost done. Then you help stop little boat?"

"Yes, we will stop little boat."

Homestead shuddered. For a long moment she balanced halfway between beam on and bow on. With a lurch she swung around to face nose up into the slipstream of the Sunrise Savior. The nets scraped the hull. Ghostly noises screeched through the ship. Then silence as Homestead dropped free from the net.

Toivo looked at the console. The green button, yes. He pushed it. A soft hum overcame the quiet and Homestead started forward.

Watch the depth, he reminded himself aloud. Slowly the numbers grew as she dropped deeper. His fingers gripped the diving control knob. Ni hadn't said which way to turn the knob to go up. He turned the knob clockwise about an eighth of a turn. The digits grew faster. Oops. He turned the knob the other way and the depth meter reversed itself. The indicator climbed until it read fifty meters. There he tweaked the knob until the digits held steady.

What about some kind of speed control? Ni had forgotten to tell him how to slow down the Homestead. What if the shepherds couldn't catch up?

A loud whoosh echoed through the hydrophones, followed by the faint whir of high-speed propellers. What was that? Something fast, running underwater. Oh God! The submarine had fired a torpedo.

"*Poika. Tyttö. They send metal fish to kill Toivo. You must turn it aside.*"

Tyttö answered. "*We will push it away.*"

Toivo strained his ears to detect a change in the direction of the torpedo. He couldn't tell. It sounded like it was still running toward Homestead. The swish of the prop swelled in the hydrophones. The torpedo reached a crescendo, then whirred passed, the sound so near Toivo could hear it through Homestead's hull.

Where were the others? Had they been left behind in the net? A clang from the forward area told him somebody was coming back aboard. He couldn't leave the controls so he waited. Finally he heard the hiss of the hatch opening. They were back safe inside.

Olga got to the control room first.

"Christ, why the hell didn't you slow this thing down?"

Toivo felt like shouting at her that it wasn't his fault. Instead he stood up, and said, "I didn't know how."

"Right here," she said and tapped a slide lever labeled "POWER."

Ici and Ni appeared around the corner.

Ici said, "Let's blow them out of the water before they think of anything else."

"I agree," said Toivo, "but we've got to deal with their submarine and the launch as well."

A distant rumble shook the Homestead. Poika's voice filled the phones. "*We pushed metal fish into a circular path. It returned to its home.*"

"The dolphins turned the torpedo around on them," translated Toivo.

"Damn," whistled Olga. "Your D's have really got their shit in order."

Toivo couldn't help laughing. Maybe it was just a tension release; maybe he was tired. "Now we've only got the Sunrise Savior and its launch to worry about."

"To get the launch we'll have to stop it so somebody can put a bomb under their hull," said Olga. "The ghost net would have been perfect to foul their prop."

"Yeah," said Ni. "But we sank it."

"How about that hunk of net we just cut out to free Homestead," suggested Olga. "I bet it would foul a prop and it's probably drifting around somewhere close. If we had a couple of the dolphins lead the launch toward the net, the rest of us could pull it up tight, close enough to the surface to catch their prop. It would stop them dead in the water."

"And I'll tape a bomb to their hull myself," said Ici. "Bring the bombs. Toivo, get on the horn and let Poika know what to do with the chain on the first bomb. Then tell him we want the D's to lead the launch over to the net so we can catch it."

Olga turned, took Toivo's hand and squeezed. "I'll see you soon."

The three of them were gone, back to the pressure lock. Toivo hardly had time to sit back down at the console before he heard the clang of the outer hatch.

"Poika, this is Toivo. We need your help. The men-who-are-fish are bringing two long pieces of metal and chain. You and Tyttö must each pull a chain up behind the big ship until it is beneath one of the propellers. Then go toward the surface until the chain catches in the propeller. Make sure you let go in time to keep from being pulled into the propeller yourself. Swim away as fast as you can. But you must hurry or else it will blow up and hurt you."

"I understand. The men-who-are-fish are here now. We will do as you ask, but Toivo, what about the little ship?"

"You must lead it toward the piece of net where the men-who-are-fish will be waiting. When the boat is close to the net, the men-who-are-fish will help you pull the net up toward the surface until the net fouls the little boat's propeller. Then get away as the men-who-are-fish will try to blow a hole in the hull of the little boat."

"What about you?"

"I must sit inside this ship until it is safe to bring it to the surface. I will be all right if you are all right."

Toivo prayed that Poika and Tyttö and the others would be all right. His feelings of inadequacy ran rampant. Everyone he cared about in the world was out there somewhere, in danger, and he sat idle, empty, powerless.

#

Poika swam away, his flukes driving him ahead with powerful strokes. Even by eyesight he could see the man-who-is-fish held two long lengths of shiny, silvery chain. Attached to each was an ugly black stick of metal. He saw a bright dot of fire that slowly consumed the cord sticking from the metal tube. Hurry, Toivo had said. Poika took the end of one chain, and Tyttö took the other. They rocketed away from the man-who-is-fish.

Humans, they are still so slow, he thought. Maybe someday they will be enough like us to survive in the ocean. Then again maybe not. They seem to take so long to discover the obvious.

The huge dark shape of the trawler was plainly visible using his sonar sight. He and Tyttö swam straight after it. Poika noticed the burning cords getting shorter. That must make the metal tubes explode. It would hurt them if they weren't fast enough. It would be close, but they would not let go of the chains. If it was time to go ahead, then he would be thankful for the life he'd had.

They were under the hull of the large ship, pulling the chains behind them. Now, up under the hull, the chains clanging noisily against the steel. Crunch, the chains caught in the huge props. It jerked from Poika's mouth and shot backward. The propeller consumed the length of chain in an instant. With a shudder and an ear splitting shriek, the propeller came to an abrupt stop.

Poika swam as fast as he could. Tyttö was right behind him. The bombs exploded almost in unison. A tremendous concussion wave caught him from behind and tumbled him around in a violent surge of angry water. The pressure waves racked him, tumbling him over and over, fouling his echo sight so badly that he lost Tyttö.

#

Toivo heard the explosion. It rattled the sonar speaker so hard the unit gave up with a squawk. The bombs had gone off. Had they gone off under the Sunrise Savior, or had they gone off too soon? He listened for Poika or Tyttö to call. Silence.

He waited a long minute. Another minute. Nothing. No dolphin talk. No one entered the pressure chamber. What should he do?

SHEPHERDS

He couldn't stand it any longer. The only choice was to surface. Toivo had to know what was going on. He spun the knob and watched the depth meter run down to zero. Almost before he felt the ship break the surface, he was at the roof hatch. He spun the wheel to undog it and clambered up the ladder out on top of the cabin. He wasn't at all sure that he'd done the right thing, but it was too late to worry about that.

Chapter 20

On the roof Toivo could see the surrounding sea plainly. Off to port, the Sunrise Savior wallowed, her stern had settled, she was dead in the water. Farther ahead, the launch plowed through the swells in hot pursuit of two tired dolphins who were quickly losing ground to the powerful boat. They were too far away to tell if Olga, Ici and Ni had gotten the net in place. The crack of rifle fire brought a sickening pain to Toivo's stomach. Where were the shepherds? Where were Poika and Tyttö? He turned to scan a full circle around Homestead. About fifty meters away he spotted the shepherds swimming underwater toward Homestead.

Aboard the Sunrise Savior men scurried around on the aft deck. Two were climbing into scuba suits and two more were hauling other scuba gear out on deck. No doubt they would be going down to inspect the damaged stern. Toivo hoped the props were blown completely off.

He looked back at the launch. It was turning away from the dolphins. The men must have seen the net they had set to trap it. He watched in horror as the launch circled wide and swung around to head for Homestead. How stupid, he should have known they would go after him as soon as the raft surfaced. At least it would give the dolphins a chance to rest.

He glanced back over his shoulder. The three shepherds were almost to Homestead. The launch was still several hundred meters away heading straight for them. He could make out the figures on deck with their deadly automatic rifles. He needed to submerge again but he didn't know how. He would have to wait for Olga, Ici and Ni to get aboard, and then they would have to submerge immediately. In the meantime, he was radioing the frigate.

Toivo waved for the others to hurry and jumped onto the ladder. He dogged the hatch closed, then dropped to the deck inside. Down the corridor, around the corner to the control room. He squeezed into the seat at the console and looked for the radio controls. There, the frequency control. He cranked it to the distress channel and picked up the microphone.

"Homestead, calling the frigate Stockholm. Homestead calling Stockholm."

He waited for a response. Instead of the expected message from the Stockholm there was a blast of static, then another voice. "Stockholm, this is Homestead. Everything has been resolved. The Martin B. is standing by. We are secure. You can break off the rendezvous."

"Voi, voi, voi," spat Toivo. The men on the Sunrise Savior were trying to convince the Stockholm that everything was satisfactorily resolved. He stabbed the talk button. "Stockholm, Stockholm, *this* is Homestead. We are under attack. Raiders are from Sunrise Savior. Repeat, raiders are from Sunrise Savior. We have not seen the Martin B."

When he released the button only a buzz of static came out. They were interfering with Toivo's transmission. Then the overpowering broadcast of the tanker drowned out everything. "Stockholm, this is Homestead. Repeat, we are under protection of the Martin B. and no longer need your assistance."

Toivo tried again to break in but the static cut him off. The receiver picked up another powerful signal, "Martin B., this is Stockholm. Are you covering Homestead? Over."

The same impostor's voice answered. "Stockholm, this is the Martin B. We are on site. No sign of raiders. All clear. No assistance necessary."

"Roger, Martin B. This is Stockholm, out."

Toivo bit his lip. He couldn't believe it. The idiots were going away. He and the shepherds were left alone to fight the raiders. To fight them with what? He heard the back hatch close and the soft footsteps told him the others were aboard.

Olga was the first one around the corner. "What are you doing in here?"

"The tanker sent a message to the frigate that we don't need any help. They said they were the Martin B. and that everything is fine. I don't think help is going to come."

"Shit," said Ici, slipping into the control room. "The launch is bearing down on us and they aren't coming to invite us to dinner." He leaned over and tapped a digital meter on the console. "Not enough juice left in the batteries for a safe dive."

Ni peeked over his shoulder. "We could go under, but we'd have to stay stationary, and we'd need the compressed air to bring us back to the surface."

An automatic rifle cracked in the distance.

"Take us down," snapped Toivo, jumping up from the chair. "We need time to figure out a new plan."

Ni plopped into the seat. "Close the door," she said, flipping a switch and turning a knob. Almost simultaneously, Homestead started to sink heavily into the waves. Toivo rushed around the corner and with Ici's help, got the back door closed and dogged down. The first wave crashed into the back of the cabin and Homestead settled beneath the waves. A crescendo of pings rattled off the steel hull. The sonar picked up the whine as bullets hit the water around her diving hull.

"Now what?" asked Ici, as he and Toivo returned to the control room. "We've got to stop that launch."

"It's a cinch we can't use that hunk of net again. It's too far away," said Ni, only half turning from the console to look at the others.

"Unless we towed it back here," said Olga.

"Yes," agreed Toivo. "With the dolphins' help you could tow it back fast enough to snag that boat—if the dolphins are all right. We can use Homestead as bait. Once the net is in place, we surface. That'll bring them running."

"Let's quit talking about it and get going." Ici was already on his way to the compression lock. "Come on," he shouted over his shoulder.

"How do I surface this thing without the batteries once the net is in place?" asked Toivo.

Ni leaned over his shoulder. "Spin this valve completely open. There is only enough compressed air to bring her up once so don't touch the valve until you are sure you want to surface."

Toivo nodded. "Don't worry, I'm not bringing Homestead back to the surface until I'm sure we're ready."

Olga looked at Toivo on her way past. "Talk to the dolphins," she said. "They need to know what we want."

Toivo nodded and sat back in the chair. He flipped on the underwater microphone. "*Poika. Tyttö. This is Toivo. I need your help.*"

A long silence followed. He hadn't heard from them since the bombs had exploded. Toivo tried again. "*Poika. Tyttö. Help.*"

Again silence. The launch had stopped chasing the dolphins when Homestead surfaced. Had they gotten Poika or Tyttö? Or had the bombs gotten them?

Finally Poika's voice came over the hydrophones. *"Toivo, I hear you. Have you seen Tyttö? She is lost."*

A lump tightened in Toivo's throat. He could hardly bare the thought of losing Tyttö. *"Lost?"*

"Yes. Ever since the explosion I have not been able to locate her. Have you seen her?"

"No. But I had not heard from you until now."

"If she has gone ahead I only hope there is time to sing with her spirit. But you wanted something."

"Poika, I wish there were time to look for Tyttö. Unfortunately, I need your help right now."

"What should I do? You have not stopped the little boat."

"I know. We will do it now. Please get the pod to tow the three men-who-are-fish to the fish-catcher. Wait while they cut off a section of the fish-catcher. Then tow them back to a place between the little boat and Homestead."

"I understand. You will catch little boat in the fish-catcher this time. Your friends are in the water now. Pungee will help me."

Toivo started to put the microphone down, then he added, *"Let me know when you have the fish-catcher ready."*

#

Poika didn't mind Toivo's mate hanging onto him. It was nice to have contact with someone so close to Toivo. The power of touch, he thought. He swam with steady strokes, not over exerting himself, but covering the distance to the aimlessly drifting section of the fish-catcher in a short time. As he swam he looked for Tyttö with his long-range sonar, but he could not find her. Already he missed her. The comfort of her sleek shape always filling a spot in the echolocation matrix was gone. Maybe forever—or at least until it was his turn to go ahead.

The woman-who-is-fish dropped off at the fish-catcher and began cutting into the strands. Poika swam to the surface and took a couple of breaths. He scouted the situation without raising his head too far out of the water. There was no sign of Tyttö.

"*Tyttö*," he called, but there was no answer.

He turned his attention to the men aboard the two ships. What were the men-killers doing? Not much. The little boat had pulled up alongside the big ship and there were men hurrying to do something around the stern. No doubt caused by the little black pipe they had put into the propeller. The whole issue seemed inconsequential. Why did men waste so much time fighting amongst themselves? Maybe that was one of the questions he was meant to ponder during his life. True, there were occasional references in past songs about the conflicts of man. However, no one had ever tried to explain why men did such things. He would have to think about that.

Toivo's mate stuck her head up next to Poika. The three men-who-are-fish had surfaced for a breath. They gulped in fresh air and dived immediately. Poika stuck his head back in the water and watched them dive to the fish-catcher with his sonar. For men, they were extraordinary, though they still had a long way to go.

Pungee interrupted his thoughts. "*The men-who-are-fish are almost ready. Where should we take them?*"

Poika sucked in a deep breath and sounded. "*We are to set the fish-catcher between the big ship and Toivo. When it is ready we must go hide behind the men-who-are-fish's raft and Toivo will surface. The men-killers will try to catch Toivo. Perhaps the fish-catcher will catch them before that happens.*"

Pungee had already picked up one of the men-who-are-fish. The other was hanging on to Slim. Now Toivo's mate grabbed Poika again. All three dolphins started forward, building speed steadily. The large section of net trailed away behind them. This was interesting, thought Poika, in a strange sort of way. I am pulling a catcher-that-kills-dolphins with the purpose of catching men.

#

It was a long wait. Toivo sat in the control room, poised, ready to bring Homestead back to the surface as soon as Poika gave the word. He worried that something had happened, that the others weren't coming back. Finally Poika gave the signal that they were ready. He spun the knob that controlled the air regulator and heard the whoosh of compressed air forcing the water out. Homestead bobbed to the surface like a cork. There was no turning back, no second chance. He was on the surface to stay this time.

Even as Homestead broke the surface, Toivo dashed up the ladder and yanked open the hatch in the cabin roof. He ran to the rail. To port, about half a kilometer away was the Sunrise Savior. She sat motionless, the bulk of her crew milling around her stern. The launch had put to on the lee side of the larger ship and was attempting to assist in making repairs.

Just as Toivo saw the men on the other two ships, they saw Homestead. Several stick figures scrambled to the cockpit of the launch and Toivo heard the motors roar. He looked for his companions.

There, between Homestead and the Sunrise Savior, he could see the faint outline of the net below the water. None of the shepherds were visible, but they had to be there somewhere. The dolphins circled and leaped, blowing and breathing on the starboard side of Homestead out of sight of the raiders.

Toivo looked back at the launch. If only he had a gun. He wished he could bring at least one of them down. Shoot them just like they had murdered his crew. But he had no gun; instead he had to appear defenseless. Basically, he *was* defenseless.

The launch was closer now, bearing down on Homestead. He still couldn't see the three shepherds, but he hoped the net would do its job. The launch came closer, closer. A shot rang out. Toivo flinched involuntarily. Better get below, he thought and dashed for the hatch.

Another shot. This time the bullet sang as it ricocheted off the steel cabin plates. Toivo dropped down a couple of rungs on the ladder so just his head was sticking up. The launch swerved, circling.

"What are they doing?" he asked, but in his heart he knew they had outwitted Toivo. They were going around the net.

Toivo ducked down into the cabin. He needed a weapon. They weren't going to get him easily. A piece of pipe, that's what he needed. He ran to the storage room at the front of the cabin. As he entered, he glanced out the forward porthole. The launch was still a hundred meters away, but closing fast. Where was a piece of pipe? There were hand tools, pieces of lumber, and under a coil of rope, a two-foot length of iron pipe. Toivo hefted it, feeling the weight. Good enough. The launch was almost alongside. His hands shook and the sweat beaded on his forehead. He never liked fighting, and even pumped by burning hatred, he was scared.

Back out in the hallway, he looked down the longer corridor toward the stern door. It was still closed and dogged shut. They would have to come down the ladder through the hatch in the roof. Toivo stood at the bottom of the ladder. He couldn't stay out in the open; they would shoot him. He ducked back through the door into the latrines, leaving the door open just a crack. Through the porthole he could see the launch pull up alongside Homestead. It thumped lightly against the port hull and rounded the cabin. The boat continued down the port side until he could no longer see it.

He heard the motors throttle back to an idle, and almost immediately the tramp of booted footsteps on the roof of the cabin. The launch engines roared to life and he heard it pull steadily away. Now the steps moved cautiously over to the hatch. Sweat trickled down Toivo's forehead. He gripped the pipe until his knuckles went white. The footsteps rang hollowly on the rungs of the ladder. There was a pause. Toivo peered out through the crack between the door and bulkhead frame. A single stocky man, dark in the shadows of the hallway, scanned the area. He carried an ugly automatic rifle. Toivo pulled back behind the door, afraid to be seen. The footsteps tiptoed toward his hiding place.

He drew back the pipe, waiting for the door to open. He didn't dare look out through the crack between door and sill again. The door started to move, opening ever so slowly. The gun barrel poked its way into the room, attached to a gloved hand. Toivo drew back. At that moment the intruder lunged into the room, spinning so he faced Toivo.

Toivo hit him in the face as hard as he could. There was a muffled groan and the man fell backwards, the gun slipping from his hands. Toivo grabbed it out of the air. The intruder hit the deck with a heavy thud.

"Hold it right there," said a voice behind Toivo.

Toivo turned his head slowly to look back over his shoulder. Two burly men in rumpled fatigues stood in the hall flanked by a black woman in green coveralls. All three had their weapons aimed at his back. Toivo fingered the gun he held but knew it was useless. He raised his hands until they were even with his shoulders. One of the men grabbed the rifle from him.

"Step away from Schmitty," said the woman, motioning for Toivo to move away from the door. "Now turn around, fisherman."

Toivo took a step away from the door and turned to face his captors. "Now what?" he asked.

"We'll wait a few minutes until the launch comes back from rounding up your friends."

Toivo flinched. He hoped it wasn't noticeable. He clenched his teeth so hard they hurt. They were going to capture the shepherds. And then what? Why hadn't they just killed them all? What did they want with them?

He heard the launch pull up alongside Homestead. Excited voices were yelling and he heard a woman scream. It sounded like Olga. His blood boiled over and he started to rush them. The man nearest Toivo slammed him in the stomach with the butt of his rifle. Excruciating pain shot up Toivo's chest and he doubled over.

"Don't try anything," snarled the black woman. "I'd just as soon kill you as look at you but Jones wants you alive."

Toivo grimaced. His breath came in short gasps and he tried to straighten. The pain was too strong. He held his stomach with both hands, afraid to show too much resistance. What did they want?

Rough hands grabbed him by the arms and pulled him to the aft doorway. One of the intruders undogged the watertight door and another shoved Toivo out onto the rear deck. The launch stood by, tied off against Homestead. On deck a half dozen armed thugs stood guard around Ici, Ni, and Olga. Toivo's captors pushed him across to join the others on the launch.

"How did they catch you?" whispered Toivo as he was force in next to Ici.

"Nets."

"Shut up," snapped one of the guards.

Standing on the Homestead's flat deck the woman yelled across to the launch, "Luis, do you want this tub sunk?"

A short, black-haired man standing next to the coxswain said, "I don't see why not. Scuttle the raft and get back aboard. Then we'll see if the Captain was right about this fisherman."

Sleena motioned to two of the men still with her aboard Homestead, said something Toivo couldn't make out and then jumped across to the launch.

"They'll take care of the raft," she said, stopping next to the dark haired man she called Luis.

He said, "Good. Now we'll find out if he can order these dolphins around or not."

A wicked smile sent shivers down Toivo's back as the dark-haired man turned to Toivo. "You, fisherman. Call the dolphins to the boat," he commanded.

"And if I won't?"

"Then we kill one of the swimmers."

What a choice. Betray Poika and the pod or watch them kill Olga, or Ici or Ni.

"Okay," said Toivo, "don't kill anyone." He looked out to sea, looking where the dolphins rolled now almost a kilometer from the launch. "*Poika, they want me to call you and the others to the boat. You know they want to send you ahead. If you do not come they will send us ahead. Maybe they will send us ahead even if you do come to the boat.*"

"*Do not worry old friend, I will not stand by and watch you sent ahead before your time. You are just now finding your family place. You should be allowed the joys your new mate can bring. I am coming. I do not worry about going ahead.*"

"*What about the others?*"

"*Do not waste time thinking about that now. Tell men-who-are-killers that you have called one dolphin to see what they wish to do to him*"

Toivo turned. A tear stung his eye. He tried not to betray his feelings but he couldn't fight it away. "I have called a single dolphin to the boat. What do you want him to do?"

The dark-haired man snickered. "Do? I want to kill him."

"Why?" asked Olga, her face drawn tight, her eyes blazing with fury.

"For money. What do you think? Some crazy assholes believe dolphin flesh will prolong their life. They will pay any price for the tiniest morsel." He motioned to his henchmen. "Move them away from the rail and get ready to shoot."

They pushed Toivo and the shepherds back away from the side of the launch. Three stout men stationed themselves at the rail, their guns ready. Over the wave crests Toivo could see Poika leaping and dancing his way toward the boat. The other dolphins had disappeared. It wouldn't be long before Poika was within firing distance. Toivo felt a burning in his stomach, the empty feeling of betrayal. He wished he could think of something to save his friend, but it seemed hopeless.

#

Poddington studied Deep as the First Mate slipped on to the bridge. Finally the two of them were alone.

"Where's Jones?" asked Deep, glancing around the empty bridge.

"Gone dolphin hunting with Sleena, I hope. I think I convinced them to trick that stupid Finn into calling dolphins to the boat so they could shoot them – if he really can talk to the dolphins. You should have seen the bitch's eyes light up thinking about all the money. I thought we needed time to figure out what we're going to do. How's the prop repairs going?"

Deep wiped beads of sweat from his forehead. "Not real well. One of the props was blown clean off and we'll have to replace it with the spare. The other one is twisted pretty badly but I think we can get it off and straightened enough to get underway again."

"Let's hope we get underway before the frigate gets here," Poddington said, nervously scanning the wheelhouse as if he expected someone to be hiding there. In a whisper he added, "Did you get a gun?"

"Yes, stashed it in the aft locker while everyone was worried about catching the raft with the net. I didn't think it was a good idea to have it on me. Too big a bulge."

"Good. When Jones and his friends get back we'll have to be on our toes."

Deep took a deep breath and grunted his agreement.

"I don't think they'll kill us while we're out to sea, but once we dock, my guess is that Jones plans to get rid of us."

"My thoughts, too. He doesn't take criticism well, does he? We should have played along better."

"Yeah, or never taken this damn job in the first place. What the hell were we thinking – a couple of fisherman running guns and drugs."

"Well, we know better now."

"Yes, we do. And I've been thinking about how we get off this tub alive. When we're coming in to port, they'll have to use tugs with the mess our props are in. One will undoubtedly be astern, and that's the one we'll get aboard through the aft cargo door. I doubt Jones knows the door is there, so he won't have anyone watching for us there.

"Once aboard the tug, we convince the Captain to fake problems with his engine and off we go to port before this ship even gets there. I've got some cash from the dolphins we sold that we'll use to bribe the tugboat crew, and if that doesn't work, well, we'll have the guns."

"Don't worry, I'll be there."

Chapter 21

Poika leaped high into the air to get a good look at the men on the launch. Yes, there was Toivo, the three men-who-are-fish, and the men who wished to kill Poika. He knew their noise-and-smoke weapons couldn't reach him yet, and he was in no hurry to get into range. He was stalling for enough time for the other dolphins to do their part. Poika had no intention of going ahead before his time, especially not on the whim of some wretched humans.

He swam lazily toward the boat. His sonar sight told him the other dolphins were deep beneath the surface and gaining on him. Soon they would start their turn upward for the surface. He hoped the men did not get lucky with any stray shots they fired at him.

\#

Toivo stood next to Olga. In the excitement he hadn't realized that he had been pushed up against her. Now he felt her hips pressed against him. He wished they were safely back aboard the Homestead.

The crowd of armed men didn't pay much attention to the four huddled prisoners. Instead, they were watching the slow progress of the lone dolphin. The last two men aboard Homestead rushed out of the cabin and jumped to the launch. Immediately the coxswain gunned the engine and backed away from the shepherds' raft. A rumble sounded from inside the cabin and Homestead staggered. With a shudder, she went under in a towering geyser of foam and spray. Toivo watched her shiny stainless steel shape sink beneath the waves, still visible for a time through the clear water as she dropped into her tomb on the bottom thousands of meters below.

So much for getting back on board Homestead, thought Toivo. She had been home for only a short time but he hated to see her go. Their last option now lay at the bottom of the Pacific. In fact, it didn't leave them much hope at all, unless they could overthrow the launch crew. Given the number of armed men aboard, that didn't seem likely. But they couldn't just stand there and wait to be killed. Maybe he could grab a gun and shoot some of them before they got him. He eyed the nearest thug. No, he was watching Toivo too closely.

Toivo looked away, checking on Poika's progress. The dolphin had halved the distance to the launch. One of the men at the rail fired a short burst. Poika dove and the bullets splashed in a flurry across the water.

"Hold your fire," snapped the leader. "It's too far away."

Toivo held his breath. Poika didn't resurface. Was that a spreading red stain? God, if they had killed Poika—or . . . He held his breath and for a moment closed his eyes. With a new resolve, Toivo opened his eyes and scrutinized the men who held him captive.

Three muscular guards stood in a semicircle around the four captives. Closer to the rail were three more, all with their weapons trained in Poika's direction. Behind the captives were two more guards standing a few meters apart from the rest. About ten meters away the leader, Luis, lounged near the radio. On the foredeck was the black woman. Damn! There were too many of them and they were too spread out.

Maybe he could knock a few of them down and dive over the side, but what about Olga? Or Ici? Or Ni? Everyone would have to dive overboard together or the ones left aboard would be shot immediately. How to tell them?

Poika jumped again, high into the air. "*Toivo,*" called Poika. "*Be ready. When I am almost to the boat you must jump. We are coming to rescue you.*" Then he plunged back into the waves.

Another burst of gunfire rattled Toivo's ears. He watched in horror as puffs of flesh burst from Poika's back and little red stains grew against the slick, gray skin. Toivo clenched his fists, wishing he could smash just one of their captors in the face. Damn them, damn every one of them. He wanted to go after the nearest one. No, wait. What was that flash in the water? Like some colored ripple that was gone almost as soon as he noticed it, Toivo caught a glitter of yellow about fifteen meters from the boat. There was another flash of gold and another and another. It was deep, a checkerboard effect. It was light reflected from the sides of thousands of tuna. Now Toivo could see the school veer sharply upward. There was no mistaking it. The herd was stampeding for the launch.

Toivo turned imperceptibly and caught Olga's eye. A sparkle was there and she winked, then glanced toward the water. Yes, she'd seen it too. He grabbed her hand.

Directly beside the launch the ocean exploded in a maddening rush of tuna hurtling forward at full speed. The water boiled with the thrashing of their fins and tails. Almost as if a choreographed unit, they smashed broadside into the hull of the launch. The boat rolled crazily against their weight. The entire crew staggered under the assault, yells of surprise and pain filled the air. Bodies flew in every direction, some of the crew hit the deck, others bounced against the rail. Several staggered to their feet only to stumble again as the boat rebounded from the initial surge.

Toivo had braced himself for the onslaught and was ready. His sea legs held against the rolls. "Now," he yelled, and ran for the stern, Olga racing along with him.

Ici and Ni pushed along right behind them, yelping with surprise and hope. Their captors reeled under the initial shock. Several cut loose with wild, aimless bursts of rifle fire but the tuna school plowed on, unhindered. Toivo reached the stern and turned to catch a glimpse behind them. Most of their guards staggered to regain their feet, yelling at each other to shoot the captives. The black woman hit the railing hard and toppled overboard where the churning tuna bodies sucked her under. The flailing fins and tails pounded her like a rock crusher, turning the water a sickly red.

Ici and Ni dove over the side a few meters to Toivo's left. He caught one last glimpse of them swimming straight down to get below the massed tuna and then they disappeared beneath the swirling blue-green water.

"Come on," shouted Olga as she dove to join Ici and Ni.

The black-haired man who had been by the radio grabbed the rail with one hand and took aim at Toivo with the gun in his free hand. Before the gunman could pull the trigger, a long gray shape vaulted over the rail behind him and slammed into his back. Powerful flukes swatted him, battering him to the deck, sending a smattering of blood flowing from cuts and abrasions. His gun skidded across the deck and splashed into the water. As if it could fly the gray shape sailed on over the deck and splashed into the ocean disappearing beside the launch.

Toivo turned to dive into the water. Just then a second dolphin sailed over the deck in a powerful leap, slamming aside another gunman, sending his automatic rifle skidding toward Toivo. Now was his chance. He wasn't running any more, he was going to pay them back. He bent and scooped up the gun. The boat still reeled from the onrushing tuna, but now the guards were regaining their stability. Toivo aimed and squeezed the trigger. Despite the powerful burst almost ripping the gun from his hand, the bullets splattered into the chest of the nearest man. Toivo felt a grim satisfaction and gripping the gun tighter he fired again. A second gunman fell backward, blood spouting from the bullet holes in his chest. Caught up in a frenzy that was fueled by his pent-up rage, Toivo held the trigger down and swept the barrel back and forth across the deck. He couldn't tell how many of the killers he hit, but in an instant the gun clicked empty. The remaining guards hesitated only a moment, then turned their guns on Toivo.

Gulping in a deep breath, Toivo dove headfirst over the rail, heedless of the teeming sea of thrashing tuna below. Gunfire rattled in his ears just before he hit the water, bullets zipping past. Then the sea washed away the sound. Instead he was surrounded by a tumultuous mass of flailing fish. Their tails smacked him in the face, in the chest, the arms and legs. Here and there he felt thin cuts as their fins sliced his skin. He tried to pull himself to the surface, his lungs begging for air. He couldn't see, wasn't sure which way the surface was, but somehow he was determined to survive, to reach the surface and breathe.

His lungs screamed for air, his arms ached from the strain, and only by willpower did he manage to pull harder. It wasn't enough. The heavy tuna forced him downward. He couldn't do it, he was losing the battle, but he couldn't give up, what about Olga? Their future? His breathing reflex tried to open his mouth to take in air, air that was still meters overhead. He choked on the saltwater that seeped in and fought to keep his lips shut tight, to force down the urge to breath. Barely he kept from coughing.

He pulled with both arms, kicked with both feet, against the rockslide of huge tuna. Powerful bodies slashed, battered and pounded on him. He was bruised from head to toe, his last bit of strength fading fast.

Suddenly, as he strained to reach the surface, he felt toothed jaws firmly grip his ankle, biting just hard enough to hold and pull, but not hard enough to break the bones. The pull was down, down into the depths of the sea and Toivo struggled to get free, but the jaws held firm. In an instant he was below the massed tuna. Free of the twisting bodies, his mind cleared and he realized Poika was propelling the two of them along with every ounce of the dolphin's strength. The gray mammal veered away from the tuna, then dashed straight to the surface. In the distance overhead, Toivo saw light flicker at the surface across the broken waves, but could he hold his breath long enough to reach it?

Up, up they soared as Poika rushed toward the surface. Toivo swallowed to keep his breath back, forced himself to hold on for just one more moment. They broached the surface, leaping above the water by half a meter and falling back with a splash. Toivo blew out with a rush and sucked in air! Sweet air! He gasped in long deep breaths and thanked God he'd made it.

Poika let go of his ankle and looked at him. "*Are you all right?*"

"*Of course,*" answered Toivo and rolled over to tread water. "*How about you?*"

"*I am fine. Their flash-and-bang weapons barely cut my skin.*"

Toivo started to raise his head up so he could see the launch, but a sporadic rifle shot made him duck. Poika dove under the water and sped toward the boat, which sat idling where the tuna stampede had intercepted her. Toivo let himself sink until his nose was barely out of the water, trying to present as small a target as possible in case one of the gunmen spotted him.

The launch was nearly empty. Only two armed men were still visible on deck tending to their fallen comrades, the others were gone. The boat sat low at the stern and as Toivo studied it, she settled lower. Another rifle shot from somewhere made him flinch. He couldn't tell who was shooting or who or what the target was. The launch shuddered, settled lower, and with a rumble and a rush of water, her bow rose skyward and she sank stern first. The two gunmen leaped away as she went under, but Toivo didn't think they got clear in time to avoid being sucked under.

Away from the boat, a man treading water held his rifle overhead with one hand, still trying to get off an occasional shot. Poika flashed past snatching the rifle from the surprised killer's grasp. The dolphin leaped high in the air, tossing the gun into a wave and both Poika and the rifle sank from sight.

Toivo surveyed the calm ocean around him. The tuna school was gone, herded away by a dozen factory dolphins. There was no sign of Ici, Ni or Olga. A hundred meters away, the few surviving gunmen clung desperately to splintered wreckage from the launch. Without lifejackets, none dared release their grip on the pieces of wood. While the others seemed intent on survival, Toivo recognized the coxswain who, brandishing an ugly automatic pistol, seemed bent on carrying on the fight.

Poika swam up near Toivo, stopping when his beak nudged Toivo's shoulder. The sleek gray of his back was broken by three puffy wounds. Toivo watched blood seep out in little red wisps that fluttered away in the rolling swells.

"Poika, you are hurt."

"Not badly. I told you the punctures are only through the muscle. I will be fine, given time to heal."

"Where are the others?"

"Tyttö is missing. I feel she has gone ahead. As soon as you are safe I will seek out her spirit and sing along with her as she departs. Pungee is leading the men-who-are-fish here. Sheriff, Slim and the others of my kind will keep the herd intact until you decide what you want us to do with the fish."

Toivo looked suspiciously at the Sunrise Savior. Like ants swarming on a damaged anthill, men still worked on the propeller. He could see them in the water with cutting torches and welding equipment. If they got the converted tanker running, then all would have been for naught. Toivo and his friends would not be able to escape again. He swiveled around so he could see the floating survivors from the launch. The coxswain had them kicking together, trying to push their collection of flotsam toward the Sunrise Savior. The man had spotted Toivo and occasionally the coxswain waved the pistol toward Toivo, threatening, but not shooting.

Toivo reached out and touched Poika on the cheek. The dolphin eased his way up next to Toivo. "Thanks," said Toivo. *"Is there anything I can do?"*

"No, if Tyttö has gone ahead then it is done. If I miss her spirit in this life I shall see her in the next. As for me, the saltwater will heal my wounds soon enough. The problem now is to get you to safety before they fix their boat."

"Safety," laughed Toivo, *"where will we be safe? The nearest land is hundreds of miles away."*

"I will tow you to the ship that is coming."

"What ship? There's no ship near enough to help."

At that moment, Ici, Ni and Olga surfaced not far away.

"Toivo," called Olga, "thank God you got away. Are you all right?"

"Yes, yes, I'm fine, for now. What can we do? Those bastards will fix the props on that tub soon. We'd better be long gone by then."

Olga looked over her shoulder at the false Sunrise Savior. "We won't be far enough, I'm afraid. They're putting over a lifeboat, and the guys waiting to get aboard it are armed."

The rest of them looked at the black boat swinging from davits at the side of the ship. A half dozen riflemen stood by ready to clamber down the sides. In a few minutes they would pick up their companions who were still swimming back to the Sunrise Savior, then they would come after Toivo and his friends.

"You guys swim for it," said Toivo. "I'll get Poika to tow me out of here."

"Toivo, my friend," said Poika, *"there is a ship coming toward us. A ship that may be the help you need. You can see it if you look over there,"* and he pointed with his snout.

"Wait a minute," said Ici, pointing in the same direction. "I don't think that will be necessary."

Off in the distance, silhouetted against the blue sky was the unmistakable shape of a U. N. warship steaming under full power toward them. Shouts from the Sunrise Savior told Toivo that her crew had seen the warship, too. The lifeboat swung around and headed back for the ship. The crew redoubled their efforts to get the propellers fixed, but it wasn't nearly fast enough. One warning shot from the frigate and the fight went out of them.

Already Toivo could see the motorized lifeboat launched by the U.N. frigate headed toward his group. It wouldn't be long before he was rescued again. For the moment, relief surged through him.

\#

Poddington glanced up from the railing and saw the frigate bearing down on the immobile Sunrise Savior.

"What now?" asked Deep, standing at Poddington's left shoulder.

The thunderous boom of the frigate's main gun answered and the high velocity naval round whooshed overhead to explode safely behind the stranded ship.

Poddington laughed despite himself. "I think it's time to toss in the towel. Maybe we can make a deal, testify against the cartel or something."

Deep nodded. "I'm with you, Captain. We're sort of running out of options."

"Hey, you idiots, help me up." Luis Jones' voice, tinged with fear, carried from the water below.

Poddington leaned over and saw the Second Mate trying to catch hold of the rope ladder that dangled over the side of the ship. With satisfaction Poddington noted how fragile Jones looked thrashing around in the water, his face cut and bloody. As the Captain watched, the short, dark haired man caught the lowest rung and started to pull himself upward. A gentle swell swatted the Second Mate and the thump of his body hitting against the side of the ship brought a grin to both Poddington and Deep.

"Come on," yelled Jones, "help me up. We'll put over the lee lifeboat where the frigate can't see us and escape."

"Escape to where?" asked Poddington.

"China. Fuji. Anywhere."

Deep laughed out loud. "The dumb shit doesn't know Fiji from Fuji."

Poddington held up one hand to quiet his friend. He struggled to hide his own smile and asked Jones, "And if we help you, what's in it for us?"

"The company always takes care of its own," was the reply.

"Yeah, we know how they planned to take care of us," whispered Deep in Poddington's ear. "I wish I had that gun. I'd shoot him."

Jones was now nearly halfway up the ladder.

Poddington yelled down to Jones, "I really don't see how you'd be any help to us escaping. I think we'll just go it alone." He turned to Deep, pausing for Jones to get a little higher on the rope ladder. "Cut the rope," he commanded.

Deep whipped out a folded, black-handled knife and, with a flick of his wrist, he snapped open the curved six-inch blade. Grabbing the rope that tied off the ladder with one hand, in two quick slashes, he severed the strands and sent the ladder and Jones crashing into the sea.

"Heeeelp," yelled Jones on his way down.

Poddington leaned expectantly over the rail, intense hatred in his eyes. He glared with glee as Jones fell backwards with a towering splash. Jones came up sputtering and coughing, fighting to keep his head above water.

The sight of the tough Second Mate, flailing helplessly in the water brought a feeling of accomplishment and satisfaction to Poddington. His lips wrinkled in a spontaneous smirk. And this was the man that had caused so much anxiety. Not any more.

"Hey," yelled down Poddington, "if the frigate picks you up, I'll see you in the brig. If not – screw you!"

Poddington turned and motioned for Deep to follow. "You get the ship's log before someone decides to destroy it, and I'll retrieve my diary. Got a few quick changes to make. Sorry I got you into this."

"Not to worry, Captain. I could have talked you out of it. It seemed like a good idea at the time."

They hurried along to the wheelhouse.

Chapter 22

Toivo sat stiffly at the captain's table. The U. N. frigate Stockholm was a welcome change to floating in the water. The crew had been a delight, helping them get warm showers, clothes—real clothes finally—and now they were all gathered in the officers' dining hall for an exquisite meal with Captain Benline, an English Naval officer serving with the United Nations.

Olga sat next to Toivo dressed in light blue seaman's britches and a matching blue shirt that was tied above her waist. She'd complained about wearing so many clothes, of course, but Toivo thought she looked grand even in such plain attire.

Toivo studied the officers' mess, noting the sharp contrast in color, texture and elegance to what he'd lived with recently. The room was a feast for the eyes, the rich, dark wood paneling, the stark white tablecloth, the silverware and the crystal goblets. Too much finery for me, he decided, and turned his attention to the wonderful-smelling pot roast smothered in brown gravy full of carrots, potatoes and peas. He forked in another mouthful and enjoyed the succulent flavor. Now this was more like it. He'd had enough fish to last him a long time.

The captain looked up from his plate. He was a large man, his crisp, white uniform offset by his fiery red hair and beard. A thin smile softened his fierce, gray eyes. He cleared his throat awkwardly and though he obviously commanded great respect, Toivo could tell he was uncomfortable with civilian visitors aboard his ship.

"It is a pleasant thing to have so many fine guests aboard the Stockholm, though I'd rather it were under other circumstances."

Nervously, he dabbed a spot of gravy from his moustache. "I'd rather talk about more pleasant subjects, but there are a few items we need to cover.

"First is the matter of the Sunrise Savior, which turns out not to be, as I'm sure you already know, the actual research vessel of the same name, but a cleverly disguised fake. As for her crew, those that are alive are all safely in irons, including the Captain, one Victor Poddington. With Captain Poddington's help we managed to secure the ship's log and his private diary, which details the gruesome events fairly well, though there are a few missing pages that cause me concern. Still, there's enough evidence to charge some members of the crew with murder. And, Captain Poddington and the First Mate seem to be in a fairly cooperative mood. With your testimony, I am sure we'll win a conviction.

"Also we found enough of the latest designer drug, PXC, on board to kill a small city. Quite the technically sophisticated operation. They had a complex series of pipes, pumps and tanks for sucking up plankton and a complete laboratory for synthesizing PXC from it."

"What about all the killing?" asked Toivo between bites of roast beef. "If they were after some kind of drug, why did they murder the shepherds and my crew?"

Captain Benline shook his head. "The first raft they sunk, the Oyster Bay, was a case of being in the wrong place at the wrong time. When the shepherds went to investigate who was sucking up their plankton, they were killed. Unfortunately, you stumbled onto the Oyster Bay, which should have been sunk, and once you'd radioed in your findings, you and your crew became witnesses that needed to be disposed of.

"If it weren't for you, they might have gotten away with it. As it turned out the criminals aboard the look-alike Sunrise Savior were still trying to fix the damage you caused to their prop and had no chance of escaping."

Olga set down the glass she'd been drinking from.

"How did you know we needed help? I mean, they sent those bogus radio signals."

Captain Benline smiled, deftly sipped from his glass and said, "That was easy. We had voiceprints of the crew of Homestead from prior radio conversations. The voice that told us to forget showing up didn't match any of them. Not to mention the fact that their jamming techniques were so rudimentary that we would have been on our way even without the voiceprints. The unpleasant part of all this is that you will have to testify at the trial in International District Court that is being convened in Hawaii. I think, however, it will be pretty much open and shut." The captain leaned in toward them, his smile faded.

"Personally, I'd like to hold the trial right here and apply the rules for a captain's trial at sea. Unfortunately they won't let me do that."

He paused long enough to take a sip of his wine. "You are probably aware that PXC is the hottest selling street-drug on the market. In the past it has been extracted from certain strains of natural plankton. Now this new plankton, developed as a superior feedstock for the factory tuna, has turned out to be a poisonous gold mine. As a starting material, it appears to produce about 50% better PXC yield than normal plankton. At first I thought it was simply one more operation of the Colombian drug cartel. Using the ship's registry, we traced the vessel back to the Colombians, just as I suspected. But, I asked myself, how did they know about this new plankton? We traced several obscure references to a research laboratory in Maryland, in the States, and discovered it was the same bioengineering lab that created the new plankton strain in the first place.

"It seems the company is in serious legal trouble. Their president, Walter Shikawa, and several other officers face long-term jail sentences for illegal experiments with human beings. As part of their research, they had developed this new plankton for the factories and accidentally discovered it was an excellent raw material for producing PXC. They kept that tidbit secret until their legal troubles started at which point they needed to raise a large amount of money very quickly. They worked a deal with the South Americans figuring that with enough money they could buy their way out of the mess they were in."

"Dr. Shikawa" snapped Ici. "He is the founding father of the cowboys."

"I thought you'd recognize the name," said Captain Benline. "Unfortunately, Dr. Shikawa didn't know how to take 'no' for an answer. He has continued his genetic experiments trying to change humans into fish—no offense—in defiance of laws against it."

"Well, I, for one, am not testifying against Dr. Shikawa," shot Ici, tossing his napkin on the table.

"You won't be," said Captain Benline quickly. "As far as we can tell, he had nothing to do with the killing. In fact, it is ironic that his dealings led to the slaughter of the very people he was trying to create."

"Then why did the ship have a cannon?" asked Toivo.

"Good question. It seems that after leaving the fishing business Captain Poddington originally was in a quite different profession – arms smuggling. However, at some point, he decided a naval piece would make a nice addition to his personal collection. He stole it from one of the arms shipments. The Colombians didn't really care what was done to the leased ship. They wanted a floating drug factory and for awhile they got it."

Ni delicately placed her fork alongside her plate. "Why did they kill all the dolphins?"

"You have to realize the caliber of men we're dealing with. Most are mercenaries, soldiers of fortune, not a man among them with a lick of moral decency. A few were fishermen—or used to be—and they had stumbled on to a market for dolphin flesh. Certain cultures believe it will prolong life and people with enough money will pay any price to get it, despite the illegality. The men aboard the tanker saw it as a chance to make an enormous profit; one they didn't have to split with anyone else. Every time they found a raft with dolphins they would kill as many of the dolphins as they could, and it also meant they had to get rid of the shepherds, too. There is a meat locker on that ship with a couple of dozen frozen dolphin carcasses. It's a sad sight indeed."

"The sonofabitches should be shot," spit Olga and stabbed a piece of potato with her fork.

"What are we going to do?" asked Ici. "Has Star-Kist said anything?"

"Yes, as a matter of fact. They have informed us that the Martin B. will be here before we finish the repairs to this phony Sunrise Savior and Star-Kist wants your herd—or all you can round up—loaded aboard. Star-Kist has agreed with our request to have the three of you," he indicated with a nod the three shepherds, "transported to Hawaii to testify against these criminals. My Executive Officer will be taking a skeleton crew onto the tanker and we'll escort her to Pearl Harbor. After the trial, there will be a new submersible raft and tuna herd waiting for you in Guam.

"More importantly, however, is the total emancipation of all shepherds by the U. N. All shepherds' debts to the factories are cancelled. The General Assembly has decided that your kind is too valuable to be endangered unnecessarily. From this day forward, all children born to shepherds will be granted a sizeable subsistence allowance until they reach adulthood. There has been quite a sum of money frozen in various Swiss and other nefarious accounts that belonged to this drug operation. That money will be used for something good. It is a shame that some of you were killed because of Dr. Shikawa's misguided dreams."

The captain looked at Ici and Ni. "They want to encourage the proliferation of your race. The only way to do that is by natural reproduction since no one is willing to lift the moratorium on genetic engineering, what with all the religious objections."

Ni nudged Ici. "I think we can help," she said.

He put his hand lightly on hers. "Let's hope so. But what about rounding up the tuna school?"

"I think the dolphins have taken care of keeping them rounded up," said Toivo. "Poika and the others have remained at their posts and the herd is nearby although food is scarce. They'll stick to it until the Martin B. gets here."

Captain Benline's weathered face softened. "I am sorry about the dolphin you lost. If we could have reached you earlier, the bomb would have been unnecessary."

"No sorrier than I," said Toivo, "but Poika is the one who should be taking it the worst. Tyttö was his mate. Instead he says he's said his good-byes to her spirit and knows someday he'll join her."

Silence engulfed the table as their thoughts turned inward, each lost in their own thoughts, each of them trying to sort out their own lives, their own priorities. Toivo wondered about going home, about buying another boat.

Finally the Captain broke the silence. "That brings me to the last topic we need to discuss. This talent of yours, Toivo, being able to talk dolphinese. I had to report it to my superiors. They are very interested in meeting with you. Several of them are waiting for us in Hawaii."

Toivo rubbed his chin. "I'd really rather not waste my time playing guinea pig for a bunch of skeptics."

"These aren't skeptics. They are members of the dolphin lobby to the U. N. They are interested in talking to you about the dolphins. About their life, culture, habits. They might ask you to testify before the General Assembly. You could be the necessary catalyst to get dolphins recognized as citizens of Earth."

Toivo leaned back. Poika a citizen? Toivo always thought of him as a person, why not the rest of the world? "Where would I have to go? What would I do?"

"Those details will have to be worked out. Right now they just want to talk to you." The captain picked his fork up. "Enough talk of business. Let's enjoy the meal."

It wouldn't get Toivo another boat, but it would give him a purpose.

#

The sun was long gone. The stars played hide-and-seek behind high, thin clouds. Toivo walked the forecastle rail. The seas ran calm and the frigate barely rolled. Only a short distance away, the tanker rode the swells, tethered on long lines. Bright searchlights from the Stockholm lit her stern where the work crews were busy repairing the damage from the homemade bomb.

Toivo hardly paid attention. His mind was elsewhere. The faces of his lost crew danced through his thoughts. Men he would never see again. Right now he would have been playing chess with Wilho. He could see them seated in the galley, the board between them, and Wilho, chin resting in his hand, studying the board. Never again, he thought, never again.

He heard the soft footsteps and turned to see Olga.

"Hi," she whispered. "I wondered where you went after dinner."

"I needed a little air," he said, turning back to the rail.

She was so beautiful in the reflected searchlights. Her short blond hair almost cried to be caressed. "What are you doing?" he asked.

"Thinking about my new freedom. Wondering what I should do. I think I'll visit my mother as soon as the trial is over."

"Good idea. Are you going to work for Ici? I heard him offer you a job."

"Yes, I think I will for a while. At least until I have some money. It will give me time to decide what I'd like to do with my life."

"A wise choice." He could feel her leaning on the rail next to him, her elbow rubbing lightly against his side. "Don't rush into things. You'll make fewer bad choices."

"What about you?"

"I will see what these men in Hawaii want from me, maybe even go to New York, to the United Nations, if that is what it takes. Eventually I want to get back to fishing if I can get another boat. Someday I'll settle down on a coast somewhere, maybe Hawaii, maybe Finland. But I'm not ready yet. I couldn't leave Poika. He is all the family I have left."

"Of course." She turned sideways, her back to Toivo. "Will I see you again?"

What could he say? Suddenly he knew how much he wanted her now that he was on the brink of saying goodbye. On the one hand he longed to put his arms around her right now. His dreams for a family were there at his fingertips, but was he ready for it? Poika's words came back to him. Why was he wasting time?

"Probably, if you'll let me visit once in a while."

"Anytime." She turned back to face him. A smile forced up the corners of her mouth, her eyes filled with happiness. "I'll call you everyday so you can't say you lost track of me."

There was a look in her eyes, soft and loving, that touched Toivo more than any words could have. It pulled at his heart. He leaned over and kissed her on the lips.

"I'll be back," he whispered. "I think I'll do my fishing here in the Pacific. That's where my dolphins will be, too."

"Then it's settled. I'll meet you back here as soon as I return from St. Petersburg."

Toivo pursed his lips. Too late to turn back now. "Yes."

She threw her arms around him and kissed him hard. Toivo kissed her back. It felt good. It would be okay, he told himself.

From the water Poika stuck his head up. Toivo saw the dolphin and, without turning from Olga, he called over his shoulder, "*I am very sorry about Tyttö, truly sorry.*"

"*Going ahead is to be expected,*" replied Poika, his smiling face incapable of showing emotion. "*She was well prepared and I found her spirit in time to sing with her before she went ahead. I will see her in the beyond. You, however, have made a good choice, Toivo. She will make a wonderful mate.*"

Toivo smiled at his friend and Poika slid back into the ocean to rejoin the pod. Toivo concentrated on holding Olga. Yes, she probably would make a wonderful mate.

If you enjoyed reading *Shepherds* perhaps you would consider posting a short review (even a single sentence) wherever you purchased your copy.

Also by J. Drew Brumbaugh

Shepherds

The Galiwee Visions Series:

War Party

Bula Bridge

Foxworth Terminus

Ten More

Girls Gone Great

(A children's book co-authored with Carolyn B. Berg)

The Tirumfall Trilogy :

Fall of the Western Kings

Child of Evil

For more information go to:

https://www.jdrewbrumbaugh.com

About the Author

J Drew Brumbaugh lives in northeast Ohio where he spends his time writing sci-fi, fantasy and suspense novels, teaching and training at the karate dojo he and his wife founded, building a Japanese garden in his back yard, and taking long walks in the local Metroparks with his wife. He continues to work on his next book and seems to always have several stories in various stages of completion. He can be reached at contact@jdrewbrumbaugh.com.

Don't miss out!

Click the button below and you can sign up to receive emails whenever James Brumbaugh publishes a new book. There's no charge and no obligation.

Sign Me Up!

[1]

https://books2read.com/r/B-A-MDC-QPCB

Connecting independent readers to independent writers.